# *Flame*

## CARMICHAEL FAMILY SERIES

## ADRIANA LOCKE

UMBRELLA
PUBLISHING INC.

*To my sweet and special reader, Debbie Doo*
*I hope you enjoy Foxx's book as much as I enjoyed meeting you.*

Sacrifice | Wherever It Leads | Written in the Scars | Lucky Number Eleven | Like You Love Me | The Sweet Spot | Nothing But It All | Between Now and Forever

For a complete reading order and more information, visit www.adrianalocke.com.

# Cast of Characters

*parents*
**Kixx Carmichael**
**Damaris Carmichael**

*siblings*
**Moss Carmichael** [Flirt]
**Maddox Carmichael** [Fling]
**Jess Carmichael** [Fluke]
**Banks Carmichael** [Flaunt]
**Foxx Carmichael** [Flame]
**Paige Carmichael** [Sweet]

# CHAPTER 1
## *Foxx*

"Are you having fun?" Banks slides next to me, a glass of lemonade in his hand. "That apple pie Honey made was the best pie I've ever had. Did you try it?"

I cock my head to the side and stare at him.

"Want me to get you a piece?" Banks asks, a wide smile plastered across his face.

I shift my weight from one foot to the other.

The air is filled with spices from the chili cook-off that took place an hour ago to benefit the local school's arts program. Conversations flow into a giant stream of noise as people catch up, recounting old high school sports games and current gossip.

*So much wasted energy.*

And in the midst of it all, my youngest brother is up to something. This isn't a revelation, nor is it a surprise. He's *always* up to something.

In the past few weeks, I've picked Banks up from jail in the middle of the night. I watched him walk across the street covered in glitter—retribution for attaching stickers of his face to every surface of our brother Jess's house. One morning, I looked out the window to witness a giant metal rooster staring at me from across the road, thanks to Banks's handiwork and toddler-esque humor.

The guy is a menace but a predictable one. His tells are as clear as day, and right now, they're *screaming*.

"I've socialized enough," I say. "I'm heading home."

"*Already*? You just got here."

"I said I'd support the cause. I didn't say I'd stay all afternoon."

"But there's still so much to do. Did you even see my calendar? And I—"

"Why do you care what I do?" I cross my arms over my chest. I'm curious despite curiosity being against my better judgment. "I showed up. Yes, I saw your ridiculous calendar. I bought a pie. What more do you want from me?"

He points at me. "Can I have that pie, by the way? You snagged the last coconut cream."

"*No.*"

He holds up his hands. "Easy, tiger. I was kidding." He grimaces. "*Kind of.* Anyway, about you leaving …"

I look at the ceiling and sigh.

This is precisely why I avoid human interaction as much as possible. I always walk away worse for the wear. I'm pushed too far or needled too much. Things are expected of me. My time and energy become commandeered, and I'm not into that sort of behavior.

It's not that I don't understand the concept behind group activities —I do. I took enough psychology classes to wrap my brain around it. People need to share their experiences and feel seen. The potential for success rises when people work together. Groups allow for high-level problem-solving and cooperation.

But me? I'd rather not be seen. I don't want to share my experiences. And I can damn well solve my own problems without someone like *Banks* weighing in.

"Are you listening to me?" Banks asks.

"No."

We turn our attention to the makeshift platform beside us. Gloria, an older woman Banks befriended in one of his silly schemes, taps a microphone. She beams from center stage.

"Ladies and gentlemen, please take your seats," she says, the microphone entirely too close to her teeth. She smiles at *me*. "It's time for the final event—the one you've all been waiting for. The bachelor auction is about to begin!"

My stomach knots at the look she's firing my way. *What's that all about? Does she think I'm Banks?*

He waves at her from beside me. She looks at him, then back at me, before returning her gaze to my brother.

*Yeah, Gloria. It's this goofy-ass guy you're after. Not me.*

Chatter breaks out through the room, and women scramble to find seats. Banks and I are nearly trampled as a group of ladies makes a beeline for the front row.

"Let's ... uh, move over here," Banks says, grabbing my elbow.

I flex my arm, and he promptly drops his hand, looking at me warily.

"Sorry," he says.

"Good life choice," I say.

"About that ..."

Banks sidesteps Marla, a silver-haired woman pushing her walker across the floor. Tennis balls cover the feet like drag slicks. Head down and shoulders back, she leans into the turn around the corner of the stage before nearly knocking over a small child to take the center seat.

"Have fun getting auctioned off," I say, turning to leave. "Looks like a good time."

"Foxx, *wait*."

The way he says my name, coupled with how he takes a half step back, has my instincts rippling with anticipation. *Something bad is about to happen.*

I square my shoulders with his. "What?"

He winces.

"I would like to welcome our four eligible bachelors on stage," Gloria says. "First, we have Shawn Daze, the surf instructor we all know and love. Welcome, Shawn!"

Cheers ring out from around the room as the first contestant takes his spot next to Gloria.

"Next, we have Chef Miguel Cotto, the reason we all go to La Pachanga," she says. "Welcome, Miguel!"

The applause grows louder.

Banks rocks back on his heels. "I need to tell you something."

"Colin Hensley, the firefighter that dreams are made of, is our third bachelor," Gloria says. "Say hello to our local hero!"

"Better hurry," I say. "You're next."

"About that …"

"And, last, our final contestant. I don't know how we got this lucky, ladies," Gloria says. "Please welcome the one and only Foxx Carmichael!"

*What?*

Cheers fill the air. Everyone in the room fixes their gaze on me. Gloria watches me expectantly.

*Oh, hell no.*

Banks grimaces, moving even farther away from my right hand.

Everything inside me stills. My jaw flexes, and my teeth grind so hard they hurt.

"Tell me she got us mixed up," I say, balling my hands at my sides.

"Look, I can't be in the auction anymore. Sara will kill me. She's dangerous when she's mad."

"And I'm not?"

"Good point." His eyes dart around the room. "Listen, Foxx, I didn't think about it until we arrived. I can't let my girl Gloria down, and none of our brothers can fill in. Maddox has Ashley, Moss has Brooke. Pippa would murder Jess if I volunteered him."

"Foxx? Can you join us on stage, please?" Gloria asks, the microphone squealing in her hand. She taps on it, making it even worse. "Can someone show me how to adjust this thing?"

The entire town stares holes in my back, waiting for me to take the trail of humiliation and occupy the spot by Colin. Hushed conversations whisper through the room. I'm sure jokes are being made over coffee and coffee cake.

"*Please do this for me,*" Banks says, holding his hands before him. "I panicked, Foxx. I didn't know what to do. You are the only one of us who's single, and I … *I panicked, Foxx.*"

"You're repeating yourself."

"It's for a good cause, and it's not like you have a bursting social calendar."

"Foxx?" Gloria asks again.

Banks grins. "You're drawing more attention to yourself by not going up there, you know."

I take a step toward him. "Sleep with one eye open, you little fucker."

Instead of looking worried, he manages to look relieved.

I don't really have a choice because, for once in his damn life, Banks is right. I'm only creating a bigger problem by resisting. The chatter among the gossips will only worsen if I duck out the back door and leave them hanging.

*Banks, you're living on borrowed time, kid.*

I straighten my shirt, stand tall, and take a long, deep breath. *Focus on revenge. It will be so, so sweet.*

I step purposely onto the stage, carefully avoiding eye contact with the audience. My heart races as I stand next to the firefighter. He gives me a slight nod, a gesture of pity, really, before turning his attention back to the women clutching paddles with numbers written in black magic marker.

Gloria drones on and on, thanking everyone who had the tiniest hand in putting the event together. Then she gives a quick rendition of the rules. While she reads the bullet points off a sheet of paper, I exhale and finally face the crowd.

The women in my family sit at a round table near the bathroom. My mother is more entertained than she should be. Dad stands next to Jess, the only brother I really like most days, and lifts a plastic cup my way. My failure to acknowledge him results in a chuckle that he's lucky I can't hear. Banks stands next to Jess and gives me a thumbs-up. I level my gaze with his, unblinking.

His smile slowly fades, and his thumb falls from the air like a deflated balloon. I enjoy a smidgen of satisfaction from that.

"Let's start the bidding on Shawn at two hundred dollars," Gloria says. "Do I have any takers?"

Paddles are thrust into the air. It's one of the most embarrassing things I've ever witnessed.

*Could I just donate a large sum of money and spare us all the trouble?*

Sweat dots the nape of my neck as the bids for Shawn increase.

"One thousand dollars for Shawn! Going once, going twice—a date with Shawn is sold to Mrs. Ferguson," Gloria says, pointing at a petite older lady with a purse embroidered with cats. "Congratulations!"

*Fuck my life.*

*And fuck Banks's life since we're at it.*

I turn to Gloria, lips parted to announce my benevolent donation, but the wind is knocked out of me.

*What is she doing here?*

Bianca Brewer stands in the entryway, chatting with a woman holding a long roll of raffle tickets like they're long-lost friends. Except they're not. Bianca has never been to Kismet Beach before.

"On to Miguel," Gloria says. "Since the last bachelor raised so much money, let's start a bit higher this time. Do I have five hundred?"

My body catches fire as Bianca moves across the room.

Landry Security assigned me to her security detail three years ago. Despite having a binder of information before meeting her, nothing could have prepared me for the powerhouse of Bianca Elaine Brewer.

She's five foot five with shoulder-length auburn hair. Her eyes are pieces of jade that can see right through you. She has high cheekbones, deep curves, and a cute button nose.

*She fascinates me.*

The woman is wildly intelligent. Watching her bring a boardroom of men to their knees is one of the hottest things I've ever seen. She's curious and confident yet humble and kind. And she doesn't give a damn about what she should and shouldn't do. She does what she wants.

Unfortunately, that can't be me.

Bianca looks up. Her green eyes shine when they connect with mine.

*Shit.*

"Hey," she says, mouthing the word from across the room.

I struggle to remain unaffected, but the corners of my lips lift. She notices. She always finds the chink in my armor. A smile creeps over her pink pout, hitting me directly in the cock.

*Get yourself together, Carmichael.*

"Going once, going twice—a date with Miguel is sold to Mrs. Daniels for twelve hundred dollars!" Gloria announces.

My brows pull together as Jason, Bianca's brother and my best friend—my only friend—enters the building. His solemn expression is replaced with amusement as he realizes what he's about to witness.

I flash him a pointed look to watch himself. It only makes him laugh.

*Maybe I don't like him either.*

"Next up is Colin," Gloria says. "Let's start the bidding at five hundred. Do I see six?"

Jason and Bianca take a seat in the back row. He folds his hands on his lap like he's settling in for a show. She takes a bid paddle from the raffle ticket lady.

This is the nail in Banksy's coffin.

"I have six," Gloria says. "Do I see seven?"

Bianca's eyes find mine again.

"There's seven. Do I have eight?" Gloria asks.

Bianca lifts a brow, pressing her lips together.

*What does that mean? Do you want a date with Colin?*

As if she reads my mind, she raises her paddle.

I raise a brow back.

"There's eight. Do I have nine?" Gloria asks the room.

Bianca shrugs innocently, daring me to react. But I don't. And I won't.

She might get under my skin like no one I've met before, but I refuse to cross that line.

I was the lead on her security detail for two and a half years, and for two and a half years the woman whittled away at my restraint. It's impossible to resist her. Her little smile and the way her nose wrinkles when she's being cheeky. Her penchant for burgers and vanilla shakes. Her perfume and her ability to wear a T-shirt and cocktail dress with the same understated elegance.

*The way she says my name.*

Our relationship shifted over time. It began strictly professionally before transitioning to more of a friendship. And then, during the past six months, we were toeing a line that shouldn't be crossed.

Conversations weren't strictly business. Smiles were exchanged when no one was looking. Our touches lingered long after contact should've been broken.

I wasn't thinking of her as my boss. I was thinking about her bent over her desk. I was imagining her in my bed wearing my T-shirt. I had visions of her in my truck, her hand in mine, doing mundane tasks like running errands.

But it was harmless. It was simply a war inside me that I was winning.

And then one night changed everything. That's the night six months ago that I asked for an immediate transfer … and I haven't seen her privately since.

"Sold! A date with Colin to Mrs. Breckenridge for one thousand one hundred dollars." Gloria peeks around the others and smiles at me. "I'm starting the bid on our final bachelor with a bid of my own at five hundred dollars. Do I have six hundred for Foxx?"

All eyes land on me. I'm not sure where to look. I don't want to see my family laughing; I want to like them tomorrow. I can't look at Banks because I'll be tempted to leap off the stage and beat his ass right here. I don't want to look at anyone bidding, lest they think I want them to spend their hard-earned dollars on a date with me. And I sure as hell don't want to make eye contact with Bianca.

"Six hundred from Marla in the front," Gloria says. "Do I have seven?"

Various paddles shoot to the ceiling. *And they stay there.*

Gloria laughs. "I see. Let's go to eight hundred?" The paddles remain in the air. "Nine? One thousand? One thousand one hundred?"

*What the hell is happening*?

"Fifteen hundred!" Marla grabs her walker to brace herself. "I bid fifteen hundred."

"Okay. Sixteen hundred, anyone?" Gloria asks. "Yes! I have sixteen hundred from the lady in the back."

Heads turn to the back of the room. Bianca sits tall in her seat, proudly waving her paddle.

I look at Jason in surprise. He shrugs as if there's nothing he can do. I send him a silent message to stop her. But instead of intervening like

I've seen him do countless times in both private and combat situations, he defers.

He's helpless and at the mercy of his baby sister.

"Seventeen hundred!" Marla shouts, her voice wavering from the force of her words.

"Eighteen hundred," Bianca fires back.

"Two thousand," Marla says, her hands shaking. She narrows her eyes at Bianca.

Out of my periphery, I notice Banks snickering.

"Two thousand, two hundred." Bianca's voice is edgier than before as she stares Marla down. "I bid two thousand, two hundred dollars."

Jason gets up and stands behind her, holding his forehead.

"Two thousand, three hundred," Marla says.

"Twenty-five hundred."

Heads swing from one side of the room to the other as bids volley back and forth.

Marla scoots her walker around so she's face-to-face with Bianca. "Twenty-seven hundred."

"Twenty-eight," Bianca says easily.

Marla's finger shakes as she points at her adversary. "Respect your elders, missy!" Her gaze whips to Gloria. *"Three thousand."*

"Someone stop this," I mumble.

Bianca stands, holding her paddle in the air, and levels her gaze at Marla. "Ten thousand dollars."

*What did she just say?*

Gasps echo through the room.

"I'm sorry, hon," Gloria says, the microphone squealing. "Did you just bid *ten thousand dollars?"*

Bianca smiles sheepishly. "It's for charity, right?"

Marla flops in her chair, defeated.

Applause breaks out as Gloria struggles through her shock, her gaze switching between Bianca and me. I feel like Gloria expects me to say something, but I have nothing to say other than *what the fuck just happened?*

My head spins.

I exit the stage, ignoring curious looks from the audience as everyone gets up to leave.

I came for pie.

*Pie.*

*What went so wrong?*

My feet falter, and I stop just short of where my brother and I stood only minutes ago.

*Banks.*

*Banks is what went wrong.*

I growl into the air.

*Today can't possibly get any worse.*

# CHAPTER 2
## *Bianca*

"What part of *let's slip in here quietly* did you not understand?" Jason asks, still holding his forehead as the locals exit the building.

I bat his hand away. "Stop doing that. You're going to get wrinkles."

He sighs, ignoring my suggestion and wrinkling his brow even more.

"Do you think I'll have bad karma for outbidding that sweet old lady?" I ask.

"It's a little too late to worry about that now. You just took her hopes and dreams and shredded them in front of the whole town."

"It's not my fault. She got my competitive juices flowing. I feel bad now that I—*ow!*"

I'm thrust forward by a metal rod bumping the back of my knee. I catch myself on Jason's arm.

"I hope you're proud of yourself, you little hussy." The *sweet old lady* sneers, scooting toward the door. "Kids these days."

"It's a charity auction." I shove off my brother. "There's no reason to be upset."

"You have no shame," she says. "No shame at all."

A part of me wants to tell Marla that I'm sorry—that this has nothing to do with her and everything to do with my unresolved feelings for Foxx. But the saucy part of me wants to tell her how shameless I can really be—which just might be the catalyst for my unresolved feelings for Foxx.

"Only you, Bianca," Jason says, shaking his head. "Only you."

"What's that supposed to mean?"

He sighs, frustration etched in the deep, *wrinkly* lines on his forehead.

Jason is my favorite out of my five brothers. He's not the most fun. He won't talk freely about anything personal, and he's not the one I'd call to gossip with about the others. But what he lacks in relatability, he makes up for with a laser-focused sense of loyalty and duty.

And sometimes that's annoying.

"You're the only person I know who can show up in a new town and have a beef with an elderly woman within ten minutes," he says.

I hold up a finger. "I didn't pick a fight. I simply placed a bid. She's the one who got all bent out of shape and tried to take me out with her walker. I was just supporting a good cause."

"A good cause which is benefiting … whom?"

"It doesn't matter," I say, laughing.

*"Because you don't know."*

"No, I don't know. But that's not the point. You're just supposed to have a giving heart. I'm just giving, Jase. What they do with the money is on them. They'll have to take that up with God."

He rolls his eyes and digs his phone out of his pocket. He glances at the screen. "Hey, I need to take this. Can you manage not to upset the locals until I get back?"

I make a face. "I'll try. But I promise nothing."

He turns to the door. *"Behave, Bianca."*

"You're no fun." I find my seat and sit again. "But that's already been established."

Adrenaline trickles through my veins as I scan the building for Foxx.

I didn't know that Jason didn't tell him we were flying down today, but the look on Foxx's face made it clear our presence was a surprise. I'm unsure whether he found it to be a good surprise or a bad one.

"Wow, that was quite a bid." A woman stops beside my chair. She's pretty with brown hair and a Smokey's T-shirt tucked into a pair of jeans. "I can't blame you, though. I would've done the same thing if I had an extra ten grand."

I smile back at her. "I mean, it *is* for charity, right?"

"Yeah. Sure."

Her laugh is gentle and kind. I instantly like her.

"I'm Bianca," I say.

"I'm Becca. I haven't seen you around here before."

"Oh, I'm just visiting for the afternoon. My brother is a pilot and thought we should do a quick getaway. Lots of family stress at home. You know how it goes."

A shadow filters across her face. "Yes, I know that feeling well."

"Excuse me, Becca. May I borrow Bianca for a moment, please?"

There's no need to look across my shoulder to see who's interrupting us. If I didn't recognize the deep, slightly aloof voice or the wood and citrus cologne, I'd know it was Foxx by the look on Becca's face. Not many men in the world can garner that reaction.

Her eyes practically have hearts drawn onto the irises as she stares at him. "*What*? Oh. Yeah. Right. Sure, Foxx. Not a problem. I was leaving anyway." She turns to me. "It was nice to meet you."

"It was lovely to meet you, too, Becca," I say.

She steals a final glance at him before disappearing into the line of bodies leaving the community center.

My insides quiver with a mix of anticipation and excitement. Slowly, I turn to face him.

Instantly, his blue eyes snatch mine up and hold them hostage. The intensity of them, *of him*, steals my breath.

*I'll never become immune to this man.*

"You want to borrow me, huh?" I ask. "Sounds like fun."

He towers over me by several inches. He stands tall and confident with dark hair on the verge of needing cut, and brows and cheekbones that define *chiseled*. His features are symmetrical, save for a slight bend to his nose. His skin is dusted with stubble, and his hands are calloused. It melts into a package of pure masculinity that turns me into a puddle.

Foxx licks his bottom lip but says nothing.

"*Or not,*" I say, pulling my gaze from his.

"What are you doing here?"

I bite back a smile. I hear it—the slightest edge of softness to his words. *That tells me all I need to know.*

Despite being removed from my security detail six months ago, nothing between us has changed.

*He's still affected by me, too.*

"Jason and I heard there was a bachelor auction down here today, so we thought we'd swing by and find me a date," I say, testing the waters.

He hums.

"I almost had two, but the firefighter looked a little too *nice* for my taste," I say, watching his reaction.

Foxx's eyes darken. He runs a hand through his hair, his eyes never leaving mine.

"Wanna sit?" I ask, taking my paddle off the chair beside me. "Jason is on a call, but he'll be in when he's done."

Foxx sits, brushing against my shoulder on the way down. It sends a blast of energy shooting through me.

"It's been a while," I say. "How have you been?"

He shrugs. "You?"

*Oh, Foxx.* I grin. "Ah, the man of a thousand words. I forgot how chatty you are."

He hangs his head, chuckling softly.

"Jason said you've been assigned to Renn lately," I say. "Lucky you. Of all my brothers, he might be the most entertaining."

He turns his head and looks at me. He wants to say something but doesn't.

We watch each other carefully, searching the other's face for direction.

I didn't expect Foxx to be game for idle chitchat—that's not his modus operandi, but I didn't expect him to say only six words either. We didn't end things, *not that there was anything to end,* on a bad note. It just … ended.

One night, I thought he was going to kiss me. The following morning, he requested a transfer from my team.

I haven't talked to him since.

*Apparently, that's the way he wants it.*

My chest tightens.

"I'm going to wait in the car," I say, starting to stand. "If Jason comes back in—"

"Wait." His palm rests against my thigh. "Just … hang on."

"Miss? Would you please bring me your paddle?" A woman waves at me from a table next to the water fountain. "The baseball team is having an auction next week, and I promised them our paddles."

I glance down at Foxx. His blue eyes are nearly green. This shade usually happens late at night, when instead of doing whatever it is he's supposed to be doing, he stays a little too long with me.

He pulls his hand away from my leg, letting his fingertips drag off to the side.

I get up and leave him behind. My brain scrambles to make sense of this, *of him*, as I reach the table.

Foxx is complicated—broody and detached. He has this vibe that says *stay away from me*. Except I've never felt like that energy applied to me. From the moment we met, when I watched him climb out of a dark SUV and slide sunglasses off his handsome face, we have been drawn to each other. We share a chemistry, a connection, which was just *there*. That *is* there.

But there are so many other things in the mix, namely Jason. Foxx's loyalty lies with my brother, and he'll never do anything to jeopardize that relationship or put his job into question. And that's why he asked to be transferred.

I don't know what I was hoping for—but it's obvious that anything more than a Foxx Carmichael shrug is hoping for too much.

I sigh. "Here you go. The paddle is returned."

The woman takes it from me. "Thank you. And congratulations on your win. That was … memorable."

"Thank you." I laugh. "I do love a good charity." *How many times am I going to say that today?*

She winks at me.

I half-smile, half-grimace, and begin to return to my chair. But as I pivot, I nearly run into Colin.

"There you are," he says, grinning. "I was hoping I'd run into you."

"Well, *I* almost ran into *you*, but I get your point."

He chuckles. "Are you from around here? I haven't seen you before."

Foxx's gaze blisters me from the side. I would love to look at him and see the look on his handsome face—*maybe it would help me understand him*—but I don't. I pointedly ignore him. He's the one that doesn't want to talk to me.

"No, I'm not from here," I say, smiling at the firefighter. "I'm just visiting friends with my brother."

"I got ya. You know, I was hoping you would save me from having a date with an eighty-year-old librarian."

I laugh. "Hey, don't knock the librarians. She might be able to teach you a thing or two."

"Maybe. But how about—oh, *hey, Foxx.*"

My insides twist as Foxx's arm slides across my lower back. Goose bumps break out across my skin as I glance up at him. His jaw pulses.

*Damn.*

I should pull away from him. I should step away and ask him what's going on—remind him that he has no right to intervene in this conversation. But I've missed his touch far too much.

Foxx doesn't say a word to Colin—not verbally, anyway. One thing I've learned about Foxx Carmichael is that sometimes words aren't necessary to convey your point.

"Nice to meet you, Colin," I say over my shoulder.

He half waves, confused, and walks away.

Foxx's fingertips press into my skin. I could so easily lean into him, relishing in the fireworks exploding in my body. But I don't. I pull myself together instead.

"What the hell is this?" I ask Foxx while we walk away.

His muscles are tense. His bicep flexes behind me, and his body is rigid as we find our seats.

He drops his arm and puts a bit of distance between us. "I could ask you the same damn thing."

"Watch this. I'll show you how to answer a question." I flash him a facetious smile. "I was flirting with a very handsome man who was all too eager to converse with me. I know you aren't super familiar with the concept of friendly conversation, but lots of people enjoy that kind of thing."

His eyes narrow. "You don't even know him."

"True. But I'm ninety-nine percent certain that I could've known him *deeply* by the night's end if you hadn't interrupted."

"You should watch yourself, Bianca."

"You aren't on my security detail anymore, *Foxx*," I say, lifting a brow. "Remember?"

He crosses his arms over his chest. "What's your point?"

"*What's my point*? My point is that what I do is none of your concern."

He smiles, but it's not out of amusement. "I beg to differ."

Anger ripples off him. I've seen him do this before. He stands tall, gets this menacing look on his face, and exudes a dangerous, broody energy. People tend to back off.

Unfortunately for him, I'm not most people.

"At least you're begging for something," I say.

He opens his mouth to respond, but Jason cuts in before Foxx has the chance.

"This day gets better and better," Jason says, appearing out of thin air.

I pull my gaze away from Foxx. "What's wrong?"

"I have a mess on my hands back home." Jason sighs. "Apparently, Dad arrived at Brewer Air this morning and tried to breach my office. It's taken care of, but he left with my assistant in tow."

My stomach drops. "What the hell, Jase?"

"I know. I know. He just gets further out into the deep end every time we turn around. We alerted your office about the situation in case he was headed that way."

I pinch the bridge of my nose. "Of course, he does this on the day we're not in town."

"I take it all things aren't resolved," Foxx says, his voice all business.

Jase shakes his head. "No. There are a lot of attorneys involved, as well as the police at this point. Dad has dug his heels in and is fighting us at every turn."

Foxx looks at me, but I don't know what to say. I give him a shrug. It almost makes him smile.

I take a deep breath and hold it in my lungs. The burn helps recenter me—helps me to release the stress of our family drama as I exhale.

A few weeks ago, our father was exposed as a cheat, liar, and all-around horrible person. It took us all by surprise. None of us saw it coming.

Mom filed for divorce with all six of us by her side. She then ousted Dad from our family's businesses, putting me in charge of Brewer Group to oversee the function of our various entities. That did not go over well. Apparently, Dad forgot about a paper he signed when accepting a loan from his father-in-law years ago. A rider in that paperwork allowed Mom to push a few buttons and take full control of the company.

Dad has spiraled even more since that became official.

"I need to get back to Nashville," Jason says, giving Foxx a look I don't understand.

"Of course," I say. "Let's go."

Jason holds up a hand before I can take the first step. "Bianca ..."

I stare at my brother.

Whatever he's about to say is going to make me mad. The wariness in his eyes and the hesitation in his voice give him away.

I grab the back of a chair and brace myself. "Yes, Jason?"

"Hear me out ..."

"I can't do that if you don't speak."

He sighs, preparing for battle. *But what are we battling? What do I not know?*

"I don't know what I'm walking into back there," Jason says. "I've talked to Landry Security and our brothers, *and Mom*, and we all think it might be best if you didn't come back with me."

I let go of the chair. "*Excuse me?*"

"Today's stunt is out of pocket—even for Dad. He's scrambling, and people are dangerous when they scramble."

"*He's our father, Jason.* I worked with him more closely than any of you for years. He's not going to do anything to me."

"Exactly. You worked with him more closely than any of us. You know the ins and outs of every business deal, every company, everything he's touched for ..." He pauses. "Hell, Bianca—you were in his office since you could walk. If anyone is a target—*it's you.*"

I close my eyes and grimace.

It makes sense. I am the interim president. I have access to every document and contract. If our father has left a trail of nefarious dealings behind and we haven't found them yet, I'll likely be the one who sniffs it out.

*Fuck.*

"Gannon will step in and keep things running until you get back. Just think of it like a little vacation. You need one anyway. This whole thing has impacted you more than the rest of us."

That's true, too. I haven't been sleeping well. I've spent more hours in the office than I have at home since Dad's betrayal. Jason had to pry me out of my office to get me to accompany him on this random adventure today.

*It has felt nice getting some fresh air ...*

I open my eyes. "For the record, I think you're blowing this out of proportion."

"Cool. I hope you're right."

*Ugh.* I pace a small circle. "Where would I go? Renn's condo in Vegas?" *Not a bad idea.* "Maybe you could have security just meet me there—"

"*You're staying here.*" Foxx's words are crisp and quick.

My head whips to his. *I'm staying here? Has he lost his mind?*

I don't know what my face does, but he rolls his eyes.

"I hardly think staying with you is the solution we're looking for," I say.

He doesn't back down. "You just bid ten grand for one date with me. Think of it as a bonus."

*Asshole.*

"So, Vegas?" I ask, letting my gaze rip slowly from Foxx as I turn to my brother. "Or Gannon has that place in Aspen. I could go there."

"Actually, I think Foxx might be right," he says.

"*What?*" I laugh in disbelief. "May I remind both of you that Foxx doesn't even want to work with me? Yet you're suggesting I stay with him for how long? A few days? A week?" I laugh again. "What's wrong with you, Jason?"

He shifts his weight from one foot to the other. "You're already here. And if something does pop off, I want you with Foxx. I trust him more than anyone in the world."

"Nothing is going to *pop off*. I assure you that you're overreacting."

"Great. Then enjoy the beach vacation, Bianca. But don't fight me on this. This is the right thing to do, and you know it."

I sit again and hold my head in my hands. *How in the world did I get into this mess?*

I want to argue my point—inform Jason that *I am* going home with him and there's nothing he can do about it. But Jason doesn't overreact. If he's insisting I stay put, it's for a reason.

But staying with Foxx? Spending a few days with him, alone, *in his house, I presume*, sounds like heaven … or hell.

Probably hell.

"Please do this for me," Jason says, touching my shoulder. "I really need to get to the airport, and we need you to be safe—just until we have a better handle on Dad's intentions."

I suck in a long, deep breath. "Okay. I guess. I … *Jason …*"

He gives me a quick hug, shakes Foxx's hand, and then bolts for the door.

I steady my breath and try to gather my wits.

The community center is empty, save for a few people picking up trash and sweeping the floor. I look around the building, letting the events of the past few minutes soak in. When I finally find the strength to look up at my new roommate, he's standing behind me with a twinkle in his eye.

"What?" I ask, deadpan.

"Looks like you're my official business now."

With that, he turns for the exit.

*Great. Just great.*

# CHAPTER 3
## *Bianca*

THE STREETS OF KISMET BEACH ARE ADORABLE. SIDEWALKS ARE DUSTED with white sand. Buildings are painted the prettiest pastels, and windsocks dangle from many of the porches that face the main drag through town. It's all a compliment to the main attraction—the Atlantic Ocean just a street away.

I rest the side of my head against the window as Foxx pulls the truck to a stop. A woman and small child pass in front of us, waving from the walkway. Foxx raises his fingers off the steering wheel in the most basic form of a wave possible. Once they're safely on the other side of the street, the truck roars to life once again.

It's been ten minutes since I followed him out of the community center. He's not said a single word. I haven't said anything either—mostly out of defiance.

My phone buzzes in my lap, breaking the silence in the cab.

I look at the screen to find our family group chat alive and well.

> Jason: Leaving the airport shortly.

> Renn: Be safe.

> Gannon: Security has been increased at all Brewer properties.

> Ripley: I'm with Mom. Walking into meetings with attorneys.

> Tate: Where's Bianca?

> Jason: Florida.

> Tate: 😌

> Jason: She's staying with Foxx.

> Tate: Bet she hates that. 🙄

I fight a grin and tap out my reply.

> Me: I'm on this thread, you know.

> Gannon: We'll keep in contact. If I need anything here, I'll call, Bianca.

> Tate: Have fun, you little rascal.

> Jason: Treat it like a vacation.

> Tate: Oh, I'm sure she's going to get a little … rest. 😏

> Jason: Can you just … not?

I snort. *Damn you, Tate.*

My youngest brother and I have had more than a couple of conversations about Foxx. He's the only one out of my siblings who I can truly be open with about things like men. That's probably because he's done so many debauched things that he can't possibly judge me. On the same note, you can't get anything past him when it comes to things even remotely involving sex.

Tate and I can walk into a full room. Within two seconds, I can find the single person wearing Oud Wood cologne. In the same amount of time, Tate can determine who's fucking and who wants to hook up.

> Me: Feel free to come down and hang out with me, Tate. I'm sure I'll be tired of talking to myself by morning.

> Tate: I'm sure you'll manage.

I laugh softly at my brother's reply.

"Everything okay?" Foxx asks, side-eyeing me.

*I win.*

> Me: Love you guys.

I set my phone on my lap. It dings five times in quick succession. That sound makes me smile.

"Yeah, everything is fine," I say. "Jason is leaving the airport soon. He was letting us know."

Foxx regrips the steering wheel.

"This is a cute little town," I say, throwing the words out there. I don't want to lose the six-word progress we've made. "Have you always lived here?"

"Yes."

I groan before letting out a long sigh.

"What?" he asks.

"I didn't ask to be here with you. To be perfectly clear, I don't want to be here with you."

He runs his tongue across his bottom lip. "Why did you come today?"

"Because Jason asked me to take a day trip with him. He said I needed to get out of the office, which is true, and he had a golf outing lined up with Ford Landry. Something happened before we got there, so he changed the plan to swing down here since we were so close."

"I see."

"So if having me around is annoying to you or is putting you out in any way, I'm happy to call Renn and—"

"Stop it, Bianca."

I flinch. "I'm sorry. Have we been apart so long that you forgot that *stop it* doesn't go over very well with me?"

His lip twitches.

We turn up a street that slips between a row of thick foliage. A green sign that reads Honeysuckle Lane is tucked under a palm tree.

The truck slows as we creep down the small lane.

Two houses are on each side and two more sit at the end of the cul-de-sac. Each home is adorable—something out of a movie—with hanging flowers on porches and tidy landscaping. A large metal rooster has been placed in one yard. But before I can ask about it, three chickens race from one side of the street to the other. They barely miss the front of the truck.

"I was trying not to talk to you," I say, chuckling. "But I have so many questions."

"*Banks.*"

I wait for an elaboration that doesn't come.

He reaches up and presses a button. Moments later, a garage door on one of the homes at the end of the circle rises. The truck engine roars as we pull into the driveway and coast into the open bay. He turns the truck off.

"Home sweet home," he mumbles, climbing out the driver's side door.

"Okay then …"

I exhale as I get out of the truck and close the door behind me.

The garage is neat, with everything in its place. Tools hang on the walls. Totes are clearly labeled and sit evenly on shelves along the back wall. Hooks hang by the entrance to the house with an array of keys hanging off them.

"I expected no less," I say, mostly to myself. But Foxx hears me.

"Expected no less of what?"

I motion toward the totes. "You're very organized, Mr. Carmichael."

"Thank you for noticing."

*What*? I laugh, following him into the house.

I've imagined what Foxx's home looks like a million times. Sometimes, I think of it as a blood-red dungeon with whips and handcuffs. Other times, it's dark and moody. It's even light gray with midnight blues and deep greens on occasion. But none of those could be further from the truth.

"Oh, *I love this*," I say, entering the kitchen. "This is beautiful."

I spin in a circle to take it all in.

The dark, bold hardwood floors pop against the warm white walls. The cabinetry is dark with gold fixtures and is capped off with white stone countertops. A window overlooks the backyard. On either side are floating shelves with white dinnerware sitting atop them.

"This is ... not what I had in mind," I say, a laugh in my tone.

"What did you have in mind?"

"Let's just say this room feels like it belongs to someone happy."

I stop moving and face him. He's leaning against the wall, watching me.

*Oh, wow.*

I've never seen him like this. Comfortable. Loose. In his element, as opposed to being in mine. *What a sight it is to behold.*

The lines on his face have eased, giving him an almost playful look. His hair is messy, and a smile toys against his lips. He's fighting it, of course—he's still Foxx—but I can see the hint of humor just behind his mask.

"Do you think I'm not happy?" he asks, lifting a brow.

"Well, I suppose we all define happiness a little differently, don't we?" I move deeper into the kitchen to investigate the massive stove. "Did you do all this? Or was it like this when you moved in?"

"Dad and I renovated the house. My parents bought all the houses on this street as they came up for sale so their kids could live close to them. They clearly have separation issues."

I laugh. "That's better than my parents' issues. My father seems to be a player in the underworld, and my mother couldn't wait to get us out of the house. But, then again, by the time she got to Tate, she had to be exhausted." I look up at him. "How many siblings do you have?"

"Too fucking many."

"That's not a number."

He shoves off the wall. "I have four brothers and a sister. Moss, Jess, Maddox, Paige, and Banks."

*Banks. Okay, that makes sense now.* "What does Banks have to do with the chickens?"

"Everything."

"You know, Foxx, I'm not asking you to engage in deep, thoughtful conversation here. But if you could use more than a couple of words at a time, I'd appreciate it."

He sits in a chair at the small table on the other side of the room. "Fine. Banks is a little shit who can't be satisfied until he pisses someone off. He was into it with Jess a while back. I don't know the specifics because I don't ask. But that huge metal rooster that you see when you turn onto this road?"

I nod.

"That was Banks. It was sitting in Jess's yard. And the parade of chickens that act like they run the place? That's also Banks's doing. There are about a hundred of the little fuckers running around here."

I cover my mouth with my hand and try not to laugh, but I fail.

Foxx rolls his eyes.

"He's your Tate then, right?" I ask.

"No. Tate has common sense. Banks has a death wish."

He stands, stretching his arms overhead. The hem of his shirt slides up, and I catch a glimpse of his abs.

*It's going to be a long few days.*

"We need to get you a few essentials," he says. "Do you want me to take you to the store or what?"

"Crap. I didn't even think about that."

He shrugs.

*Him and that damn shrug.* "Well, I could rent a car while I'm here. That might make things easier."

"Since you're supposed to be laying low, it would probably be a good idea if you weren't out gallivanting around by yourself."

"I hardly think going to the local grocery store is out gallivanting around." I put a hand on my hip. "And, when you put it like that, it makes me want to do it even more."

"You are such a pain in the ass."

"I can go to Vegas …"

The look he gives me begs me to try it. I know it's supposed to make me have second thoughts about Vegas, but all it really does is turn me on.

"I can have my assistant send me things," I say. "But I won't have them by morning."

He glances at the refrigerator. "We probably need to get some groceries, too. I don't have any Greek yogurt or bananas."

I grip the edge of the counter as my insides melt. He's just stating facts, going through a list of what he has and doesn't have to eat. But the fact that he just named the two things I eat for breakfast every morning has me in my feels.

*I need a few minutes to get myself together …*

"If you don't mind, I need to make some calls before we do anything else," I say. "I need to check in with Astrid and let her know I'm not returning right away. She can get a package together to send me. And I need to call Mom and make sure she's okay."

Foxx buys it. "Not a problem. I have a couple of things I need to do, too."

"Great."

He furrows his brow. "Are you good with hanging out here while I take care of something?"

"If you're good with it, I'm fine with it. It's your house."

"Make yourself at home." He clears his throat and gestures to a doorway. "There's a bathroom through the living room and down the hall. It's the second door on your right. The third door is the guest room in case you want some privacy."

*Fabulous.* "Sounds great."

"I'll give you a tour of the place later."

I nod.

We watch each other for a few seconds. The room shrinks around us, and the air gets hotter. I can hear my heartbeat as it pounds steadily and feel my chest rising and falling rapidly as I work to keep myself calm.

"I'll be back," he says finally.

"I'll be here."

He dips his chin toward the floor and leaves through the garage door.

As soon as he's gone, my knees buckle. I exhale a harsh breath and fall back against the counter.

*How am I going to survive this? How can I possibly stay at Foxx Carmichael's house for a few days and come out on the other side unscathed?*

Lord, help me.

# CHAPTER 4

## *Foxx*

"BACK TO SQUARE FUCKING ONE."

I step onto the driveway and tip my face to the sun.

When I was a little boy, I was obsessed with the sun. Its size. Its power. The color and eclipses and the way it could light the sky with purples and oranges just before sundown—it all felt magical. I loved everything about it.

*If only life were still that simple.*

"How did I wind up here?" I ask, the question carried off by the breeze.

I did the right thing, *the hard thing*, and separated myself from Bianca. I ensured she had someone undistracted and focused watching her back.

Because that man couldn't be me.

But here we are, six months later, and I'm not sure I made the right decision because it sure as hell doesn't seem like anyone is watching her back.

Fury rolls through my veins again today. Only, this time, I'm alone. This time, I don't have to hide it.

I've intentionally avoided having anything to do with Bianca since I left her security detail. If I hear her name, I tune out. If we're in the same place, I ensure I'm the farthest away from her.

It's for the best. For all of us.

But now she's here, in my fucking house, and it appears it's where she should've been all along.

*Are these motherfuckers dropping the ball?*

I massage my aching jaw from clenching my teeth all day.

We knew there was a threat to Bianca the day Rory left Reid. We also knew that threat grew when Rory appointed Bianca as Brewer Group's Interim President—Reid's former position. If that threat has continued to grow, and it appears it has, why in the fuck was she without security today?

*Am I the only one that cares about her safety?*

The idea that there are men sitting around a table somewhere half-assing a security plan for Bianca fills me with rage. I've kept it packed away all day. I couldn't let it boil over until I was alone and had time to think it through.

Now that I have, I want answers.

I pace a circle along the side of my house and yank my phone from my pocket. I find Ford Landry's name and hit call. It rings three times before his voicemail picks up.

"Hey, it's Carmichael. I have a couple of questions about Bianca Brewer. Give me a call when you can. Thanks."

I slam my finger against the red button on the screen.

"You okay, Foxx?" I look up to find my mom walking up the steps to her house. She waves with a curious, if not slightly concerned, face.

*No.* "Yeah."

She hesitates as if she's considering heading my way. So I quickly cut across my yard and into hers, meeting her at the stairs.

"Do you need a glass of tea?" she asks as I swing open the back door.

"Nah. I'm good." I hold the door open for her. "Seen your son lately?"

She laughs. "Well, I have five of them. But something tells me you're talking about my youngest."

"Where is that little fucker?"

Mom leads me to the kitchen. "I take it you weren't aware that you were participating in a bachelor auction today."

I stare at her.

"Oh, Foxx." Mom laughs again. "I know you don't think this is funny—"

"It's not."

"—but who would've thought Banks would be able to con you into something like this?"

"Me." Jess comes in with a hat that reads Proud Chicken Daddy. "Found Sparkles yet?"

Mom points a finger at him. "Jess, you stay out of this."

"Sorry, Mama. *No can do.* I've waited my whole life for this."

"For what?" she asks.

Jess snickers. "For Banks to have enough balls to finally fuck with Foxx." He sighs happily and turns to me. "I take it you haven't found him since the … charity event."

His amusement isn't amusing. *The list of people I don't like is growing by the hour.*

"No," I say. "But I about ran over three chickens a little while ago."

He gasps. "Greta, Iris, and Rita?"

"Who?"

"Was it Greta, Iris, and Rita?"

I sit at the table. "I feel like this conversation went left, and I took a right."

"We're talking about my chickens."

"You named your chickens?" I ask, somehow surprised. "Who names chickens?"

"People who wear Chicken Daddy hats," Mom says, laughing.

Jess glares at her, snatching a glass of sweet tea out of her hand. "You've been spending too much time with Maddox. You think you're funny."

Mom swats at his shoulder, making him laugh.

"At this point, Moss and Maddox are the only two of you who I don't fear are losing their marbles," Mom says. "The rest of you are starting to concern me."

I hold a palm in the air.

"You were in a bachelor auction today, Foxx," Mom says. "That's concerning."

"Tell me about it."

Jess downs half the glass of tea before shoving it back in Mom's hand. "Thanks for the drink. I have to go find the girls before dinner."

He marches out of the house like a man on a mission. *What the fuck is happening here?*

"He's not right," I say, shaking my head.

"*He's happy.*" Mom gathers a stack of notebooks off the counter and heads to the table. "One day, you'll understand."

"I don't mean this the wrong way, but I hope to hell not."

She grins. "You will. Trust me."

"If I ever get chickens and refer to them as *my girls*, I'm not happy. I'm ill."

She laughs, shaking her head while she organizes her notebooks. "Sometimes you just need to be reminded about the things that make you happy. That's Jess right now. He was always slightly goofy and fun-loving." She looks at me briefly before going back to her books. "You'll see what I mean someday."

*Or not.*

I should get up and go home. I should check on Bianca and figure out how I'm going to maneuver the next few days without losing everything—my sanity and my career. But there's something centering and calming about sitting with my mother at her kitchen table.

"So," she says, easing her way into a conversation she's clearly nervous to broach. "Are we talking about the beautiful young lady who bid very aggressively to win a date with you today?"

"No."

She stops, a notebook balanced in her hand.

"*No,*" I say again, this time with more emphasis.

"It was Jason Brewer's sister, wasn't it?"

"How in the hell did you know that?"

"I've seen him a few times, and that bone structure doesn't appear out of thin air, Foxx." She smirks. "And I saw him there today, so I put two and two together."

*Oh.*

"She looked pretty enamored with you," Mom says, her voice far too ... *hopeful* ... for her own good.

"Stop it."

She puts the notebook down. "What's wrong with a woman being smitten with you? It's a completely natural thing—"

"Can we not do this, please?"

"Sure." She shrugs. "Are you here for advice, possibly?"

I sigh. "*No*. I am here for Banks, and I know exactly what I need to do with him. But thank you for your concern."

She smiles to herself.

My phone buzzes. I jerk it out of my pocket and look at the screen, hoping it's Landry. But the text is from a number I don't know.

> Unknown: Foxes are solitary animals. They are not pack animals. They live by themselves or in small family groups called skulks (not skunks). These usually include a mama fox and around six cubs.

"Is that written in English?" Mom asks. "Because you're looking at it like it's not."

I toss my phone on the table. It spins as it slides, coming to a rest against Mom's books.

"Someone thinks they're cute and just sent me random facts about foxes," I say, unamused.

"You, too, huh?"

"What do you mean?"

"Your brothers get texts like that. They all get a different animal. Of course, you get a fox."

"Someone is *so* witty."

She grins. "I think it's cute."

"You would." I stand and grab my phone. "I need to get home. If you see that kid of yours, tell him I'm looking for him."

"My gut says that he already knows that."

I turn to leave.

"Foxx?"

I look at her over my shoulder.

"In all seriousness, I know you don't need my help or advice," she says, her words solemn. "But I'm here. If you can't hear your heart, you can come talk to me."

I knock on the table with my knuckle. "No worries. My heart is loud and clear, and it's telling me to find Banks and remove his spleen."

"Just don't get blood on the carpet or furniture. You'll never get it out."

I shake my head, chuckling. "Love you."

"I love you, Foxxster."

Just as I turn to leave, the front door opens. Banks stops, freezing in place with his eyes wide as dinner plates.

"*Oh, shit*," he says, spinning on his heel to flee.

I cut the distance between us in half and pluck the back of his shirt, yanking him backward.

"Mom!" he yells.

"Don't yell for Mommy," I say, shoving him into a corner. "You and I are going to have a little talk."

"Foxx, buddy, pal—just listen to me with an open mind …"

"Shut up." My phone buzzes in my pocket. I manage to get it out and into my hand without dropping it. *Ford Landry* flashes on the screen. I look up and point at Banks. "Stay put, or it's going to be worse for you."

He nods slowly.

I press the green button. "Carmichael."

"This is Ford. I got your message. What's up?"

Anger begins to build inside me again.

I point at Banks to back up closer to the corner. He holds his hands up and presses himself flat against the wall.

"I want to talk to you about Bianca," I say, my jaw aching from clenching so tightly all afternoon.

"Of course. What about her?"

*Stay calm.* "Why in the hell was she on a plane with Jason and no backup if you know there's an open threat?"

He sighs. "All right. Calm down. Let me explain."

"I'd love for you to explain. I'd love for you to explain to me why the protocol is being ignored." I suck in a breath. "Where was her security detail? Where was Troy? Dominic? Calvin? You had no one escorting them? Jason is flying a fucking plane with her on board, and there's no backup?"

"Everyone had another assignment—"

"No one called me."

"*You* asked to be removed from her detail."

I'm breathing fire. "I ask to be reassigned. That doesn't mean I'm unwilling to rejoin her team if there's no one available."

Banks starts to slip away from the wall.

I lunge at him, and he slides right back into place.

"You're not affiliated with that plan," Ford says. "You know how this works."

"I know that she should never be allowed to fly around the country alone when someone is making threats against her," I say a little too loudly.

Banks's eyes go wide.

"She wasn't alone. She was with Jason. And let me remind you that Jason isn't a normal civilian. He's as trained as you are. He's as capable of protecting his sister as any of us, and he took responsibility today. *He* called Dominic off."

"You're dropping the ball, Landry."

There's a moment of silence—long enough for me to *try* to regain my composure.

I kick myself for getting too close to Bianca in the first place. I kick myself harder for not being able to handle it. I bust my ass for asking for the detail transfer and allowing these assholes to leave her in harm's way.

I fucked this all the way up.

"Foxx?" Landry asks. "Are you okay?"

I tug at my hair with my free hand. "I'm fine. I'm ... *fine.*" I blow out a breath and drop my hand to my side.

"Bianca is with you now, correct?"

"Yes."

"Is that okay with you? If not, I can send someone—"

"I wouldn't advise it," I say through clenched teeth.

The door slams. I jump just in time to see Banks jetting down the porch.

"I have a call with Jason this evening," Landry says. "I'll confirm that you're to remain with Bianca."

"*It's confirmed.*"

Papers shuffle in the background. "We have a conference call tomorrow morning at nine. I'll have a link sent to your email."

"Fine."

"Okay." He pauses. "I know you're frustrated. I know you had this thrown into your lap today. But I also know how much Jason respects you and appreciates your loyalty."

I nod, even though he can't see me.

No one understands the bond that Jason and I share—not even Landry. He knows that Jason and I both worked for Fenton Abbott at Mandla and were on the same rescue mission in Africa. But what Landry doesn't know, *that no one knows*, is that Jason saved my life that night.

And I'll never forget it.

"Jason asked that you be appointed the lead on Bianca's detail if you want it …"

*He did*? I suck in a breath.

Bianca is sitting in my house a stone's throw away, and her entire security plan is being thrust into my lap. Things will have to be strictly professional between us—no matter what.

*Can I do this? Can I do this with her in my home? Can I trust myself to stay focused on the task at hand and not her?*

But as I think about it and weigh the pros and cons, it becomes apparent that there's really only one choice. Because if I don't do it, I'll be distracted anyway, wondering if the threat against her has escalated. I'll be of no use to anyone. Hell, *I'll* be the weak link.

I can't risk that.

*Especially now I've breathed the same air as Bianca again.*

No, I *won't* risk that.

"Let's talk about it tomorrow," Landry says. "Get some sleep. I'll see you at nine."

"Goodbye."

"Goodbye," he says, ending the call.

The weight of the world settles on my shoulders as I stare out the window toward my house.

Earlier, I was wrong.

Today could get worse.

And it did.

*It sure fucking did.*

# CHAPTER 5

## *Bianca*

Don't be nosy. Don't be nosy. Don't be nosy.

I frown.

*But I really want to be nosy.*

The house is absolutely silent. It's not uncomfortable or eerie like my house can be at certain times of the day. If I hadn't designed and built it, I would've sworn someone was murdered in the guest room downstairs. I have to pass it to reach the kitchen at night for a snack, and I've almost tripped more than once after a few glasses of wine in my attempt to reach the pantry without getting attacked by ghosts.

I stroll through Foxx's "unhaunted" kitchen and poke my head into the living room.

*Oh, very nice.* A large plant has been placed beside a picture window. There are two brown leather chairs with a small table between them. The sofa is made of the same material and houses three large fluffy pillows in various shades of blue. The hue picks up the colors in a painting hanging above the fireplace.

Everything about Foxx's house is cozy.

My friends always joked that I lived in a museum because everything was for show, not for use. There were busts of poets, signed first editions of books, and vases from my parents' trips around the world that were worth far more to them than the sculptures my brothers and

I made in elementary school for Mother's Day. As I've grown older, I've realized that my home feels quite the same as theirs. It's beautiful and tasteful. Very elegant—except for the ghosts. But it's also cold and hollow—probably because of the ghosts. It probably doesn't help that I'm almost never there.

I sit on the couch and rest my head against a soft pillow. I check my texts to see if there have been any updates at home.

There's one.

> Jason: Are you doing okay?

I type out a quick response.

> Me: I'm alive.

> Jason: Good to hear.

> Me: Is everything okay back there?

> Jason: For the most part, yes. My assistant put in her letter of resignation, but I expected as much after hearing that she left with Dad. We're going through her computer and things now to see if anything is amiss.

> Me: If there's anything I can do from here, let me know.

> Jason: I think the less you have to do with anything, the better. Just for now. I need you to trust me.

I sigh. "You're overreacting, big guy."

Me: Don't I always?

Jason: If only our siblings took direction as well as you.

Me: Never thought I'd hear you say that about me.

Jason: It's odd, isn't it? 😉

Me: I'm going to call Mom. She always calls my work cell phone, and I left it in the office THANKS TO YOU.

Jason: You're welcome for that. And Mom is still in meetings. I could kill Dad for putting her through this.

Me: Get in line, bud.

I pause, waiting to see if my heart will hurt. But it doesn't.

I keep expecting it to happen—to have a breakdown out of sadness or an outburst of anger or a meltdown from mental exhaustion over everything that's happened. I'm ready to give myself space to feel and honor whatever emotions arise. Except, none of them do. Not toward Dad, at least. Fuck him.

Down deep in the recesses of my soul, I knew something was off for a couple of years. I watched the man I knew growing up—the one I loved and idolized—change before my eyes. It was so subtle that it was hardly noticeable. But I noticed. I just didn't do anything about it.

And, if I had, maybe some of this bullshit could've been prevented.

Jason: I'll call you tomorrow. Let me know if you need anything.

Me: I will.

Jason: Thank you for cooperating today. It means a lot to me.

Me: I expect a huge Christmas present for this inconvenience. HUGE. MASSIVE. EXPENSIVE.

Jason: Brat.

Me: Ha. Love you.

Jason. Love you, too.

I set the phone on my stomach and close my eyes. But it buzzes again. This time, Tate's name is on the screen.

Tate: So I'm sitting beside Jason right now and I was reading your texts over his shoulder. I just want to point out that this trip could be a gift if you play your cards right.

"Oh, Tate," I say, laughing.

> Me: I would tell you to mind your business, but you'd ignore me.

> Tate: You know me well. Gotta go. The tech guy just came in and nothing he's saying is registering with Jason. How can he fly planes and run an airline and be so technologically incompetent?

> Me: Go be a hero.

> Tate:

I wait to ensure he doesn't send anything else. After a few moments, I lock my screen and settle into the cushions again.

My mind goes to work—budgets, contracts, and negotiations flood my brain, reminding me of the many tasks required of me. I envisage the unread emails, the piles of papers on my desk, and the voice messages waiting to be returned. And I don't want to do any of it.

I lay my hands on my stomach to help ease the guilt eating through my insides.

All I ever wanted to do in life was to run Brewer Group. Everyone who has ever known me knows this singular fact. I followed my father to work while the other girls took dance classes. I asked for a briefcase when my friends at school wished for dolls. While they followed movie stars and celebrity marriages, I watched the stock market.

It was who I was.

It's who I am.

But I'm not so sure it's who I want to be.

And I'm also not quite so sure what to do about that.

*Oof.* I stand and stretch, trying to jostle the anxiety out of my bones. Then I pick up my phone and dial the number of the one person I know can help and distract me.

My assistant answers immediately. "Hey, Bianca."

"Hi. What's going on with you?"

"Let's just say that Renn is getting much better at asking me for help with things," she says, laughing. "I took his reluctance to request help for granted for so long."

I laugh, too. "Well, I have a few things that I need help with, and I need you to prioritize my stuff over my brother's. Okay?"

"Don't I always?"

*You do. And that's why I adore you.* "You know that I flew to Florida with Jason this morning ..."

"Right ..."

I pace the room. "And it turns out that I'm not coming home for a few days."

You could hear a pin drop on the other side of the phone.

"Astrid?"

She clears her throat. "And you made hotel reservations for yourself on the beach somewhere with a cabana boy?"

I grin. "Only if the cabana boy is named Foxx Carmichael."

*"Get out of here."*

"I'm kidding, but I am staying with him."

"You're staying *with him*, as in *you're staying at his house*? Or in a hotel room? What's happening, Bianca? Expound on this subject, please."

I peek in the kitchen to ensure Foxx hasn't snuck up on me.

"Long story short," I say, "Jason didn't want me to go home for a few days. There's some fuckery afoot with Dad, and they want me out of sight for a little while."

"But I thought you didn't work with Foxx anymore?"

I stop next to the window and look over the backyard. There's a pool with a diving board and a few chaise lounges. I wonder how often Foxx uses them. Beyond the decking, there's a landscaped yard that leads to a tangle of trees and grasses at the far side of the property.

It's so different from what I'm used to in Nashville. But I kind of love it.

"I don't. But it was Foxx who basically told Jason and me that I am staying with him until this mess is figured out," I say.

Hearing that aloud makes me smile.

"*Okay* ..." I can hear the grin in her voice. "What's that mean?"

"It means he's doing my brother a favor."

Slowly, my smile fades from my lips.

That *is* what he's doing. He's being there for Jason. As much as he's attracted to me, and I know he is, he can walk away from the attraction. *From me.* He's unable to walk away from his loyalty to my brother, and I need to remember that.

"Have things been weird?" she asks. "You haven't seen him in six months. What was his reaction when he saw you?"

I blow out a breath. "At first, he looked happy, I guess." I pause and decide not to tell her about the auction. "Then he was super quiet and pulled the noncommunicative bit on me. I took him to task about it, and he eased up a little, but he's Foxx. What can I say?"

"Are you okay with staying there?"

I mosey through the living room and back to the kitchen. I take in all the little bits of Foxx buried in the details.

The salt and pepper containers are equally spaced on the counter. There's a historical biography, his weakness, on the table. A pair of sunglasses sits next to a bowl by the door. Aviators. His favorite.

But even as I take in the nuances of Foxx, I realize that I know so little about him. I didn't know he has five siblings. I didn't realize he lives on the same street as his family. That surprised me, actually. And I don't know his bedtime routine, or what grocery stores he likes to shop at, or what he looks like when he wakes up.

*How can I feel so close to someone yet be so far removed?*

"Bianca?" Astrid asks.

"Yeah. I'm sorry. What did you say?"

"I asked if you are okay with staying there."

I mull that over for a long moment before answering her. "I am. Maybe this is what we need to sort of wrap up whatever this was or wasn't between us. Do you know what I mean?"

"I do. He up and quit you out of nowhere. You deserve closure from that, especially with how close you two were getting."

*It wasn't out of nowhere. It was the morning after the night I thought he was going to kiss me.*

"Well, I'm not holding much hope that he'll sit down and pour his heart and soul out to me," I say, chuckling. "But I'm hoping that in a couple of days, I'll go home and be able not to think about him every day."

"I know what would also help that."

"Tell me."

"Fuck his brains out."

"*Astrid*!" I laugh too loudly. "Where did that come from?"

She giggles. "Look, as your only friend—and I say that with all the love in the world—it's my job to give you girlfriend advice. The same advice I'd give my other friends."

"You mean, the other friends that don't pay you to like them?" I shake my head. "I'm so pathetic."

"It's only pathetic because you don't leave your damn office long enough to have friends. When was the last time you went somewhere with people your own age that you didn't have to go?"

I narrow my eyes playfully. "I don't pay you to be mean to me."

"The truth hurts. And so will you tomorrow if you follow my advice."

I laugh again. "You know what, Astrid? I like this new side of you."

"Oh, no. This isn't new. This is a side of me that doesn't need to come to work very often. This is the first time in five years that you've needed *this me*. I can be *this me* whenever you need her—and I hope you need her more."

The lightness in my body makes me feel the same. *I hope I need* this her *more, too.*

"So since we're talking about me needing you, can you get me a few basics for a few days? Clothes, my thyroid medicine, a bikini?"

"Absolutely. Aside from the meds, anything specific you want?"

"Not really. You know what I like. Wait. Do you remember my red bikini with the triangular top?"

"I do."

"Can you dig that out? If not, it's fine. But I'd really like to have it down here." My stomach twists as I remember Foxx's reaction the last time I wore it in front of him. I grin mischievously. "And that see-through cover-up I got in Bali last year."

"Got ya, boss. I can overnight it, but you won't have it until Monday morning. Can you figure things out until then? I can get your doctor to call you in a couple of pills somewhere local to you, so you should be able to get those tonight, if a pharmacy is open wherever you are."

"I'm in Kismet Beach, Florida. And, yes, that all works great. Thank you, Astrid."

"Of course. If you think of anything else, just call or text me. And feel free to do the same if anything else happens that's noteworthy."

I laugh. "I'm pretty sure he's ruled out anything *noteworthy* from happening. But I might have a little fun torturing him back since he left me without saying goodbye."

"That's my girl!"

"Goodbye, Astrid."

"Goodbye, Bianca."

I end the call just as the garage door opens. Foxx walks in, looking a little worse for wear. His shirt is slightly askew, and his forehead is marred with lines like he's been in deep thought.

My brows pull together. "Are you all right?"

He runs his hand through his already-mussed hair and sighs. He stares at me for a moment, and I think that he might answer me.

But he doesn't.

"Did you get your calls made?" he asks.

I start to point out that he's ignoring my questions *again* but stop short of opening my mouth. Something tells me now isn't the time to screw with him.

"I did," I say.

He nods. "Okay. Do you want to run to the store and pick up a few things?"

I don't. I want to sit here and look at him, wait for him to remember that I'm not his enemy. I'm not someone who is happy staying on the other side of the wall he's built around himself. That at one point a few months ago, things between us were … special.

At least, to me. *He walked away as if there was nothing between us at all.* I frown. *Maybe I need to adjust my thinking, too.*

"Yeah, I'm ready," I say instead.

He holds the door open for me, and I walk out of the house.

# CHAPTER 6
## *Bianca*

"What's wrong?" Foxx asks, grabbing a shopping cart at the front of the store.

"What do you mean?"

"You're looking around like you've never been in a grocery store before."

I wait for him to untangle the cart from the others and join me before I answer. Finally, he frees the buggy—not without more than a few profanities muttered under his breath—and meets me at the apples.

"I don't know the last time I was in a grocery store," I say, falling in step with him. "It's the little things in life that you don't realize you've missed so much until you do them again."

"Do you remember how to do this? Or do you need a refresher?"

I bump him with my shoulder. "Are you being cheeky, Mr. Carmichael?"

He tries to appear unamused, but there's the faintest twinkle in his eyes. *Thank God.*

The ride to the store was quiet. Foxx seemed preoccupied—somber but not grumpy. He glanced at me over his shoulder now and then, his brows pulled together. I didn't push or crack a joke. I just sat still, giving him a small smile when I caught his eye and gave him room to work out whatever was going through his head.

By the time we pulled into the parking lot, his shoulders were much more relaxed. The lines around his eyes had lessened. And he'd stopped clenching the steering wheel so hard that I could see the whites of his knuckles.

I want to ask what was bothering him. But, knowing Foxx, he would just retreat further inside himself.

I pick up a bundle of bananas and put them into the cart. "I've been having groceries delivered or having Astrid pick things up for me. And I've been ordering out a lot—too much, really."

"Have you been taking care of yourself?"

"What do you mean?"

He reaches for a bin of blueberries. "You know what I mean."

"No, I don't."

He adds the berries to the cart and exhales.

"What do you mean, Foxx?"

We move lazily down the aisle. I'm curious about what he has to say. *What does he know about me taking care of myself?* He hasn't been around in months. He has no idea what my life looks like now.

"I know you've had a lot on your plate lately," he says carefully. "The stress. The pressure. Not wanting to let your family down and thinking it all rides on you to some extent."

*Well, you nailed that.* I grab the edge of the cart handle, refusing to look at him.

"I wonder if you've been getting enough sleep. If you've had Troy or whoever is with you, stop to get you a cheeseburger and milkshake sometimes."

His voice is steady, but his tone is soft. It's as if he doesn't want anyone to hear him besides me.

I watch him choose a pack of hamburger meat from the cooler and wonder if he's thought about me before now. *Has he wondered how I was doing? Has he worried about me?* The thought makes me grin.

"What?" he asks, dropping the meat next to the berries.

"Actually, Calvin has been really sweet with me," I say, enjoying how his jaw pulses at the information. *I see you, Foxx.* "I feel really comfortable around him."

"You do, huh?"

"Yeah. I asked Jason to make Calvin the lead on my detail," I lie. "I feel like he really understands me and my needs, you know?"

He hums. The sound tumbles across my skin, landing in my core.

"Hey, wait," I say, turning back to the personal care aisle. "I need a few things down here."

He's stewing behind me. His discontent hits me full force, rippling off him in waves and pounding my back. I'm glad he can't see my face. I wouldn't want him to see my grin.

I take a package of razors, a bottle of face wash, and a toothbrush off the shelves. It takes a second to find a decent moisturizer, but I finally locate one on the top shelf.

"Astrid is sending me a few things on Monday," I say, dumping the items into the cart. "But this will get me through until then. Except for clothes. Is there a place to grab a few things in town?"

"No." He sighs. "We'd have to go to Breakwater for that, but the shops there are probably closed by now."

I look at my phone. "At seven o'clock on a Saturday?"

"This isn't Nashville, sweetheart."

My gaze flips to his. I'm all too pleased with myself. "Sweetheart, huh?"

"It's an informal term of address."

"It's also a term of endearment," I say, even though I'm aware he didn't mean it like that. Still, it's fun to watch him squirm.

He pushes the cart by me. "Maybe for some people."

"For a lot of people," I say, catching up with him. "I would even venture to say that it's used more as a term of endearment than an informal term of address or whatever you said."

"I think we've established that I'm not like a lot of people."

"You're not like a lot of people, or you don't like a lot of people?"

He reaches for a bag of granola. "Both."

"That was the hardest part about working with you," I say as we continue through the store. "But Calvin, on the other hand—"

"Say another word about Calvin, and I'll ensure he never works with you again."

He stops abruptly, causing a woman to nearly ram her cart into us. Foxx doesn't bother to acknowledge her. His focus is on *me*.

My body tingles as I search his narrowed eyes. He lifts his chin, warning me to back off.

He should know me better than that by now.

"I love that you think you have any say whatsoever about who I work with," I say, grinning like he's not getting to me. "The only control you have over that is when you walked away."

His nostrils flare. "Let's not do this here."

"Oh, so we'll do it later." I wink at him, only to wind him up a bit more. "I mean talk. Not … *it*."

We have a stand-off next to the crumb cakes. I'm not sure which of us is going to break first. Just as I think he's going to give in, a woman with a name tag hanging from her chest walks by.

"Here to pick up another key, Foxx?" she asks, laughing.

He looks up, glaring at her.

She keeps walking without breaking stride. "Have a good evening."

"A key?" I ask.

He heaves a breath and pushes the cart once again. "Don't ask."

"I already did."

"My keys have been coming up all over town," he says.

"Really? That seems out of character for you."

He side-eyes me. "That's because I didn't lose them."

*Huh*? "So someone is stealing your keys and dropping them at the grocery store? That doesn't make any sense."

"Because that's not what's happening."

He adds a gallon of milk and Greek yogurt to the basket. I toss a package of imitation cheese slices into the mix.

"I'm trying really hard to follow you on this, but I'm lost," I say. "Your keys have been coming up all over town, but you aren't losing them, and no one is stealing them. What am I missing?"

"Someone is fucking with me. They have labels on them just like the ones I use."

"You label your keys?" I flinch. "Of course, you label your keys. It's you. Sorry. Continue with your story."

He shakes his head. "*Anyway*, instead of being numbered as my keys are, they have my phone number on them."

"But they're not your keys?"

"No. They're not my keys."

"Did you try them in your locks?"

He sighs, exasperated. "Yes, I tried them in my locks. Do you have any other bright ideas?"

"I don't know. Give me a minute. I'm still mulling this over."

He rolls his eyes.

I point my finger at him. "I'll figure this out."

"I won't hold my breath."

"Ye of little faith." I pull my phone out of my pocket. "Oh, perfect timing."

> 555-555-5555: Bianca, 1 rx has been filled at
> MILLER'S PHARMACY AND WELLNESS.
> Please call 555-555-5555 with any questions.

"Where is Miller's Pharmacy?" I ask, sliding my phone back into my pocket.

"Here. Why?"

"I need to pick up a prescription."

"It's at the front of the store. We can grab it on the way out," he says.

"Perfect. Now, back to the keys—do we have any suspects?"

He turns the corner into the ice cream aisle. I smile when he reaches for the vanilla ice cream. I want to call him out and ask him if it's for milkshakes, but I don't. I'll let him surprise me later.

*I hope.*

"Are we thinking it's Banks?" I ask.

"That's the obvious answer. But, no, I don't think it's him."

"Why?"

"Gut reaction." He stops at the end cap. "Regular chocolate syrup or dark?"

"Regular. Why does your gut say it's not Banks?"

He drops the bottle in the cart. "Because this is a long game. Whoever is doing this didn't expect to get a quick reaction. This has continued for over a month now, and I don't think Banks has that much patience. He likes instant gratification."

"Don't we all?"

He ignores me. "There's something I'm missing with this. I just can't figure it out, and it's driving me crazy."

"Who are the other suspects?"

"This isn't something you can solve in the middle of Miller's," he says, chuckling.

"You don't know what I can do. I listen to true crime podcasts while I run on the treadmill in the mornings. I know all kinds of tips and tricks about how to solve crimes."

Foxx slows the cart and faces me with one hand on the cart. "When did you start running on the treadmill?"

I stare up at him. *After you left to cope with the sting of rejection.*

"We can't forget hamburger buns," I say.

"You didn't answer my question."

I shrug, scooting him out of the way and pushing the cart myself.

"Oh, I see what you're doing," he says, amused.

"What am I doing?" I look at him over my shoulder. "Am I Foxx-ing you?"

*"When did you start running on the treadmill, Bianca?"*

"Do you have Dijon mustard?"

His lips twitch. "Bianca ..."

I shrug, grinning. "I'll take that as a no." Then I pivot down the condiments.

He's no more than a few feet behind me. I can feel him matching me step for step. My palms sweat against the handle, and my heart pounds harder the deeper we go into the mustards.

My body sings, happily reverting to muscle memory and how it used to be with Foxx. The easiness. The push and pull. The only place in my life where I felt truly safe.

"Here it is," I say, grabbing a random bottle off the shelf. I toss it in the basket. "Do we need anything else?"

I turn to find him standing beside me, his hands shoved in his pockets. His face is unreadable, a mixture of annoyance and amusement. *God, how I want to kiss it right off him.*

"When did you start running on the treadmill?"

"What does it matter?"

His tongue swipes across his bottom lip. "Please answer me."

I want to bury my head in his chest and have him hold me tight against him. I want something from him that I can't have—that I'll never have.

Because he values Jason more than he wants me.

*So what does it matter if I'm honest with him or not?* It won't change anything either way. And it's not like he doesn't know I want him, just like I know a part of him wants me, too.

*Fuck it.*

"I started running a few days after Calvin showed up," I say, standing tall. "I needed a way to cope with my life that didn't involve my family."

He takes a half step closer to me.

"And, as you know, I have no friends who aren't on my payroll," I say.

Foxx's eyes darken as he searches mine.

"And the one person I trusted, although he was on my payroll, left me because we almost kissed one night."

The words barely escape my mouth. My throat burns, and my mouth is dry. I swallow hard to try to relieve some of the discomfort.

"Is that why you think I left, Bianca?"

My chest constricts, and a well of tears, which I didn't know were in me, threatens to spill over my lids. *What the hell?*

I don't cry. I especially don't cry over men, and I *absolutely* don't do it in public.

And I damn well will not do it in front of Foxx Carmichael in the middle of his hometown grocery store.

"I have to get my prescription before I forget it," I say, stepping around him. "Don't forget the buns."

*"Bianca."*

I jet to the front of the store without looking back.

It won't matter if I turn around.

But it *will* matter if I *don't* turn around because then, at least, I can maintain a little bit of dignity.

# CHAPTER 7
## *Bianca*



"THAT WAS DELICIOUS, FOXX."

He rests back in his chair across the table from me, tossing his napkin next to his empty plate. Moonlight streams through the window, casting moody shadows across his face. It's fitting. The vibes this evening since our return from Miller's have been moody, too.

Foxx started dinner while I sat in his office and made a few calls. They could've waited until tomorrow, but I thought we needed some space apart. The ride home was fine. To his credit, Foxx attempted idle chitchat. It's the one thing I've found that he truly cannot do well. And, considering the plaques and awards hanging behind his office door, it seems as though it might be the only thing in the world he doesn't do well. By the time I finished my calls with Gannon, Mom, and a quick check-in with Astrid, dinner was ready.

He lifts his wineglass, studying me like he has most of the meal. We managed to keep things superficial and polite. But I think the stress of walking around the elephant in the room is wearing on him as much as it is on me.

"I'm glad you enjoyed it," he says.

A dollop of mustard is all that's left of the cheeseburger and sweet potato fries. I want, *need*, to acknowledge that he cooked my favorite meal for dinner. It wasn't accidental. *But how do I do it without making him clam up and ruining the progress we've made?*

*How do I move us beyond this awkwardness?*

I sit back, too. "It was probably even better than the burgers that Calvin makes for me."

*Bingo.*

He takes a long drink, watching me over the brim of his glass. The intensity of his stare sends a chill down my spine.

"I hope you enjoyed Calvin's burgers because you'll never have them again," he says, setting his glass down with a thud.

"I love that you think you have a say in it."

He lifts one brow. It says more than words ever could, yet at the same time, it says nothing at all.

"Calvin has never made me a burger," I say, standing. I gather our plates and carry them into the kitchen. "I was just winding you up. But I am curious about something."

He hums, carrying our glasses to the island.

"Why do you care?" I ask.

The question hangs heavily in the room. It sits on us like a heavy fog as we work silently together to tidy up dinner.

He takes so long to answer that I'm not sure he'll even dignify the question with a response. When he speaks, it makes me jump.

"Calvin isn't there to make you dinner."

That's it. That's the response.

I look at Foxx over my shoulder. "You weren't there to make me dinner either. But it didn't stop you."

"But I had the wisdom to step back."

I drop the plate in the sink and turn to face him head-on. "So that's why you left? Because you were doing too much for me?"

"Stop it, Bianca."

"Stop what?"

He runs a hand through his hair, refusing to make eye contact.

My heart pounds as I watch him fight whatever he wants to say. I hate this about him. I hate that he won't just speak from the heart. He refuses to speak the truth.

"You know, I don't want to tiptoe around this for the next couple of days," I say, my chest pinching. "So we can either resolve my questions, or we can fight about it, and I can go to Vegas whether you like it or not."

His hand falls to his side. "What questions can you possibly have?"

"There's a list."

"Fine." His jaw flexes. "Then you'll answer mine, as well."

"I'm an open book, baby."

He snorts. "Great. I'll start."

Instantly, I regret being so cocky.

"Have you been taking care of yourself?" he asks, squaring his shoulders to mine.

He looks down at me with ferociousness wrapped in a tenderness that takes my wits and tosses them to the wind. I don't know which to grab on to, which side he means more. I also don't know why in the hell he cares.

"We already discussed this," I say.

"You didn't answer me."

"Oh, *that's rich*."

"Answer the question, Bianca."

"*Fine*." I mimic the look he's giving me, knowing all too well that it's falling flat on its face. "Yes, Foxx. I have been taking care of myself. I have been doing the best I can while working twelve to fourteen-hour days, uncovering illegal and damaging deals that my father engaged in before he left and trying to minimize those. All the while, being a daughter to my mother, a sister to my brothers, and a human who takes showers and brushes her teeth." I narrow my eyes. "I'm doing great. Thanks for asking."

"Funny. I didn't ask a damn thing about work."

My brows pull together. "What are you talking about? You asked me if I'm taking care of myself, and I answered you."

"You just gave me a laundry list of shit that you have to do, but never once did you tell me how you are taking care of *you*."

I blink.

He takes a step toward me. "You're putting in long hours—for whom? You're—"

"That's my job."

"—fixing your dad's fuckups—"

"To save the company, Foxx."

"—and you're supporting your mom and your brothers." He takes another step my way, his chest rising and falling like he's run a mile. "But who is taking care of *you*?"

My breath trembles as he approaches me. Every cell in my body is on high alert. I can't process his question because the look on his face—the severity, the agitation, *the anger*?—demands attention. *He* demands attention.

I suck in a lungful of air and hold it. He stops moving inches in front of me.

"For two and a half years, I watched you kill yourself for everyone around you," he says, the words filled with grit. "You're brilliant, Bianca. Strong. You've never met a challenge you can't conquer."

"*Except you.*"

His blue eyes flash, melding into green. "That works both ways."

I lean back until my back presses against the counter. Foxx matches every move, maintaining the small distance between us. My head spins as I try to make sense of his words. *Of his actions.*

*Why is this so important to him? Why does he insist on sliding into my personal space when I thought he wanted distance?*

"Your relationship with everyone in your life is based on the fact that they need you or want something from you," he says, lowering his voice.

"Not true."

"And you keep giving, feeding your magic to better their lives while never bettering your own."

"That's *not true*." *It's absolutely true.*

"And you're so damn good at it that I wonder if they even realize what's happening. You make it look so easy," he says. "But, my God, Bianca, how long can you do that before you break?"

I lift my chin. "I'll never break."

"*Everything* breaks."

There's a lot to unpack in this conversation. There are a lot of truths that I have no interest in uncovering in front of Foxx. So I divert.

"My turn," I say.

He smirks, knowing exactly what I'm doing. But I don't care.

"Why did you leave me?" I ask.

His smirk fades away.

"Is it because you were doing too much for me?" I ask, unable to keep the frustration out of my voice.

"No."

"Was it because we almost kissed?"

"No."

I cross my arms over my chest, my gaze unwavering. "Was it because you actually—probably accidentally—opened up to me the tiniest bit?"

"No, Bianca."

I pause and wait for an explanation that, unsurprisingly, doesn't come.

"This is the part where you elaborate," I say, talking slowly as if I'm talking to a toddler. "This is where you set the record straight and explain yourself."

"You really don't know?"

I throw my hands up, almost smacking him in the face. He leans back just in time.

"*No, I really don't know.* Do you think I'd keep asking if I knew?" I ask, realizing I'm trapped in the bend of the counter. I press my hands to his chest to guide him out of my way, only to realize that touching him is a very, *very* bad idea.

A shot of fire races through my veins as my eyes connect with his. I gasp, my lips part, as I watch him absorb the connection as forcefully as I do.

His irises burn so green that they're nearly yellow.

He takes a half step toward me. I try to move a step back but am stopped by the stone countertop. He moves again, even closer—so close that the fabric of our clothes dust each other.

The air is filled with the woodiness of his cologne. My fingers dip into the cotton of his shirt, skimming his hard chest beneath it. He breathes shallowly but roughly, and every breath he takes causes my heart to strum faster.

My tongue swipes across my bottom lip. His attention drops to my mouth. He widens his stance, caging my feet in with his, before returning his gaze to my eyes.

"*This*." He bends, gripping the counter with both hands.

I'm confined, fenced in by both his arms and legs. It's heady and intoxicating—dangerous and foolish.

And I'm just dumb enough and brave enough to do something I know I'll regret.

I wad his shirt in my hand and give it a gentle tug. His eyes sparkle as he's jostled another inch closer.

My insides buzz—deliciously zinging from the close contact and proximity to the man I can't stop thinking about.

"I didn't leave because I almost kissed you." His tone is rough and raw, scraping against my emotions. "I've stopped myself from kissing you every day I've been near you." He licks his lips, his gaze dropping to mine. "It's taken every ounce of control I can manage not to kiss you, fuck you, make love to you, and everything between for three years."

"*Foxx* …"

My knees weaken. My stomach drops. The bottom of my belly burns with a need for him that scalds me.

"I left because I couldn't stand by and watch another man get to have you," he says.

I flinch. "What are you talking about?"

His eyes narrow, and his shoulders stiffen. "*Quade Kellaway.*"

"Renn's old teammate from Australia?"

I have no idea what he's talking about. *Why would he bring up Quade? Where the heck is he going with this?* I let go of Foxx's shirt.

"He came over that night, remember?" Foxx asks, staring a hole through me. "His arrival is what interrupted us."

I scramble to remember. "Yeah. Maybe." I think back. "Okay, yes, I remember that. He had been over earlier that afternoon with Renn and left his passport on the table."

"I had to go let that motherfucker in, and he was all too happy to tell me about how you called him earlier that day, and he was coming by to fuck you before he went home."

A laugh falls from my lips quickly—too quickly. Foxx is not entertained.

"I'm not laughing," he says.

"Well, you should be, and if you believed him, you should be laughing at yourself."

He stills before pushing away from the counter ... and me.

I heave in a breath as Foxx walks away, circling the island with his hands behind his head.

"You seriously thought I was going to have sex with Quade Kellaway?" I laugh, the thought so funny that it's a relief.

While Quade is quite good-looking and has charisma in spades, I've never been interested in him. And that probably has something to do with the man pacing in front of me. I haven't been interested in anyone, despite trying to distract myself with my hot, new neighbor—and failing—since Foxx walked into my life.

"You did, though, didn't you?" I ask.

He turns the corner and faces me. His hands drop to his sides. "Yeah. I did."

"*Foxx.*"

"I watched him walk inside your house with that cocky fucking swagger of his and convinced myself that I had no right to piece that fucker apart."

That should not be hot ... *but it is*.

I move across the kitchen and stand in front of him. "So what you're saying is that you didn't quit because we almost kissed. You quit because you thought someone else was kissing me."

"Yes."

"Well, not that it's any of your business, but I didn't kiss Quade that night or any other night." I smirk. "He's not my type. Unfortunately, rugby players remind me of Renn, and I just can't get into it."

Foxx's shoulders fall. He almost smiles.

"I'm so happy to know I've spent the past six months thinking you hate me when, instead, you were just jealous."

The corner of his lip lifts. He tries so hard not to let the other follow suit.

My grin slides into a full smile. "I usually hate jealousy." I take a step back, and he takes one toward me. "But, my God, it looks good on you."

He cages me in again. This time, he leans toward me.

"But everything looks good on you," I say, touching his cheek.

He leans into my palm, his long lashes shutting briefly. The lines are gone from his face, and the tension in his body floats away. It's a quick, precious moment that records in my heart as a core memory.

"What would've happened if Quade hadn't shown up that night?" I whisper.

He raises his head and opens his eyes. A war is taking place inside them—a battle I don't understand.

His attention flickers to my lips, and I think he's *finally* going to kiss me.

I drag my hand across his jaw, down the side of his neck, and across his muscled shoulders. He doesn't pull away and doesn't object.

He lowers his lips. I lift on my toes, raising my arms to encircle his neck, when his phone rings on the table.

*Oof.*

Foxx stands tall, shaking his head as if coming out of a trance. I fall against the cold counter and drag in a hasty breath.

He turns and leaves me … *stunned.*

My emotions swirl, going from turned on, to confused, to excited, to *desperate.*

"Foxx …" There's more need, more want, more pleading in my tone than I care to acknowledge.

My heart races just as quickly as my head, leaving me loopy and frantic.

He strolls across the floor like the composed, untouchable Foxx Carmichael that he is with everyone else. *How can he be so calm and cool now?*

*"I watched him walk inside your house with that cocky fucking swagger of his and convinced myself that I had no right to piece that fucker apart."*

My eyes fall closed for the briefest moment.

*He'll come back. He'll need to discuss this as much as I do. How could he not?*

*Just breathe.*

Foxx grabs his phone and looks at the screen and then at me. Lines mar his forehead.

I force a swallow down my throat.

"We can't do this, Bianca. And it has nothing to do with you."

*What the hell?*

I shove away from the counter, my jaw hitting the floor. My face is hot—my temper even hotter.

"What do you mean, *we can't do this, and it has nothing to do with you*? What the fuck is that supposed to mean?" I ask, staring at him in disbelief.

"I have to take this call," he says, heading for the door.

I pick up my jaw, my teeth clenching so hard they hurt. There's no way he's ghosting me. Not again.

"Tell me you're kidding me right now," I say, barely able to get the words out.

He pauses in the doorway. "There's nothing left to discuss."

"You think you're going to stand here and tell me all that and then walk out?" I laugh angrily. "*Again?*"

He takes a long, deep breath. I expect him to slide his phone in his pocket and return to me. But he doesn't move—not toward me, anyway.

"I'll put something for you to sleep in on the counter in the guest bathroom," he says, resolute.

"Don't bother."

The phone stops, then begins to ring all over again. Irritation flashes through his eyes, but I'm not sure if it's because of me, the call, or both.

"What's that supposed to mean?" he asks.

I can see it in his eyes—he's locked me out. Only, this time, he can't call off the job because he's home. I'm the one in his space. Regret is painted all over his face. *Fuck you, Foxx.*

"Your phone is ringing," I say, glaring at him.

He looks at the screen again, then back to me.

The world pauses—it stops spinning on its axis—as I await his reaction. Internally, I beg him not to leave. *I beg him to stay.* But externally, I'm not about to give him that satisfaction.

He sighs and walks out of the kitchen.

Tears fill my eyes out of rage … and pain. *Fuck. You. Foxx.*

I listen as his footsteps fall down the hallway and then as a door clicks shut.

My lungs strain for air. My heart squeezes tight. My brain sorts as fast as it can through everything that just happened.

And everything that didn't.

And everything that won't.

I grab my phone off the counter, find the number I'm looking for, and hit the green button.

*You want me to take care of myself? Will do.*

# CHAPTER 8

## *Bianca*

> Astrid: The car is 10 minutes away.

> Me: Thanks.

> Astrid: Let me know when you're at the airport.

> Me: I will.

> Astrid: I would feel a lot better if you let me loop Landry Security in on the plan.

> Me: Absolutely not.

I find my purse on the counter and fish out the auction receipt. *At least it was for charity.* I leave it beneath the Dijon mustard, finding some satisfaction that I won't have to think or say that charity line again.

The house is still as I pull open the front door and shut it softly behind me. Balmy air kisses my skin, but I shiver, nonetheless. *This day has been so messed up.* I just want to go home, climb in my own bed, and sleep until I've forgotten this happened.

*Who does Foxx think he is, ghosting me every time he gets uncomfortable?* I scoff. He thinks he can preach to me to take care of myself—act like he's worried that I'm not in a good place—and then turn around and dismiss me like I'm inconsequential. He acts like he knows me so well. He doesn't know me that well at all, or else he would know I'm not putting up with this bullshit.

"Well, hello." A voice off the side of the deck makes me jump. "Easy, there. I'm Kixx, Foxx's dad."

My heart thunders, and I grip the railing for dear life.

Kixx steps out of the shadows and into the light from Foxx's porch. *Oh, the genes in this family are strong.*

From the striking resemblance, I could've picked this man out of a lineup as Foxx's father. The same build—broad shoulders, strong arms, sharp bone structure. Heavy brows. Adorable yet sexy grin.

He rests his forearms over the railing on the other side of the porch, careful to keep a respectful distance.

"I didn't mean to scare you," he says. "I was taking out the trash and discovered that my grandchickens shit all over the concrete slab where I keep the waste containers. Had to clean that up." He makes a face. "They're almost as bad as Banks."

I grin. *Banks again? This guy must be a handful.* I want to ask him about him, but considering I'm pissed at one of his other children and don't want the conversation to venture in that direction, I leave it alone.

"Grandchickens?" I ask instead.

"It was probably Rita. She just laid her very first egg this week and thinks she's big stuff."

I laugh softly. *Why can't Foxx be this easygoing?*

"Where's Foxx?" he asks, his brows pulled together like his son's do when he's curious.

"Oh, he's inside taking a call. I'm just waiting for my car."

"Do you need a ride somewhere?" He jabs his thumb over his shoulder. "I can get Damaris, that's my wife, and we can give you a ride somewhere. But be warned, she listens to nineties country music in the car and really feels herself when Lorrie Morgan comes on."

"No," I say, returning his smile. "But thank you. I've already called for someone to pick me up."

He shrugs like it's no big deal either way. "You're Jason Brewer's sister, aren't you?"

"Yes. How did you know that?"

"I saw you with him at the auction earlier today. When you bid an astronomical amount for a date with my son." He smirks. "Was that what was happening here—your date? Because I sure as hell hope I taught my son how to date a woman properly."

My insides twist. "Oh, no. No date. And it was more of a charitable donation than anything. We—"

"What's going on out here?" The porch shakes as Foxx steps out onto it.

Clearly, he's talking to me. Obviously, I'm ignoring him.

Kixx glances at us, quickly assessing the situation. "Oh, I was just doing my chores and thought I'd—"

"Not you, Dad."

"Oh."

"Why don't you come inside, Bianca?" Foxx asks, his words sharp.

I smile as brightly as I can. "That's okay. My car should be pulling up soon, so I'll just wait out here."

Kixx holds his hands in front of him. "Kids, I think I'm going to go. It was very nice to meet you, Bianca."

"You, too, Kixx. Enjoy your grandchickens."

He chuckles. "I will. Be safe in your travels."

"I will."

Kixx slips into the shadows. As soon as he's out of sight, my annoyance with his son slips right back over me.

"You don't need to wait out here with me," I say, turning to the road. "I can do this alone."

His energy slams into me from behind. "What are you doing?"

"All right. I'll rephrase. Leave me the fuck alone."

"All right. I'll rephrase. *Get back inside the fucking house.*"

*Oh no, you don't …*

A set of headlights shine up the road.

"That's my ride," I say, glaring at him over my shoulder. "I can't do this, and it has everything to do with you."

He glares back at me, his facial features severe in the low light. His temple pulses as he works his jaw back and forth. "Who is in the car?"

"That's really none of your business."

"I'm going to ask you one more time."

"You can ask me a dozen more times for all I care."

Foxx's brows shoot to the sky. "Excuse me?"

"You're excused."

I turn to leave, but he spins me around to face him.

A small gasp spills from my lips. I'm not sure if it's from him touching me or the redirection, but my blood pressure skyrockets. I grip the railing for support.

"You aren't getting in that car," he says, peering down at me.

"Bet me."

"Let's not forget the reason you're here."

I narrow my eyes even more. "Cool. But let's not forget the reason I'm leaving, either."

The car pulls to a stop at the end of the driveway. I give the driver a gesture to wait a moment.

"You are *not* getting in that car," Foxx says, his voice icy.

I fire him the most hateful look I can manage and pivot. But I don't even get one step to the stairs when Foxx steps in front of me.

"*Move*," I say.

"Over my dead body."

"Keep standing in my way, and we can make that happen."

He wants to smile.

"*Stop this*," I say, my tone as close to a growl as I've ever heard it.

Sweat dots the back of my neck, and I yank my hand away from his. But I don't step back. That's what he wants me to do.

"I don't know why you think it's acceptable to do this to me, but it's not," I say. "And I find it incredibly ironic that you just gave me a lecture about taking care of myself and then fuck with my head in the very next breath." I lean away from him. "I'm taking *your advice* and doing something good for me—and I'm leaving."

He cuts me off again. "You can either turn your ass around and walk back inside, or I'll pick you up and carry you."

"*You wouldn't dare.*"

"Is that a bet you really want to take?"

A horn echoes through the small neighborhood, making me jump.

"In the house. *Now*," he says, eerily calm.

"Foxx—"

"Someone out there wants to hurt you, Bianca. Now, get in the fucking house."

His tone is not to be messed with. But I am not either.

"There's someone in front of me that apparently wants to hurt me, too," I say, keeping my eyes glued to his. "Considering I know how badly it'll feel when this person does it, I'll take my chances on the other. I—*ah!*"

I'm swept off my feet and tossed over Foxx's shoulder in one fluid movement. He holds me down with one arm over the backs of my legs and the other pressed just above my ass.

"Put me down!" I yell, smacking his back.

He doesn't flinch. He doesn't react at all.

My purse dangles from my fingertips as I try to kick my feet. He's too strong, too determined. I simply can't move.

"Hey, lady! Are you ready or not?" The driver sticks his head out of the window. "I'm not sitting here all night, ya know."

"Sorry about that," Foxx tells him. "She changed her mind."

"Foxx, you better put me down right now ..." I say through clenched teeth.

"She's still paying a pick-up fee," the driver shouts.

Foxx waves at him. "Sounds good. Charge her double for the inconvenience."

"*Damn you, Foxx.*"

He swats my backside with a *pop!* "Have a good night."

I'm not sure if he's talking to me or the driver. Either way, the contact sends a ripple coursing the short distance from where his hand landed to my core.

My face is hot as blood pools in my head.

We spin around, my hair trailing behind us in a half circle. He carries me the short distance across the porch and then through the doorway.

His grip eases, and I slide slowly, *painfully slow*, down his front. My heart beats so hard that I wonder if he can feel it against his chest. He peers down at me with eyes so wild that it takes the rant right off the tip of my tongue.

I pant, unable to get my thoughts and emotions in order.

"Don't make me do that again," he says.

And that's it. I'm me again.

I take a massive step back. "I think you've forgotten who you're talking to, pal."

He presses his lips together—essentially making fun of me. "Okay."

*The audacity.* "What is this, Foxx? *Huh*? Are you trying to prove some point? Are you some kind of a masochist who enjoys thinking you emotionally dominate me?"

He recoils.

"If that's what this is—"

"Of course, that's not what this is. Who do you think I am?" he asks.

If I thought he actually had emotions, I might think his feelings were hurt. And if he hadn't just hurt mine, I might also care.

"Good question. I don't know who you are because you won't be honest with me. You won't let me in." I laugh angrily. "But don't worry. I know it's not about me."

He lifts his face to the ceiling and groans.

My breathing is so quick, so hot, that I have to work to control it. Losing my temper isn't going to help anything. It won't find me a way out of here.

I take a long, paced influx of air and exhale evenly.

It doesn't help.

"The way I see it, we have a few problems here," I say, dropping my bag to the floor.

He dips his chin until we're eye to eye.

"You don't actually want me around," I say, biting back the bitterness of the words. Instead of spewing them, I use them to fuel my rage

—the rage flooding me so completely that my hands shake. "But then you volunteer—actually, you demand to have me here, although I have other options."

He rolls his tongue around his lips.

"Then you get me here and proceed to fuck with me," I say, instinctively moving toward him. "You screw with my head like it's some kind of deluded game to you."

"It's not, Bianca."

"You tell me to take care of myself, and when I try to do that— when I try to get away from you—you hold me hostage."

He stiffens. "That's not what this is."

*"The hell that's not what this is."* I glare at him. "But why? Why don't you just let me leave? If you care so much about Jason—because you obviously don't care about me—then let me call someone else. I'll call Troy or Renn or Ford Landry or Calvin—*oof.*"

His mouth crashes against mine.

My knees buckle. He slides his arm around the small of my back and hauls me into him *where I melt.*

Anger and frustration—the force of denial and restraint snaps and flows into the way his lips press against mine.

His hands cup my cheeks, and he holds me still like there's a chance in hell I'm going to pull away.

I can't pull away. I can't believe this is happening. I can't do anything but stand in place while he deepens the kiss … and then breaks it.

*Everything breaks.*

His eyes search mine as I wobble on my feet. He drops his hands slowly, watching me carefully as I back up.

*Oh my God.*

Flames lick outwards from my core. Explosions rattle off in my head. I struggle to breathe and to remember how we got here. To Foxx kissing me.

*Oh. My. God.*

I touch my lips with my fingertips, composing myself as quickly as possible. As fast as I get myself together, he slips away from me.

"What was that?" I ask, almost afraid to hear the answer. A part of me expects another bullshit response, and I don't know how I'll react if he pulls a stunt like that again.

His chest rises and falls. For the first time since I met him, the shield between us is completely gone.

*There he is. The man I considered my friend. The kind, thoughtful Foxx.* I grin. *And he gave me the best kiss of my life.*

"That was what I think about every minute of every fucking day," he says. "Not an hour goes by that I don't think about you—about kissing you, listening to you laugh, seeing your smile. About holding you, making you dinner, running you a bath with the little bomb things you love so much."

Tears gather in the corners of my eyes.

"I think about lying beside you and listening to you tell me about your day. I imagine making love to you, fucking you—being so damn deep inside you that it's impossible to tell where you end and I begin."

My fingers itch to reach for him, to offer him a reminder that I'm here. But a hesitation in his honesty holds me back.

He smiles sadly. "But that's not possible. I know that, except it's so hard to accept it. And when Jason said you might be in danger, and I watch as Landry Security doesn't send anyone ..." He wipes a hand down his face and exhales. "I can't trust you with them." He swallows. "But I can't trust you with me, either."

"Why not?"

He looks at the floor.

"Why not, Foxx? Just tell me. Let's get this out in the open now so we can move on."

He nods, lifting his gaze to me once again.

My breath stills in my chest. I almost want to tell him not to speak —not to answer me. Because if the tightness in my stomach means anything, and it usually does, I might not want to know after all.

"I met your brother years ago when we were both working for Fenton Abbott," he says. "We were on an operation together in Africa, rescuing a doctor who had been kidnapped by a terrorist organization."

I nod, remembering when that happened. We didn't know Jason was on the team that went into Zimbabwe until they had returned. It was a national story, although the media never broke the names of the contractors involved beyond Mr. Abbott.

Foxx clears his throat. "We landed the bird in front of this small compound. We'd been over this layout for a week, memorizing every wall, every door, every corner. We knew the plan frontward, backward, and inside out."

I shiver as I listen, the hollowness of his tone breaking my heart. Jason has never talked about this—not to me, anyway. And this is the most I've ever heard Foxx say. True, he was warmer with me and the tiniest bit more open with me, but he was never a talker. Not like this. I wonder if this is the first time he's shared this experience with anyone.

*Has he kept this bottled up for years?*

"So we get into position, and I remember thinking how much darker and quieter it was than I expected. Our intel said there were five guys on-site, and our target was on the third story of the center building." His words come faster. Clearer. It's almost as if he's reliving the moment. "It felt like a trap, but it was now or never. We came after this kid, and we weren't leaving without him. So we make it to the middle of the compound and start up the stairs. It was so fucking eerie."

"What happened?" I whisper.

He licks his lips. "We get to the top, and the doctor sits cross-legged in the center of the room. He sees us, jumps up, and starts shouting. But before we can figure out what the fuck he's saying, a door bursts open behind these drapes, and bullets start flying."

My heart drops to the floor. The tears that threatened earlier tumble down my cheeks.

"Fenton grabs the kid, shoving him toward the door. We're taking gunfire from behind us now, too. It was pure chaos ..." He closes his eyes and takes a deep breath.

"Foxx, you don't have to say anything else."

He looks at me. "I'm the last one out of the room. Completely out of ammo. Just as I put a boot on the steps to go down, a bullet grazes the side of my helmet from the top of one of the other buildings. Then hellfire follows. I'm pinned against this half wall, unable to fire back. The guys are back at the bird by now. How the fuck I got separated from them, I'll never know. But I look down and see Jason coming back."

My tears fall harder at the pain in his voice. Imagining my brother and Foxx in this position creates a fissure down the center of my chest. The ache is almost unbearable.

"I shout at him to go, to leave, to get the fuck out of there. I don't know if he has any bullets left or what his plan is. Because there's no way I'm getting out of there, all I can foresee is either he takes a hit on the way to me or gets stuck next to me. And there's no sense in us both dying."

I reach for his hand. Instead of letting me take his palm in mine and supporting him, he wraps his hand around mine.

"He had two bullets left," Foxx says, smiling to himself. "But he only needed one." He looks at me, the smile fading. "I owe your brother my life. He risked it all for me that night. He saved my mother from burying her son. And I will never forget that."

It all makes sense.

I give his hand a final squeeze and then let it go.

"Bianca, this is my fault."

"No, Foxx. It's not."

"I should've stopped this before it got to this point. But ... I couldn't."

I want to hug and hold him—to have him hold me. But I can't do that, and that's the problem.

My world slows. The fog of emotions begins to clear. Suddenly, I see his predicament clearly.

"There is nothing I want more than to be with you, Bianca. You're the first woman I've ever wanted like this. But if I get involved with you, that puts my entire career and friendship with Jason into question. My bias is compromised. I can't make good, rational decisions when I'm thinking about fucking you or wondering what someone else is doing with you. Bianca, if something happened to you, especially on my watch, because I wasn't focused ..." His face pales. "Jason ... your family ... would never forgive me. And I would never, ever forgive myself."

His last words are almost a whisper. But they roar through me, touching every last part of my heart.

*My God.* What a selfless, compassionate, amazing man.

The river of tears down my cheeks is hot. They taste like salt. But the real pain sits in the middle of my chest because this isn't fixable. And I understand and respect why.

I clear the cobwebs from my throat. "Can I stay here tonight? And we'll figure this out tomorrow."

"I don't want you to leave."

I smile at him. "I know you don't. But you know I have to. Unless you can come up with some brilliant plan to solve this impossible puzzle, I can't do this."

He nods without trying to reply. It's just as well. If his voice breaks like I think it might, I don't want to witness it.

"Thank you for being honest with me," I say.

I tuck my chin to my chest and head down the hallway.

He stands in the foyer and watches me go.

## CHAPTER 9

### Foxx

"Fuck this day already." I run my hand over my chin and look in the mirror. "Carmichael, you look like shit."

I don't know what I expected when I peered in the glass, but this is at least accurate of how I feel inside.

Dark eyes. Blotchy skin. A crack down the center of my bottom lip. My cheeks are dusted with stubble from not shaving, but I couldn't possibly care less. The only thing I care about is in a room across the hallway, probably mad as hell at me and making calls to get herself out of here.

And I can't blame her.

*"Can I stay here tonight? And we'll figure this out tomorrow."*

*"I don't want you to leave."*

*"I know you don't. But you know I have to. Unless you can come up with some brilliant plan to solve this impossible puzzle, I can't do this."*

I grip the counter and hang my head. "I'm trying, Bianca. I'm trying."

There's no obvious solution to this *impossible puzzle*. I signed a code of conduct with Landry Security when, at Jason's urging, I started working for them. I assured Jason that I would be there for him and his family—that he could count on me. That I wouldn't fail him just like he didn't fail me.

But in that code of conduct, I can't fraternize with the people I'm sworn to protect. And even if it wasn't written in black and white, it's unethical. How can you remain steadfast and unbiased, thinking clearly and logically, when you're in a relationship with someone? Of course, emotions would be involved, and in my field of work, emotions are dangerous. They're a weakness. I can't risk it.

I can't be the weak link.

I groan, picking up my phone beside the toothpaste.

Landry: Please have Bianca join us for the meeting if at all possible.

"Great."

I type back my response.

Me: I'll let her know.

I check the time before locking the screen. *We have ten minutes before it starts.*

I've put off leaving my bedroom because I know the countdown to her departure begins as soon as I see her. The thought of her walking out makes my heart beat out of control. If she leaves, she won't come back. It'll likely be the last time I see her without being in a room full of other people.

This will be it. And I'm not ready.

*Think. Figure out how to fix this. There's always a way.*

"Here goes nothing," I mutter, releasing a long sigh before opening the door.

"Wear a bell or something." Bianca slaps a hand to her chest and huffs out a breath. "You scared the crap out of me."

*Oh, holy fuck.*

My eyes nearly fall out of my head.

The T-shirt I left on the bathroom counter for her is the only thing covering her body. It hits mid-thigh, skimming her curves. Her nipples are hard, poking against the thin material, and I immediately get hard.

Her hair is piled on top of her head in a messy knot. Her face is bare and fresh. Sleep clings to the corners of her eyes. A soft pink line runs from her temple diagonal to just short of her lips, and I wonder what crease she slept against.

I'm glad she slept. I'm just pissed it wasn't with me. *That it will never be with me.*

She raises a cup of coffee and then continues to the guest room. "I didn't think you were up, or I would've gotten dressed."

"Hard not to be up when you haven't been to sleep."

Her steps stutter. She stops, pressing a hand against the wall, but doesn't turn around. "I didn't sleep well either."

Relief gushes from my lungs. It makes me a dick to be relieved she didn't sleep either, but I can't help it. It does.

"Landry sent me a text a few minutes ago and asked if you could join us for our meeting this morning," I say.

"When?"

"In about eight minutes."

Her shoulders fall. "I might as well. We need to figure out where I will go, anyway."

My heart falls, too.

"Let me get some clothes on, and I'll meet you … in your office?" she asks.

"Yeah."

She nods before disappearing into the bedroom.

I stomp down the hallway and into the kitchen. Every cabinet door I open is closed harder than necessary. I slam my finger against the button to start the coffee. I glug the creamer into the mug and accidentally add about triple the amount I like.

But fuck it. *Fuck it all.*

Every part of me screams not to go into my office. I fight myself every step of the way. This is going to be it—the last moments I'll probably ever see the woman who I'm certain will be the one that got away, and there's not a damn thing I can do about it.

My pity turns to frustration, which lends itself readily to anger. Anger at myself. *Anger at the world.*

I haul an extra chair around my desk, then sit in mine. Bianca comes in just as I find the email from Landry and click the button to join the meeting.

She gives me a measured smile, dropping into the seat next to me. She's still in my T-shirt. I think she's put a bra on, though. I'm not sure if she has pants on or not, and the possibility that she's sitting here with nothing beneath that shirt makes me crazy.

I'm acutely aware of everything about her. The natural, warm scent of her body. The softness of her knee as it brushes my hand. The determination in her eyes can't hide the disappointment that takes its place when she doesn't think I'm looking.

"Let's get this party started," she says quietly.

*Let's not.*

"Good morning," Ford Landry says.

Other boxes populate, and Jason and Gannon appear on the screen.

"Good morning," Bianca says.

*Oh yeah.* "Good morning."

She shifts in her chair. "Hey, guys. How is everything at home?"

Jason and Gannon sit side by side in the Brewer Air offices.

"It's going," Gannon says. "How are you?"

"I'm going." It's a joke, but she quickly realizes the truth she inadvertently admitted. Her smile melts off her face. "I'm fine. So what brings us together this morning?"

Landry coughs, picking up a sheet of paper. "I asked you to join us this morning, considering this meeting concerns you."

"I appreciate it, Ford."

"We got a piece of intel this morning," he says. "It seems your father is close with a man named Bobby Downing. Does that name ring a bell to you, Bianca?" Landry asks.

Bianca stills. "Close? I'm not sure I'd say they're close. But we have done business with him on several occasions. He assisted us with the purchase of the Tennessee Raptors hockey team years ago. Dad also called him when the purchase of the Arrows franchise got stuck in baseball red tape hell. Why? What's going on?"

*Yeah, what's going on?*

Her knee wiggles up and down—an expression of her worry. I reach over subtly and lay my palm on her thigh. She gasps but stills. Then slowly, she lays her hand on top of mine.

The weight of her palm and the heat of her bare skin send a burst of energy straight through me. This is what I'm not supposed to be doing. The fact that I want to do this is why we're here—it's why she's telling her brothers she wants to leave. And maybe that's why I got ballsy and touched her. Maybe it's because I know it'll be the last time I can.

Maybe. But it's definitely why I want to shut this computer off, take her in my arms, carry her to my bed, and never let her go. *Because even one taste of her is better than none.*

"When Dad inked the deal for both the Raptors and the Arrows, he put them in a trust," Jason says.

Bianca nods. "That's right."

Jason's eyes flip to mine. He doesn't need to say anything. *This is going to be bad.*

I give Bianca a gentle squeeze of reassurance and brace for whatever he's about to unload on us.

"There is an amendment to the trust that was inked six months ago," Jason says.

Her brows pull together. "I haven't seen an amendment."

"The legal team found it while they were readying the new trusts for all Brewer companies," Gannon says. "It's a good thing they insisted on it despite Dad losing interest. If they hadn't—if we had let the old trusts stand—we never would've discovered this."

"What does the amendment say?" Bianca asks.

Jason hesitates. "It says that on your twenty-seventh birthday, you become the sole beneficiary of the Brewer Sports Trust."

Bianca struggles to process this information. So do I, but I think it's for different reasons. She's wondering why her father favored her. I'm waiting for the other shoe to drop. Reid Brewer may be many things, but benevolent he is not.

"*Me?*" Bianca balks, obviously surprised. "That's not … that's not how it's set up. We're *all* the beneficiaries of Brewer Sports. We all inherit them equally."

Jason takes a deep breath and looks at Gannon.

Gannon leans forward. "The amendment goes on to read that if you're not married on your twenty-seventh birthday, three-quarters of Brewer Sports goes to Charlie Downing."

*That's what I was waiting for. Holy shit.*

Bianca's feet fly to the floor, knocking my hand off in the process. She scoots to the edge of the chair. "*What*? What are you talking about?"

"That's supposed to be Bobby's kickback for the work he put in for Dad. Dad is giving Bobby's son three-quarters of the trust," Jason says.

*The fuck?*

I've never liked Reid Brewer. He was shady and off-putting from the moment I met him. I couldn't believe a man like that fathered Jason. But this is beyond anything I could've imagined he would've attempted.

*Fucking over his children to this degree? Wow.*

My attention switches to Landry. "Need me to find him?"

His chin sits between his steepled fingers. He shakes his head.

"We would lose control of the trust," Bianca says, putting the pieces together. "We'd effectively be removed." She lifts her gaze to her brothers. "What are we going to do?"

My attention meets Jason's through the screen. We exchange a look, one I'm afraid to name.

"Wait a second," Bianca says, holding her forehead. "I don't understand how this would work. I mean, what was Dad going to do if he were still around, and I wasn't married next month on my birthday? Just not mention it? We would've found out one way or another."

"Bobby would've started getting paid on your twenty-seventh birthday, but he would not have any overt power until Dad triggered an action. That action must happen within three years, or it goes to Bobby by default," Gannon says.

Bianca stands, tugging the shirt down. The fabric drapes over the globes of her ass cheeks, making it clear she doesn't have anything on under it.

*I'm too weak for this. Somebody better save me.*

"What's to say that Dad won't amend it again?" she asks. "Are we certain he hasn't?"

Gannon nods. "Yes, we're sure. His ability to change anything ended when Mom enacted her option from Granddad's bailout. He could've before then, but he hasn't."

"Can we just void it?" Bianca asks, her voice growing frantic. "I'm assuming we have attorneys on this already."

"We do," Jason says. "But it'll have to go through the legal system, and that—"

"*Will take longer than a month*," Jason and Bianca say together.

Bianca laughs in disbelief. "I'm actually shocked. He shocked me. Dad finally went so far that I can't believe it."

"We'll figure it out," Gannon says. "Just sit tight."

"Sit tight and hope that the legal department can figure out how to undo this mess when you know Downing is going to fight it tooth and nail?" Bianca asks. "Please forgive my language, Ford, but fuck that."

Landry smirks.

Bianca sits again, perching on the edge of the chair. "What happens if I'm married? Then what?"

"It looks like Dad didn't have faith that would happen," Jason says.

Her back straightens. "What are you saying?"

Jason glances quickly at me. "I'm saying that if you get married, the deal falls through. The amendment stands as is, meaning they get nothing."

"We're not sure if they overlooked that option or if Dad expected to be here to keep us from finding out and thereby keeping it from becoming an issue," Gannon says. "But yes. If you get married, the amendment is essentially void."

Papers shuffle in front of Landry. Thoughts shuffle inside my head.

Bianca takes a deep breath and blows it out steadily. She's holding it together well. For now.

*But how the fuck do you deal with that level of betrayal? My father would burn in hell before he'd ever betray us at all, not to mention like that.*

A swell of heat rises in my chest, and I cover my face with my hands. There must be a way to ensure this deal is thoroughly fucked, especially if that means it's a *fuck you* to Reid Brewer. It seems like

Bianca marrying someone is the easiest solution. But she would have to trust that person to have that level of responsibility. That sort of sway. That kind of trust is hard for anyone, but even harder for Bianca. Such trust is—

*"And the one person I trusted, although he was on my payroll, left me ..."*

—hard to find.

I glance at her out of the corner of my eye. Her bottom lip quivers ever so slightly. She's scared, feeling alone—feeling betrayed.

My gut sours as the few times that Bianca has mentioned marriage as a non-option for herself sneaks through my mind. I'm not certain why she feels that way, and I certainly wouldn't want her to do anything she doesn't want to do. I wouldn't want her to resent me.

But as I watch the wheels turn in her head and how defiant she is about not letting this go through—and the shimmer of fear hiding in her beautiful green eyes ...

There's a serious chance she does something big, something like marriage, to stop her father. And the thought of her marrying some other asshole with bad intentions makes me want to fight.

*Here goes nothing.*

"Okay, I have the solution," I say.

Their attention turns to me. The weight of their gazes, their curiosity, is hefty.

This is ridiculous. It's downright asinine. And after our argument last night, I won't be surprised if Bianca laughs in my face and tells Jason to send a plane for her immediately.

And I won't be surprised if Jason never looks at me the same again, either.

I have no idea what marriage to Bianca, fake or not, would look like, and I don't know how I'll manage without driving myself mad. But the fear in her eyes puts my needs in the back seat. Even if she blows me off and Jason pulls me aside to ask me what the hell is going on—I must do this for her.

I must try.

She grins softly. "I wish you did."

My heart swells in my chest.

*"Unless you can come up with some brilliant plan to solve this impossible puzzle, I can't do this."*

"What are you thinking, Foxx?" Jason asks.

I square my shoulders to the computer monitor and brace myself.

"You can't kill Bobby or Charlie," Bianca says. "Love how you think, but it's a hard no."

"That's not what I was thinking."

The tension is thick between the five of us—a thousand miles be damned. Everyone's eyes are on me. I just hope their swords aren't ready to be drawn.

"Let's hear it," Gannon says. "How do we fix this?"

I look at Landry. He crosses his arms over his chest and grins.

I look at Jason. He's holding his breath.

I look at Gannon. *Is he smirking?*

Finally, I turn to Bianca. She licks her lips, her foot tapping against the floor.

*This woman.*

I smile as confidently as I can. "Marry me."

# CHAPTER 10

## *Bianca*

"Marry you?"

I blink once. Then twice.

My lungs burn from the breath I'm holding. He's kidding—he has to be. But the words, sounding so unbelievably serious, nail me in the heart.

I've never wanted to get married, and I actively avoided a proposal by the one boyfriend I had in my early twenties whom I feared was on the verge of asking me to be his wife. Nothing about marriage has been attractive to me. What is it about having another person in your life to take care of, to consider—*to manage*, makes people want to do it?

But my reaction to Foxx's proposal isn't what I felt when I imagined Peter proposing years ago.

I don't want to run. I want to fall into his arms.

I don't feel vulnerable. I feel safe.

I don't feel like a heavy, dark cloud just fell upon me, and I'm struggling under the weight. I feel … joy.

I'm not scared of it.

I want it.

*Oh God.*

"Marry you?" I ask again. The words come out in a laugh injected with disbelief. "Did you just ask me to marry you?"

Foxx shrugs.

I have no idea if he's serious or not—and that shrug of his tells me nothing. *But he can't be.* He just told me we can't be together at all, and now he's proposing marriage? This is a sick, terrible joke.

"Why would you say that to me?" I ask under my breath. "Now isn't the time to find your funny bone."

He scoots to the edge of his chair and twists so no one besides me can see his face. A mischievous glimmer twinkles in his eye.

"Think about it," he says softly. "It's a *brilliant plan to solve an impossible puzzle.*"

My heart races.

"Well, what do you think, Bianca?" Jason asks.

I realize my brother can't see me. I've stepped off-screen.

I sit beside Foxx, bumping his knee with mine. "I think Foxx picked a really strange time to try to find his comedic side." I clear my throat. "Let's figure this out because there's no way in hell Dad is getting away with this. And if he thinks the road to getting what he wants is by exploiting me—he's wrong."

Jason folds his hands together on his desk. "I'm going to be really honest with you, B." He glances briefly at Gannon. "Foxx doesn't have a bad idea."

My mind is blown.

My brother suggested that I marry his best friend—the same best friend who just told me he couldn't have anything to do with me because it would be a giant offense to my brother.

What the hell is happening with these people?

"Of course, we aren't pressuring you to do anything," Gannon says. "And we're fully prepared to fight this out in court. But I think we need to take a second and breathe here and really take a look at this logically."

Foxx is bizarrely calm beside me.

"This is a family issue, but may I join this conversation?" Ford asks. "Can I help break this down into manageable chunks?"

"Sure." I shrug helplessly. "Why not?"

He smiles. "You have two options, Bianca. The first is to put it all into the hands of your legal team and hope for the best."

My stomach knots. *The time. The money. The stress. The uncertainty.*

"You do have a fantastic legal team behind you," he says. "And I have faith they can find a way to undo this mess. But we would be remiss if we didn't consider the alternative, which is marriage. I know that's not the most moral or appealing choice, but you're not exactly dealing with an ethical situation."

I bury my head in my hands.

If this had happened yesterday, before Foxx and I had our little blowout, this might feel very different. But I'm not sure now, having endured our conversation last night, that Foxx isn't taking pity on me. Or, maybe even worse, that he's not volunteering to marry me in another show of loyalty to Jason.

While marrying him doesn't feel like a terrible option for me, it's a completely different thing if being married to him will amount to more arguments like the one we just had.

I can't do that. And considering the details he shared only hours ago, I can't see it going any other way.

"Regardless of what you choose," Ford says, "I do *highly suggest* that we increase your security until this all shakes out. I would imagine the Downings are waiting with bated breath for your birthday to come and go, and I would also imagine your father is scrambling from the pressure."

"Hey, B? Are you okay?" Gannon asks.

I lift my face slowly and look into the monitor. My brothers sit shoulder to shoulder, waiting for my reply.

I sit up straight and shake off the shock of the past few minutes. *This is business, Bianca. This is bigger than just you. Think.*

There's no way I can let our father get one over on us. He has hurt our family so deeply and cost us so much in every way. His antics have been a cancer that has infected every part of our life, and I'll be damned if his sneakiness is going to steal anything else from us.

Not on my watch.

I suck in a breath.

"Can I have a minute alone with Bianca?" Foxx asks.

Jason nods. "Sure. Absolutely. Take your time."

He clicks a few buttons. The screen goes black, and a red line crosses the speaker icon.

The room shrinks as he turns to me. The air gets hotter. I can barely breathe as he begins to speak.

"I want to make something clear," he says.

"What's that?"

His Adam's apple bobs in his throat. "I'm not doing this for Jason. I'm doing this *for you*."

I sink against my chair. The fuzziness cocooning me to protect me from the shock starts to wear off, and tears gather in my eyes.

My father has fucked me over. *Me*. Specifically *me*. This wasn't a generalized hit on our family but a manipulation of his only daughter. The one man who was supposed to love and protect me from the world is the one person I'm scrambling to protect myself against.

"I'm sorry for last night," Foxx says. "I should've handled things differently."

I smile at him. "I didn't exactly give you a lot of room to figure it out."

He smiles back.

"Are you serious?" I ask him, holding my breath. "Are you really willing to marry me?"

His gaze softens. "I'd do anything in the world to help you and protect you."

"But you'd *marry me*? Even if it wasn't real? You'd do that?"

"You shouldn't have come down here with nothing under my shirt."

I tilt my head, giving him a look to be serious. "I love that you chose this situation to try to be funny."

"I'm not joking." He smirks, sitting back and stretching his legs out in front of him. "What are you going to do? Tie this up in the court system for years?"

The thought of that makes me want to die.

"I don't want to take it to court," I say. "And I don't want my dad to win."

"And I don't want to see you try to go through that."

The sincerity in his features slays me. *He's such a good man.*

"What would a marriage look like between us?" I ask, shoving a strand of hair behind my ear. "I can't believe I just said that."

He chuckles.

"But after everything you said last night, I can't see how this would function in a healthy way," I say.

He leans forward, resting his elbows on his knees. "It's convenient."

"True."

"And it's essentially in my job description."

"Also true."

He reaches over and lays a hand on my bare thigh. "And when I woke up this morning and thought about you leaving today, it tore me apart."

I use the neckline of my shirt to dab beneath my eyes. *Stop it, Foxx, before you show me every reason it hurts not to be with you.*

"I'm sorry," I say, laughing and sniffling. "My allergies are acting up."

He laughs, squeezing my leg before withdrawing his hand.

I sniffle, gathering myself once again. "Okay. So let's pretend we do this. I'm guessing you still feel the way you felt last night and that's going to make our fake marriage a little tricky."

"We get the answers as we go. Take this one problem at a time."

I stare into his bright eyes. "You'll really do this?"

"What do you want? Do you want me to get down on one knee?"

My laughter feels like it carries some of the weight off my shoulders. The man beside me picks up the rest of it.

I push the button to bring my brothers and Ford back on screen. A shiver snakes down my back as I turn the mic on. *Is this really happening?*

"Before you say anything, I want to clarify one thing," Jason says, scooting his chair forward. "I made a quick call to the legal team while you two were discussing this. They don't love the idea of a fraudulent marriage but agree it's the easiest solution financially and contractually. But if you do this, it must look real. It must be believable. If they were to get an idea that you were getting married to bust the contract, they could try to sue us for breach."

"They could go to the people you know—your family, for example. They could subpoena them to see if they knew the marriage was a sham," Gannon says.

*Oh shit.*

I look at Foxx for his reaction.

He shrugs. "We can make it work. If that's what you all want, we can make it happen."

"You're the only person in the world I would trust with my baby sister," Jason says. "If you hadn't offered, I would've taken marriage off the table."

"What if I wanted to marry someone else?" I ask.

"Too bad," Jason and Foxx say at the same time.

This gets a laugh from everyone—including me.

My fear and shock fade away, and excitement takes their place.

"Can someone get a prenup together?" Foxx asks. "We can get it signed today."

Jason beams. "We'll have someone email it over this afternoon."

"Does it need to be a public wedding?" I ask. "Or can we just … do it?"

"Just do it," Gannon says. "The faster, the better. Mom won't be thrilled she can't come, but she'll get over it. She has bigger fish to fry at this point, anyway."

Ford Landry grins cheekily. I want to ask him what that's about, but I don't know him well enough to call him out like that. Besides, I don't want to waste time on him.

I, too, have bigger fish to fry.

Jason gathers papers and taps the edge of them against the desktop. "Let's end this now so Foxx and Bianca can get themselves sorted. If you two need anything at all, call us. And we'll have that prenup over to you shortly, Foxx."

"Sounds good."

Jason holds his gaze, grinning. "Welcome to the family."

Foxx chuckles. "Thanks."

We exchange hurried goodbyes before I end the Zoom call.

I stand, too energized to sit and lean against his desk. He sits before me—knees parted, hands clasped, and a shit-eating, satisfied smile on his lips.

"What's that look about?" I ask, unable to get the same one off my face.

"Which one?"

I laugh. "The one on your face."

"*Oh*." He sits upright. "So how real are we making this?"

"What do you mean?"

He shrugs. "How real are we making this? Are we going to the courthouse? A church?"

I hadn't considered this, and the question is bigger than I imagined. "I've never really thought about it because I never imagined I'd be getting married." I take a quick breath. "And I know this is a marriage of convenience, but it feels weird to think about getting married in a courthouse." I stand tall. "But that probably makes the most sense since—"

"No courthouse."

I want to reach for him—take his head in my hands and hold it to my stomach. And even though we're apparently getting married, it's too soon for that.

"What kind of ring do you like?" he asks.

I shake my head. "You do not have to waste money on a ring—"

"*What kind of ring do you like, Bianca?*" He lifts a brow. "They said make it real, remember?"

"Fine. Something cheap and simple."

I can tell he wants to roll his eyes. Somehow, he refrains.

"Where do you want to go on our honeymoon?" he asks.

"Foxx, no. Let's not ..." I quickly backtrack after seeing the no-nonsense look on his face. "Somewhere simple—you absolutely don't need to think about this too much. But I don't know anyone here. I don't know how I'm supposed to arrange for a dress because all I have are the clothes I showed up in yesterday. And how do I find a chapel? And where even is the courthouse for a marriage certificate?"

"You're not alone." He leans forward. "You don't have to do this alone. Let me carry this for you. Let me help."

Out of all the times I've been attracted to Foxx Carmichael, this one takes the cake. There's nothing sexier or sweeter than him seeing what I need and stepping in to improve it.

A slow smile stretches across my face. A red-hot burn spreads through my body.

"I have a question of my own," I say.

He hums.

"I didn't grow up going to church every weekend," I say, watching his eyes darken. "We'd go on the big holidays and other times if one of my parents felt guilty about something. But I do know that marriages aren't deemed legal unless they're consummated."

A devious smirk settles against his lips. "I don't think that's true."

I grin. *"But it could be."*

Foxx grips the sides of his chair.

I turn away and begin to round the corner of his desk. I'm fully aware that his shirt has bunched at the small of my back and that the bottom of my ass is peeking out from beneath the hem.

I glance at him over my shoulder. "Are we consummating this marriage, Foxx?"

A smirk kisses his lips. "They did say it had to be real, didn't they?"

I turn to face him, one hand on the corner of his desk. My nipples bead in anticipation of his reaction to my next question.

The insides of my thighs are sticky, and my breath is hot. All I can think about is him touching me, kissing me—breaking the invisible barrier between us that we've both wanted to knock down for so long.

I smile at him. "Do we have to wait?"

# CHAPTER 11
## *Bianca*

"Who do you think I am?" he asks, feathering a finger across his lips.

"What kind of a question is that?"

He drops his hand, smirking. "You just had all that information thrown on you, and you want me to fuck you now?"

"Uh, yes. That's exactly what I want to happen."

He stands slowly, his brows pinched together. Hesitation is written all over his face.

One thing I love most about the man is how considerate he is regarding me. He's kind and thoughtful, and I adore that quality. *Usually.* Now, it's proving to be one very, very frustrating characteristic.

I've never been able to be so outright with him—so open. Sure, we've danced around this topic many times, but it was always within the confines of the limits of our relationship. And it was a relationship centered around work. Not a personal relationship and definitely not one on the precipice of marriage.

"For the record, I wanted that to happen yesterday, too," I say.

"So what you're saying is that this isn't a call for help."

My core tightens as he comes closer. "I don't know. A part of me does need a lot of help right now."

He grins. *Oh, my heart.*

"You're the one who said you'd marry me," I say, my heartbeat quickening as he approaches. "You had to know that sex was a part of the marital contract."

"I love how you're suddenly serious about marriage vows."

I swallow hard. "What do you mean? I've always taken marriage seriously."

"Really?" He smirks. "What about all that shit about you not getting married unless your life depended on it?"

"At the moment, Mr. Carmichael, my life sort of does depend on it. Ironic, I know." Reality trickles into my psyche again. It takes a bit of wind out of my sails, and a wave of anxiety slides through me. "Do you think my father or Downing will do something to me if they know I'm getting married? I mean, seventy-five percent of the value of Brewer Sports is … *a lot* of money."

He stops before me, brushing a strand of hair out of my face. The back of his hand sweeps against my cheek in the sweetest, most tender way. And if I weren't already smitten with him, I would be now.

"No one will touch you as long as you're with me," he says softly. "I promise."

I'm not sure if it's his promise that hits me so hard or how he says it. It could be how he looks at me—with what looks like reverence. Whatever it is, it takes me aback. I have *never* had anyone look at me the way Foxx looks at me.

No one has ever made me feel like this before. No one has ever done something so grand, so selfless to protect me. To show their respect or their affection.

I always wanted my father's approval. He was the most powerful person I knew. Growing up as the only girl in a brood of boys, I was forgotten. My interests took a back seat to my brothers, and the only way I found to gain approval, *to gain visibility*, was to excel in an arena they were expected to dominate. *The office.*

But with Foxx, I don't feel like I have to earn anything. Maybe it's out of loyalty to Jason, to our family—or to me. But it feels so honest and raw and pure.

And I believe him.

"But what about you?" I ask, biting my lip.

"What about me?"

"Will *you* touch me as long as I'm with you?"

His eyes hood, and he growls a laugh.

"What?" I ask, giggling. "It's a serious question. I need to set my expectations."

He licks his bottom lip, watching me carefully. We stand this way for a few long seconds. The energy between us is so heated, so fueled with anticipation, that it crackles.

"I want to make sure that you have a moment to process this," he says. "Today was pretty heavy. You're choosing to get married to save your family's business. That's a lot to put on someone in one day."

I stand taller. "You forget whose daughter I am. I've had a lot of heavy days over the years. But instead of looking at this like I have to get married to save my family's business, I'm looking at it like at least there's an option to win." I take a deep breath. "And at least I can take that option with you."

He reaches for me, cradling my face in his hand. His eyes are so bright, so blue—so clear. I've never seen them like this. I've never seen *him* like this.

"Let's make a deal," he says, thumbing my jawline.

I lean into his hand, letting his touch reverberate through me.

"What kind of a deal?" I ask.

"We have a lot to figure out. Let's do that—let's get that behind us before we try to complicate things."

I laugh, pulling away from him. "You think *not* touching you will somehow *un*complicate things? Explain that."

"It's easy." He shoves his hands in his pockets. "As soon as that happens, as soon as I know what it's like to be inside you, things will never be the same."

*My God.*

He grabs the desk on either side of me. His face is inches from mine as he stares into my eyes.

"But you will find out what that's like, right?" I ask.

He licks his lips before they part into a wicked grin. "It is a part of my job, and I do pride myself on doing a complete, thorough job."

"Just how thorough?"

"You'll come on my fingers, face, and cock. You'll take me so deep, you'll come so fucking hard that you'll realize no one has ever really fucked you before."

I suck in a shaky breath.

"But I want to give you a little time to make sure this is what you want," he says.

I take his hand and hold it between us. Slowly, I bend each finger down except the second one.

His breathing is labored, his eyes wide, as I place it on my sternum. Holding his gaze, I drag his finger between my breasts, down my stomach, and beneath the hem of his shirt. I grin as I slide his finger through my wetness, sinking my body against it.

Fireworks shoot through my core, exploding at the apex of my thighs. Wetness coats his fingers as I pull them between us again.

"Does it feel like it's what I want?" I ask.

He drags both of our hands to his mouth. I gasp as he pops his finger into his mouth, sucking on it before he pulls it back out.

I shiver, my legs threatening to give out.

"The next time I taste your pussy, my face will be buried in it," he says, the gravel of the words prickling my senses.

"Fuck me now, Foxx. Dammit. Stop being a dick."

He leans forward, his breath scented with my sex, and grins. "*No.*"

I plant both hands on his chest and shove him away. He takes a step back, chuckling.

"I hate you," I say, walking toward the doorway. "We're not even married yet, and I hate you already."

"I've heard makeup sex is the best, anyway. We're off to a good start."

He follows me into the kitchen, stopping at the counter while I pour myself a glass of water. I can barely think straight. Everything is so convoluted, so jumbled together in a thick fog. Not to mention feeling so needy—so incredibly turned on. *And he's barely touched me.*

The glass is cool in my hands. I press it between my breasts to help cool my body. Foxx's attention settles on my chest.

"I should take this shirt off right now and torture you," I say.

His eyes darken.

"But then—*what the heck is that*?" I set the glass down and point out the window overlooking the street. "Is that a … chicken on a leash?"

Foxx looks at the ceiling. "You've got to be kidding me."

I scoot across the room and peer out the window. A man about Foxx's size, with a bandanna tied around his forehead, walks down the street with two chickens on a leash.

"Who is that?" I ask, looking at Foxx over my shoulder. "And am I seeing that correctly? He's walking two chickens like you would dogs. Right? Or am I really losing my mind?" I pause. "That would make sense—the mind loss and not the chicken walking. I just thought we were getting married. Clearly, I'm losing it."

Foxx exhales, clearly perturbed. "That's one of my brothers. Jess."

I glance out the window again. "Jess is kind of cute."

I barely get the words out of my mouth before Foxx is behind me. His fingers dig into my waist as he spins me around.

My breath is stolen by the heat boiling off him.

"Say that again, and you'll be sorry," he says.

"What? That Jess is hot?"

He laughs angrily.

"*He is*," I say, resting my hands on his shoulders. "He's not as hot as you are, but I'm currently overwhelmed with needs to be met, and my fiancé refuses to meet them. It could just be a haze of desire that's clouding my vision. You could fuck that out of me, you know."

Foxx studies me. The mischievous grin he wears makes me regret talking shit.

"Fine," he says, giving me his trademark shrug. "Guess what happens now?"

"You peel me out of this shirt and slam your cock inside me?"

He rolls his hips against me. He's rock-hard, and the sensation makes me whimper.

"No." He pulls away. "I'm not fucking you now until our honeymoon."

I drop my hands. "*You wouldn't dare.*"

"Oh, sweetheart. You have a thing or two to learn about me." He turns and moseys into the kitchen like our exchange didn't happen. "When do you want to get married?"

"To you? Maybe never now."

He pours a glass of tea like he doesn't have a care in the world.

I'm clearly going to lose this battle. I might be able to wage a solid war if I had my shit together. But my emotions have been shredded and strewn today, and getting a solid plan together to screw him back is a little out of my capabilities this afternoon.

I slump into a seat as exhaustion settles into my bones. I'm frazzled and overwhelmed and just want this part of it to be over.

"It's really hard for me to figure out the logistics of this wedding without knowing anything about this area," I say. "Hell, Foxx, I still don't even have clothes here."

He takes a sip of tea and then sets his glass down. "We'll get you clothes today. Do you want to arrange to bring some of your things here from Nashville?"

I hadn't thought of that. "I mean, yeah. I'll want a few things, but I'll coordinate that with Astrid. She's already sending me a care package, but I'll need a lot more. I'll call her in a little bit."

"What are we telling people?"

"That we're getting married, right?"

"It must be believable. We must have a consistent story, so it's not questioned."

I grin. "Want to say we've been having a hot affair behind closed doors, and you fell so madly in love with me that you can't take it anymore?"

"They do say that lies are more believable when they have truths built into them."

I'm not sure what he means by that. But I am sure he's not going to tell me.

"That's fine. Let's say that," he says, moving along before I can question him. "We'll say we've been in a quiet relationship for a couple of years, and we decided to get married."

"How do we do that? Get married, I mean?"

He leans against the counter. "You don't want to go to the courthouse, right?"

I shake my head. "No. I understand that ethics at this point are moot, but it's important to me."

"I'll go talk to my mom and see what she recommends. But be prepared. She's going to love this. She can be … a lot."

"The woman who bought all the houses on her street so her kids would stay close to her? That's surprising."

He chuckles.

"Can I meet her?" I ask.

He runs a hand down his face. "Let me talk to her first. Let me break the ice and ease her in."

"At least you're easing into one of us."

He frowns.

"I'm kidding." I roll my eyes and stand. "I need to call Astrid and my mother before she hears this from my brothers. I don't need that drama."

"And I'll go talk to my mom and see what we can get set up. Sound good?"

I nod.

"Then we'll get you some clothes and whatever else you want for here."

The breeziness in which he says that tugs at my heartstrings.

"Okay," I say.

He gives me a bashful grin. "I'm going to set the alarm when I leave. The code is seven eight nine eight if you need to turn it off. The keypad is over there." He motions toward the wall. "It's basically the same system you have at home."

"I got it. I'm not going anywhere, anyway."

He taps the counter. "All right. I'll be back."

"I'll be here."

He starts to say something else but stops himself. Instead, he shakes his head and makes a beeline for the door.

I exhale as soon as I'm alone.

*I'm marrying Foxx Carmichael.*

*Me. Marriage. I'm marrying Foxx Carmichael.*

How is this my life?

I laugh in disbelief all the way to the bathroom.

# CHAPTER 12

## *Foxx*

*SHE'S GOING TO LOVE THIS WAY TOO MUCH.*

There's no way to break this to Mom easily. She's going to *lose her shit* when I tell her I'm getting married.

A small grin touches my lips as I approach her porch. I never thought I would be doing this—telling Mom I need to plan a wedding.

Strangely, I'm not mad about it. Not even a little.

"Things could definitely be worse," I mumble, opening the door. "Yes, they—*don't you fucking move.*"

Banks whips around from the kitchen table. He's startled to see me. His eyes dart from me to the hallway leading out of the back of the kitchen, trying to determine whether he's quick enough to escape.

He's not.

Fueled by irritation, I cut through the living room and stand across the table from him before he can finish his calculations.

"If you break anything, you're replacing it," Mom says, shaking her head while stirring a pot on the stove. "I'm making potato soup for dinner if you want to come by, Foxx."

I ignore her.

"Hey, Foxxy," Banks says. He tries to juke to the right like he's reliving his high school fullback days. Unfortunately for him, I'm a step ahead.

I grab the table and slide it at an angle to cut off his exit. His eyes go wide. I continue to push.

"Whoa," he says as the edge presses against him, and he's pushed back.

The chair legs squeak against the hardwood as they move. The other chairs fall to the floor in noisy crashes. I keep pushing until Banks is in the corner with both sides blocked off.

"No one is leaving here until that's cleaned up," Mom says.

My palms smack the tabletop, and I glare at my little brother. "Now give me your puppy dog eyes and say something witty before I *beat your fucking ass.*"

Banks starts to talk, but Mom casually slides a sandwich down the table to him.

He smiles at her. "Thanks, Mom. This looks great." He lifts the top piece of bread. "Oh, and you didn't forget the pickles. You're a gem."

*This motherfucker.*

He looks up, giving me a cocky smirk before taking a bite of his sandwich. Then he returns it to the plate like he has all the time in the world.

"Want a snack, Foxx?" Mom asks. "We have ham and turkey."

Banks puts his phone next to his plate. "The ham is excellent." He touches the screen, and a video begins to play.

*He has to be kidding me.*

I place two fingers on the side of his plate and drag it slowly to the side of the table.

His mouth falls open. "What the fuck?"

I hold his gaze and place the same fingers on his phone. Then I drag it across the table, too.

He gasps. "What the fuck do you think you're—*ah!*"

I dive across the table and tackle him into a pile of chairs. The little shit manages to slide far enough to the side to avoid a direct hit. He grabs my shoulders from behind, sliding one hand under my chin like he thinks he can pull off a chokehold.

"Aw, is this what you wanted," he mocks, fighting to keep in position. "Did Foxxy want to cuddle?"

I'm not sure if it's the auction that has me the maddest or the audacity of him thinking he can fight me. Either way, he's only hurting himself because now I'm not going to take it easy.

I scramble to the side. My ribs slam into a chair. *Oof. I'm too old for this shit.*

Somehow, I manage to get an arm through his legs and another arm around his neck and shoulder. We tussle until I get him right where I want him. In one quick burst of motion, I bring him over my shoulder and slam him onto the table.

"Oh, for heaven's sake," Mom mumbles.

Banks squirms, sensing his mortality. I pin him to the table with my hand on his throat.

"I'm sorry," he says, writhing around. "I'm sorry for putting bird-seed in your backyard so the birds shit everywhere."

My jaw clenches. *I knew that was him.*

"I'm sorry for borrowing your hammer drill and then losing it," he says, gagging.

*You little motherfucker.*

I squeeze harder. Tears begin to fill his eyes.

"I'm sorry for … humiliating you … in front of the whole town … and Bianca," he says, barely able to get the words out.

I grab him with both hands and lift him off the table. He's clawing at my hands to let go as he lands on his back again.

"You never stop running your mouth," I say, shaking him. "For once in your life, stop fucking talking."

Jess and Maddox come in the back door. As soon as they see what's happening, they start to laugh.

"Looks like we're late to the party," Jess says.

If I weren't busy strangling Banks, I'd tell him that any man walking a chicken has no business laughing at anyone.

"Don't antagonize them, Jess," Mom says, sighing. "Are you boys hungry?"

"*Help me,*" Banks hisses before I increase the pressure again.

"Sure. Do you have ham?" Jess asks.

Maddox picks up Banks's sandwich from the edge of the table. "I'll have this one. It looks good."

Banks continues to flail. Maddox takes a bite of his sandwich and comes closer to investigate.

"I think purple means he can't breathe," Maddox says, pointing at our brother.

I ease up enough to fade the purple to a shade of red.

"You're going to promise me on our mother's honor—"

"Don't bring me into this," Mom says.

"—that you aren't going to pull this kind of shit anymore," I say. "You're going to mind your business. Right? You'll promise that?"

I stare at him, warning him not to play games with me. Then I ease the pressure around his neck.

Banks hauls in a long, deep breath. Then another.

"Promise me," I say, repositioning my fingers around him.

He stills. "Okay. I agree. I promise not to hook you up with rich, beautiful women ever again." He smirks. "Good enough?"

I squeeze until he starts to choke again. He turns his head simultaneously as Dad comes into the room. "Dad!" he says hoarsely. "Help!"

"Oh hell, Foxx. What did he do now?" Dad asks.

Jess strolls up to the table and takes a bite of his sandwich. "Don't stop them, Dad. This is good entertainment. I got a free meal and a show."

Dad grins. "So I'm guessing Bianca left?"

*Fuck.*

I push hard against Banks one final time and then let him go. He wastes no time in rolling off the table and getting to Mom.

Jess smacks his lips. "Bianca is at your house?"

I glare at him. He grins back.

*I hate all of them, I think.*

"She said she was leaving last night," Dad says, screwing with me. "I'm guessing that's why Foxx is a little testy today."

"As a matter of fact, I came over here with news." I cross my arms over my chest. I might as well just tell them all at once and be done with it. "I'm getting married."

Mom drops something. The clanging sound rattles through the room.

My heart begins to pound.

Maddox cocks his head to the side. "Did you just say you're getting married?"

"Who is getting married?" Moss comes in, stopping in the doorway, confused. "What the hell did I miss in here?"

Jess takes another bite. "Foxx just tried to kill Banks."

"Oh. That's fair," Moss says.

Mom shuffles around the island and stops by Dad. Her eyes are wide.

"Did you just say you're getting married?" she asks as if she's afraid to say the words.

"*Who*?" Moss asks.

"I might've missed something because I thought Foxx said he was getting married," Maddox says. "But that can't be right."

I sigh, rolling my eyes. "I'm getting married. You heard right."

"To whom?" Mom asks.

"If it's to Bianca, I want an apology!" Banks yells.

I wipe my palms down the front of my jeans. I didn't expect to be so nervous. I'm not used to feeling this way. It's … strange.

"I'm marrying Bianca," I say, warning Banks not to say another word. He holds up his hands. "As soon as possible. I was coming over here to see if you, *Mother*, could help me figure things out."

She races across the room and pulls me into a hug. Jess chomps on his sandwich, amused. Moss pours a glass of tea, warning Banks to keep quiet. Maddox picks up a chair and takes a seat.

"I'm glad you're all so entertained," I deadpan.

"When did this happen?" Mom asks, her excitement building. She pulls away. "I didn't know you were seeing her."

*Here we go …* "But, if you do this, it must look real. It must be believable."

I clear my throat. "We've been seeing each other for a while and decided to get married. We don't want to go to the courthouse. So I was thinking maybe you knew a pastor or a preacher who could come over to my house and perform a quick ceremony. Nothing fancy."

"Can I at least meet her first?" Mom asks. I think she might cry. "I'm so happy for you, Foxx. I … When can we meet her?"

"I can bring her to dinner tonight."

Mom's eyes light up. "That would be wonderful."

"So the preacher?" I ask, my skin feeling too small for my body. *I need to get the hell out of here.* "Can you help me?"

"Yes. You know I can. I'll have options tonight at dinner."

I nod, relieved. "Thanks. When do you think you can get it done?"

"Well, you'll need to go get a marriage license. But I don't see why you can't get it done tomorrow, probably. Tuesday at the latest."

*Perfect.*

"Do you need help with anything else?" Moss asks.

"Can I throw you a bachelor party?" Banks asks.

"*No,*" everyone in the room says.

Banks sighs, dejected.

"Pippa and I know this great place not too far from here," Jess says. "We've gone there a couple of times. Great hotel. Great food. Lots of stuff to do if you're into that. If you want the information for a honeymoon or something, let me know, and I'll hook you up."

Beyond fucking her brains out, I haven't thought about the honeymoon. The only thing I could think about as she taunted me with her sweet little body was needing to be inside her. I nearly came when I felt how wet and tight she was after she dragged my fingers down her sinful body.

There were no brain cells available to find a honeymoon location. *But damn if I don't want to take her somewhere that would blow her mind.*

"I'd appreciate that, Jess. I'm thinking just a night or two somewhere close."

He nods. "I'll text you when I get home and see Pippa."

"What about flowers?" Mom asks.

I hold out a hand. "Slow down."

"Did you get her a ring?" Maddox asks.

*Fuck.* I scramble to come up with an excuse. "Actually, no. We've been talking about marriage for a while but decided to do it as soon as possible this morning."

"I got a ring for Ashley for her birthday in Breakwater," Maddox says. "I'd be happy to go over there with you if you want."

Moss slides a chair out and sits beside Maddox.

"Does she need a dress or anything?" Moss asks. "Brooke has all kinds of shit she could borrow. Or I'm sure she'd be happy to take her shopping. God knows she knows every shop in Eastern Florida."

I stare at my family and feel a strange twist in my chest. I'm unsure what to say to them or how to respond to their offers. The whole thing makes me twitchy. Yet, especially considering Reid Brewer's contemptible betrayal, I can't help but be grateful for my family. They might drive me nuts and make me want to hide from them most days, but we always take care of our own.

*Always.*

Even Banks.

"I'll get back to all of you. I appreciate you," I say, looking at Mom. "So you'll call around for someone to marry us? And you'll let me know at dinner?"

She scurries back to the kitchen. "I'm on it right now."

*Well, okay.* I take a deep breath. "Well, then, I'm going home. I'll see you all tonight at dinner."

"Come bearing an apology!" Banks shouts.

I'm too preoccupied to respond.

My family is ready to help me plan a wedding.

And my soon-to-be wife waits for me at home.

*What in the hell is going on?*

*And how did I get so damn lucky?*

# CHAPTER 13

## *Bianca*

"THIS IS NOT HOW I EXPECTED TO END THE WEEK," I SAY, LAUGHING AND walking down the hallway to the guest room.

It seems like only yesterday that I was sitting at my desk and Jason came in, asking me to join him on a daytime adventure. *That's because it was yesterday.*

My life has taken a one-eighty in the last twenty-four hours. That should bother me. I should be concerned that things in my life, *massive things*, are changing at the speed of light. People go to therapy over this level of change in this short period.

*So why am I excited about it? Invigorated? Refreshed, even?*

It's a sensible question, but one I can't answer.

The last exciting thing that happened to me was the realization I could buy pumpkin spice creamer year-round and that my favorite pens were available in bulk.

But marriage, when you were fine being a bachelorette, isn't a coup like scoring a case of individual creamers you can keep in your office. And getting married to protect your family's legacy, and not for love, isn't exactly a reason to celebrate. Neither of those things would make a rational person feel … *free.*

I suppose I'm not rational.

The way I see it, this is the opportunity I've been longing for—a way to fight back against my father for all the shit he's put us through. For all the shit he's put *me* through. Mom has taken the biggest toll emotionally. Her husband was a fraud. My brothers are using their various specialties, ranging from schmoozing personnel, shoring up contracts, and poring over finances and security. But me? The bulk of the actual work—that's been on me.

I've coordinated efforts to ensure every piece of our lives is clear of Dad. I've been taking calls from furious partners, nervous investors, and curious clients. I've been working more of the day than not—and all weekends—rebuilding teams, building confidence, and restructuring contracts and commitments to minimize the hit we're taking as a whole.

That was the basis of my anger with my father before yesterday. It wasn't personal.

Today, *it's personal.*

To think he had the gall to use *me*, his only daughter and the child that has had his back more than any other, in a scheme to sell us out.

Did he assume he could control me so tightly that he could safely bank on the fact that I wouldn't find out? Did he bank on my previously unquestioning trust? And how had he been so sure that no one would want to marry me?

Sure, I'd said I wouldn't marry several times over the years. And, granted, the odds that I'd get out, find a man, and marry him in a few weeks weren't great. But it's the point of the matter.

Putting me in this position, using me like this for some unknown backdoor deal—it's unforgivable. And if marrying Foxx Carmichael is the only way to fuck Dad over, then I guess I'll suck it up. *Is that really such a sacrifice for me?*

No, not really. But it is for Foxx.

A swell of gratitude hits me hard. This could have gone down much differently. The amendment *was* discovered before my birthday, in plenty of time for us to thwart it. And Foxx willingly put his life on hold for my family … and me. *He's* making the sacrifice. He's going out on a limb, signing himself up to be a divorcée and pressing pause on his own personal life to help eradicate this heinous betrayal.

He's really such a good person. Such an amazing man.

My chest tightens, and as much as I hate to admit it—I need a hug. *I hate needing a hug.*

My phone is on the bed, so I pick it up and dial Mom. A bubble of anticipation ripples in my stomach while I wait for her to pick up.

"*Bianca,*" she says, relief thick in her voice. "How are you?"

I sit on the edge of the mattress. A cloud settles on my shoulders, making me feel silly for thinking this conversation would feel like a hug.

"Well, I've been better in some regards and worse in others. How are you?" I ask.

"*Oh, Bianca ...*" She sighs heavily. "I can't wait for this mess to be over."

"I know, Mom. Me, too. So how are things going?"

"The police are still looking for your father. Jason said he filled you in on the Brewer Sports situation. I am so, *so sorry*, honey. I wish I could say something to avoid this happening, and I wish I would've seen it coming."

I smile sadly. "This isn't your fault. You trusted him."

"And I shouldn't have."

"He was your husband. Of course, you should've."

She sighs again.

My hand shakes around the phone, so I move it to the other one. I'm not sure if she knows about my impending marriage. I'm also unsure if this is the right time to bring it up.

"I called you twice yesterday," she says. "Did you not get my messages?"

"My work phone is in my office. I'm in Florida."

She pauses. "Did I know that?"

I laugh softly. "I don't know."

"I don't even know what day it is, honestly."

"Well, since you didn't know I was in Florida, I have some other news you probably don't know and probably aren't expecting."

"What's going on?"

I get up, too amped to sit. "I came down here with Jason yesterday and wound up staying. He got the call about Dad showing up at

Brewer Air and decided to keep me removed from circulation until Landry Security could determine if there was a true threat."

"That's a good call, I think. But I wish someone would've told me this. I know you're all adults now, but I do like to be in the loop, you know."

"I know. But it was truly a game-time decision."

I look out the window and watch a man and a woman wash a Jeep. I wonder which one of Foxx's brothers it is and what he's like. *Is he anything like Foxx? Is he a chicken walker like Jess? Is he kind like their father?* The thought makes me smile. *There's so much to learn about this family.*

"Where are you staying?" she asks.

My smile widens. "With Foxx Carmichael."

"*Ooh …*"

I laugh. "What kind of *ooh* is that?"

"Exactly the kind of *ooh* you think it is." She laughs, too. "How is *that* going?"

"Well …" My laughter shifts. "I have something to tell you."

"Okay."

I take a deep breath and brace myself against the windowsill. "Foxx and I are getting married."

The line is silent.

"The official line is that we've been having a secret relationship for a couple of years and decided to get married soon. Like, we're probably getting married tomorrow kind of soon."

"You're getting married tomorrow, and you're just now telling me? *Bianca.*"

"Hang on. Don't get all crazy on me."

"Oh, child. You haven't seen anything yet."

I chuckle. "The real reason we're getting married is because Jason and Gannon found a loophole in the Brewer Sports amendment. I'm assuming they told you about it."

"They did. I almost hunted your father down myself and held him to task." She scoffs. "I'd like to say that this is the most surprising thing he's done, but I'm afraid it would be setting the table for him to one-up it again."

Sexual misconduct. Threatening his son's girlfriend. Selling Brewer Trade for well below value. Firing our chief financial officer for no cause—no *legal cause*. Purchasing a professional baseball team, the Tennessee Arrows, on a whim.

Well, maybe not on a whim. Maybe to benefit the Downings. *But why?*

"It does feel like that's how it's been working," I say.

"Your brothers only told me they resolved it, but not how. I was in the middle of a meeting about the Arrows baseball team—I'm struggling to find a GM—so I took them at their word. But what does a loophole and you getting married have to do with each other?"

"Well, if I don't get married before my birthday, then our only option is to fight it out in court. We may be able to do that, but not without a fortune spent—both monetarily, time-wise, and emotionally. And none of us love that option."

"No, we don't."

I pace the room. "Alternatively, if I get married before my birthday, the amendment is void. Even if we shift the trust to a new document—which we're doing, as you know—the Downings could have a legal leg to stand on. But if I'm Mrs. Carmichael, it voids the entire thing."

She groans. "Are you sure? This seems so barbaric. And the fact that it was your father who put you in this position infuriates me."

"Well, the infuriation line starts behind me."

"I am so sorry, Bianca." She pauses. "I just want to put this out there—if we lose Brewer Sports, we'll survive. We don't need the money, and our portfolio is—"

I stop pacing. "That's not the point."

She doesn't speak and waits for me to expound.

"Obviously, we don't need the money. It's the principle of the matter. And I would rather sell it for pennies on the dollar than hand it over to the Downings." I grit my teeth. *I will not let Dad win this one.* "And it's personal for me at this point. *He wagered my marital status, Mother.* He hinged his hideous plans on something so private. And don't think it's a coincidence that it was whether I was married and not Gannon or Ripley. He thought he could manipulate me like he does every other woman in his life—no disrespect intended."

"It's the truth either way."

*Sadly.*

My heart hurts for my mom. She's been pushing forward every day —one foot in front of the other—to clean up the mess her husband made. I hope one day she can stop, pause, and have the space to find what makes her happy. I don't think she's been happy in a long time, and that breaks my heart.

"Is there anything I can do?" she asks. "I feel so helpless. I want to go to war for you, baby girl, but I don't know where to start."

I sit on the bed again and consider her question.

*Can she do anything?* No.

*Would I want her to do anything if she could?* Also … no.

I ignore the swirling sensation in my stomach and focus on the wall across the room. "This is probably going to sound like I'm having a stress reaction, but … I'm okay, Mom. I'm really okay, I think."

Her tone softens. "Do you want to talk about anything?"

I read through the lines. And I can't help feeling like a little girl for a beautiful split second.

Since graduating from high school, my mother and I haven't discussed anything besides business. I can't recall having anything other than a superficial conversation with her about men, feelings, or face creams. She's been a great mother in many ways, and I don't blame her for the lack of depth of our relationship. I'm just as much to blame. I've spent my whole life following in my father's footsteps and neglected … everything else. It wasn't until he was unmasked, and I saw the destruction his choices have had on his life and ours that I paused to take stock of my own life.

And realized how unhappy and unsatisfied I really am.

I'm unsure what will make me happy and satisfied, but if this conversation indicates anything, getting to know my mother better would be a good start.

"One day, Mom, I'd love to talk about many things," I say. "When we have time to sit down and have a drink and really have a conversation."

"I'd like that, too."

My heart swells.

"Can I come to the wedding?" she asks.

"It's just going to be a quick, little thing with a preacher. Nothing fancy. If you'd like to come, I'd love that. But you should probably check with Jason first. I'm supposed to be laying low."

"I didn't think of that. I'll definitely check with him. But I cannot imagine you getting married and not being there."

"At worst, we can video call with you," I say. "I know it won't be the same, and I want you here, too. But it's not a real marriage, so …"

My face falls, and I'm not sure why.

"Bianca, I'm getting a call from Jason. Let me take this, and I'll call you back this evening, okay?"

I nod. "That's fine. I love you, Mom."

"I love you, too. More than you know."

I end the call feeling more relaxed … and content than I have in a long time. *She would've made an effort to be here. That makes me happy.*

There is too much going on to worry about work, and while this situation isn't a walk in the park, it is a nice change of pace. When I left the office yesterday, I would've said this was impossible. I would've sworn that the only way to keep me from thinking about work was if I was six feet under.

But I haven't thought about it at all today. I've thought about myself. I've made plans. I have something to look forward to that doesn't involve a computer screen. Granted, it's for a wild and convoluted reason, but it's fun to remember I'm a whole person again.

And it's not so bad to think about marrying Foxx.

I grin as I dial Astrid.

"Hey," she says. "How's Florida?"

"Florida is surprising."

"Oh really? Surprise me. What's going on?"

I peel off Foxx's shirt and dress in yesterday's clothes. "Well, I need you to send me a few more things."

"Okay …"

I grin. "Do I have anything in my closet that I can get married in?"

Silence. Absolute silence.

"Astrid?" I ask.

"I'm sorry." She laughs. "I thought you asked me if you had

anything in your closet to get married in. It took me a minute to realize you asked if you had anything in your closet to be *buried in*. Do I even want to know what's happening now?"

I laugh. "Is it that crazy I'd need something to get married in?"

"Considering it's you—*yeah*. So why do you need burial clothes, and who must I track down and inflict revenge on?"

"I need something to get married in, Astrid." I pause for dramatic flair. "I'm marrying Foxx."

"*What?*"

I laugh. "I don't want to get into it. But I need you to believe that we've had a hot love affair for a couple of years behind the scenes. And now we've decided to make it official and start a life together."

"Wow. Okay. I'll believe that. It's certainly possible, considering the chemistry between you two. But I have questions ..."

"And I'll answer those later. For now, that's the story, and I need you to propagate that if anyone asks. Okay?"

"You got it. But can I spice it up a little? Can I tell people I'd come in to work and find you handcuffed to the bed? Or hear you screaming—"

"No." I laugh so hard I snort. "I mean ... you know what? You do you. If you want to create some sexy backstory for me, just promise me you'll make it good."

She snickers. "Do you even know me? Of course, I'll make it good. Don't forget that I've seen that sexy-as-hell fiancé of yours, and I'm certain he knows his way around a woman's body. Those hands. Those sexy lips. That body."

She must stop, or I'll combust here and now just thinking about him ... and what's to come. *I hope.*

"Now, what do you need from me? How can I help you?" she asks.

I walk down the hallway and into the living room, listening to her babble.

"You'll need a dress. Flowers. Lingerie for the honeymoon." She groans. "I'm so damn jealous of you."

My cheeks ache from my smile.

"When is this going down?" she asks.

"I'm not sure. As quickly as possible. He's talking to his mother now to see if she can help us set it up."

"Okay … Aha! I just found that Halcyon is opening a shop really close to you."

I make a face. "They are? I love that store."

"Let me make a call and see if I can pull some strings. They always have really cute stuff, and if I'm lucky, I can get you a few more outfits and maybe even a dress for the wedding. I sent you a care package that'll arrive tomorrow, but there's probably not enough in there to get through a wedding, honeymoon, and … wait. Are you living down there? *Do I still have a job with you?*" She groans. "If not, please don't refer me to Tate."

I burst out laughing.

"I'll stay with Renn. Hell, I'll assist Gannon if that's the only other option. But *do not give me Tate.*"

"Don't worry. You're still my assistant. This is a marriage of convenience, remember? It's not for real."

"Mmm—"

"It's not!"

"I know. It's not … right now. So let me call Halcyon and see what I can do," she says over my objections. "I'll call you back."

I sigh. "*Fine.*"

"*Fine.* Talk soon."

She wastes no time hanging up on me. It's a good thing because I hear the alarm chirp that Foxx is home.

# CHAPTER 14

## *Foxx*

"How did that go?" Bianca asks, rounding the corner. "Was your mom *a lot*?"

"I'll put it to you this way—we'll be married tomorrow."

Her eyes sparkle as she follows me into the living room. I sit on the sofa. She curls up with a pillow next to me.

This almost feels like an out-of-body experience. It's so beyond anything I ever imagined that I have difficulty believing this is real. Bianca is sitting on my sofa. We're discussing our wedding. In a few hours, she'll be with me in front of my family and introduced as my fiancée.

Her smile digs right through the fog and slams into my chest.

I should be more upset about this. There should be a notion of panic. *I should be thinking that being married will crimp my lifestyle and be worried about just how wrong a divorce, even from a fake marriage, will be.* At the very least, I should be looking at this situation as an extension of my employment and not finally knowing what it feels like to have this woman in my arms.

But I'm not.

At all.

"What?" she asks, amused.

"I was just wondering if I'll get an end-of-the-year bonus for having to marry you."

She gasps. "That's no way to talk to your wife."

"You're not my wife yet."

"*Oh, good point.*" She sits back, tossing her pillow at me. "You better be careful. I haven't decided what kind of wife I will be."

I place the pillow beside me. "Do I have options?"

"No, but I do." She laughs. "Do I want to be the doting housewife? I'll have your laundry done and your dinner made when you get home."

"I've seen your attempts at cooking, so I hope not."

She shoves my arm, making me chuckle.

"Then I might be the nag. I might be on your ass all the time about the trash and your socks on the floor and watching too many sports. I might constantly beg for your attention."

"I can safely say you will *never* have to beg me for attention."

She smirks.

I can see where this is going. If I don't redirect this conversation soon, she's going to be bouncing on my cock. And as much as I want those giant titties in my mouth and her pussy wrapped around me, I need to give her time to process this. I need to give her the chance to back out.

Even if it kills me.

Groaning, I adjust myself as discreetly as possible. "How did the call go with your mother?"

Her smirk dwindles. "It went okay. She was surprised, I think. And really upset that I'm in this situation."

My curiosity rises as her gaze settles on something across the room. I don't know a lot about Bianca's relationship with her mother. And I've never worked on Rory Brewer's security team. But something tells me their mother-daughter bond isn't what I see with my mom and my sister, Paige. They're thick as thieves. In fact, even my mom and brothers' better halves have a closer relationship than I ever saw between Bianca and Rory.

"She wanted to come tomorrow, but I told her to ask Jason," she says, drawing her attention back to me.

Pools of emotion cloud her pretty green eyes. It makes it hard not to grab her and pull her onto my lap.

"Do you want her here?" I ask. "Because if you do, I'll make it happen."

She takes a breath to speak, but something holds her back.

"Is everything okay, Bianca?"

She exhales slowly. "I can't tell if I'm being rational or if this whole thing has made me more emotional than I'm aware."

"Wanna tell me and see if I can help?"

A smile ghosts against her lips. "I've never said this out loud." She laughs to herself, almost in disbelief. "Okay, I'll say it like this. I don't want my mom to be here when we get married." She shifts in her seat. "I know that sounds horrible, and you must think I'm some brat for feeling that way. But—"

"Hey." I lay my hand on her thigh. "That doesn't sound horrible. And I think you're a brat anyway."

A grin filters across her face.

I wink. "You just had a lot of shit thrown at you from inside your circle. You have every right to want to take a step back and protect yourself." I give her leg a little shake. "And you're going to have a husband who gives no fucks about telling people to back off. So if you need someone to help with boundaries, you're marrying well."

"I think I'm marrying well anyway."

"My mother does seem to think I'm a catch."

She laughs. I'm relieved. Despite her return to laughter, there's more to her feelings than she shared. I want to know what they are, but I don't want to push her. Not now.

If I'm completely honest, I can't believe I care this much. It's not that I was ever an asshole to Bianca—not intentionally, anyway. But I didn't suggest talking about emotions and sharing personal shit or deep matters with each other. Yet ... it doesn't feel uncomfortable.

*Who knew?*

I hide a grin. *As long as I don't turn into Banks and be all about emotions, I'll be okay.*

My phone starts ringing. "Ah, hang on." I dig it out of my pocket. "This is my sister, and if I don't answer it, she'll just keep calling. And if I turn my phone off, she'll send someone over here to order me to turn it back on and answer her."

"I like her already."

"You would." I roll my eyes as she bumps my shoulder. "Hi, Paige."

"Foxx Callum Carmichael—you better tell me that our mom is a big fat liar."

I chuckle. "I'm good, Paige. How are you?"

"*Are you getting married tomorrow?*"

"We're trying to get married tomorrow."

"And you didn't think to tell me? Even Maddox had the decency to tell me so I could be there. How can you do this to me? I'm getting a new sister, and I don't even know her. How am I supposed to know what kind of memes to send her?"

I laugh. "That's what you're worried about?"

"*Sir,*" she says as if the word is a whole sentence. "Memes are the language of the times. You would know that if you weren't an out-of-touch, cranky old man."

I grin. "And you wonder why I didn't invite you to my wedding."

"Jerk. Is she there? Can I talk to her?"

In a perfect world, I'd rather not let Paige talk to her yet. I'd rather she meet the family one at a time in a controlled environment. But something gnaws at me, making me wonder if it wouldn't help Bianca to know there's a big family of slightly crazy but supportive people who will rally around her with no questions asked. So she can relax here. So she can feel safe.

"Bianca hasn't even met Mom yet," I say. "I'm afraid you'll scare her off."

"I'll be on my best behavior. Swear."

I sigh, looking at Bianca. Secretly, I'm glad Paige is being a pain in the ass. This might take one element of anxiety away from my fiancée.

"This is my sister. Do you want to talk to her? You can say no."

"*But please don't say no!*" Paige shouts.

Bianca is unsure but holds her hand out for the phone. I place it in her palm and hope for the best.

"Hello," Bianca says, sitting tall. "Yes, I'm really marrying your brother." She listens for a moment—too long of a moment before laughing. "Absolutely. And, no, I won't tell him."

She looks at me and winks.

"Give me that back," I say, holding out my hand.

"Talk to you soon," Bianca says before returning the phone to me. "She's so sweet."

I roll my eyes. "Happy now?" I ask my sister.

"I couldn't express my current level of happiness if I tried," Paige says. "I'll let you go. I just had to find out if you wouldn't be a solitary animal any longer. And, Foxx, I already really like her."

"Well, I'm glad. I can go through with the wedding now."

"Asshole." She laughs. "Love you."

"Love you, Paige. Goodbye."

I rest my head against the cushions and turn my face to Bianca's. Instead of feeling a ripple of anxiety, a wave of contentment washes over me.

She sits sideways on the sofa with her shoulder against it. She studies me.

"What?" I ask.

"I just can't believe you're doing this for me."

I smile. "It's really putting me out."

She narrows her eyes but smiles, too. "Do you want to get married one day? For real?"

I hum, looking at the ceiling and pondering that question. It's not an easy question to answer.

I've purposely avoided relationships that I thought could develop into something serious, mostly because I didn't want to go through the drama of having it end. Women, *people*, annoy me. I dislike most of them. That's not a great character trait, but at least I'm honest with myself. I get a negative vibe from most of the people I meet—something that tells me they have a vein of dishonesty or laziness or disloyalty. I can't override my gut instinct. I spent too many years relying on it.

Would I have felt differently had I been with the right woman? If I'd been with a woman who made me laugh, who challenged me, who kept me on my toes? Someone intelligent, and brave, and beautiful ... would I have considered a path to marriage?

Would I have considered a real marriage if it had been with Bianca Brewer?

My chest tightens as I turn my attention to her again. I don't want to answer her inquiry.

"I think we need to start watching our language," I say, satisfied with the detour. "We are getting married, and for all anyone knows, it's a forever kind of thing. We need to practice speaking to each other like we're, you know ... in love."

Suddenly, I'm less satisfied with the detour.

My lungs constrict so hard they burn. *Like we're in love? Carmichael, come on.*

A chime rings through the room, alerting me to a message in the group family text. I generally silence my notifications as soon as I hear that noise. But today, I appreciate the distraction.

Maddox: Ashley and I ran over to Breakwater. Do you want me to pop into the jewelry store and send you pictures of rings, Foxx? I'm just sitting in the car while Ashley is in the store next door.

I read the message three times.

I'm not quite sure how to interact in this dynamic.

Me: Yes.

Me: Thanks.

Maddox: I'll go in now. Do you have anything in mind?

I glance quickly at Bianca.

The first word that comes to mind is *sexy*, but I don't think there's a category for that in rings. The next thought I have is *class*. And although she does have a ton of money and a personal assistant at her beck and call, she's not pretentious.

> Me: Something simple yet classy. Nothing flashy.

> Maddox: Got it. Gimme a few.

> Jess: Okay, honeymoon is booked. Silver Springs tomorrow night with a Wednesday check-out because you asked for just a couple of nights. You can extend it if you want. Just let me know.

*What?*

"What's wrong?" Bianca asks, studying me.

"Nothing. Hang on."

> Me: What do you mean it's booked?

> Jess: We all went in and paid for it. It's our wedding gift to you.

> Me: I don't even know when the wedding is.

> Jess: It's tomorrow. Mom was finalizing details.

*Oh.*

Excitement creeps up my spine.

"What's happening?" Bianca asks.

I chuckle. "Apparently, my brothers just booked our honeymoon."

She flinches. "What? Where? How?"

I scroll up through the messages until I find the location. "Silver

Springs. Just a couple of nights." *To bide me some time to think of something that's worthy of you.*

"I don't want anyone out of pocket for this," she says. "I'm happy to pay for everything. I feel bad, considering this is … not real."

Her words fall on the last two words.

"Don't," I say. "Language, remember? This is real, for all intents and purposes. And there's no way I'm letting my wife pay for anything." I tap her on the nose. "I don't care if she has a lot more money than I do."

She giggles.

"Speaking of that, the prenup is in my email," I say. "We need to get that signed tonight and back to Gannon."

I pull my gaze away from hers and go back to my texts.

> Me: I didn't expect you to do that. Thank you.
> That was very thoughtful.

Three pictures load one after the other. I turn so Bianca can't see my screen and flip through them. The third one—emerald cut diamonds along a gold band—is the one.

> Me: Number three.

> Maddox: Size?

> Me: No clue.

> Maddox: The lady here says the average is
> between a five and a seven. So let's say a six,
> and you can have it resized later if needed?

> Me: Sounds perfect. I'll pay you back tonight.

> Maddox: I'm paying for it now.

"A delivery person is on their way with things that Astrid found at a shop in Breakwater," Bianca says, looking up from her phone. "She thinks she found me something to wear for our nuptials."

She stands, her clothes clinging to her curves.

"What about for the honeymoon?" I ask.

Her eyes widen in surprise. A sexy little grin slides over her lips. "Oh, thinking about the honeymoon, are you?"

"I've been thinking about the honeymoon since I asked you to marry me."

She stands in front of me, dragging a finger along my jawline. The contact sends goose bumps across my skin and a bolt of heat straight to my cock.

"You didn't ask me," she says. "You demanded it."

My throat is dry. "That won't be the only thing I demand."

Her chest rises and falls. "Want to get in a practice session?"

I lean forward as if I'm going to kiss her. But instead of going through with it, I grab her by the waist and move her backward as I stand.

"*No*," I say, walking around her.

"Ugh. Why are you like this?"

"Because I can be." I peek through the curtains and find a car parked on the road. "Did you say someone was delivering your things now?"

"Yes. And tomorrow. But Astrid found a place to get me clothes today and some options for the wedding, and they said they'd deliver now."

A man gets out and then opens the back door. He grabs several bags with Halcyon stamped on the front in pink font.

"They're here," I say, opening the door.

She jumps up and races outside. "Stay inside! Don't look."

"I can't see through bags," I say, laughing at her.

She chats with the deliveryman, who is clearly smitten with her. *Can't blame you, man*. Then she carries her loot by me and down the hall.

"I'm going to be a while," she says. "You should probably find something else to do unless you want to see me naked." She stops in front of the guest room door. "But if you want to see that, I won't complain."

She blows me an awkward kiss with the bags in her hands before ducking inside the bedroom.

I chuckle and head for my office to get the prenup. As soon as I sit at my desk, my phone buzzes again.

Banks: Hey, did you eat that pie? If not, can I have it?

I silence notifications and swipe out of the text app.

# CHAPTER 15
## *Bianca*

"SHOULD WE HOLD HANDS?" I ASK, GRAVEL CRUNCHING BENEATH OUR shoes. "What's an appropriate level of PDA at your parents' house? Are we supposed to be cuddly or hands-off?"

"I don't know."

"How can you not know? What do your brothers and their girl-friends do?"

He rolls his eyes as if I'm ridiculous for asking him to have noticed his siblings' behavior and then shrugs.

A shrug is not an answer. Yet it's a classic Foxx answer.

But as I start to prompt him to actually give me a response, a realization occurs to me. He might not have answered me with words this time, but he has spoken more in the past twenty-four hours than I've ever heard since I met him. *Interesting*.

He fidgets with his collar. *Foxx doesn't fidget*.

"Stop," I say, coming to a halt at the base of the steps leading to his parents' porch.

He faces me. "What?"

I give him a look not to be contrary and make a show of fixing his collar despite it not needing it. My stomach is a mess of butterflies without his sudden bout of nerves. Now that he's acting nervous, the butterflies start to spread.

"If you don't want to take me in there—"

"No." He leans back to look me in the eye. "I'm proud to show you off to my family."

I pat his chest and take a step back. "It certainly seems like it."

He gazes over my shoulder at the house I assume he grew up in, and then pulls his attention back to me.

"I've never done this before," he says, clearing his throat.

"You've never done what before?"

"I've never brought a woman to a family dinner, least of all the one I'm marrying."

A cheeky grin settles over my lips. "Is that so?"

"Don't get cocky."

"I would've but you refused to let me have it."

He shakes his head, chuckling.

"Are you sure I look okay?" I ask, running my hands down the black linen shorts and emerald-green shirt that Astrid had delivered. "Am I underdressed? Overdressed? I have no idea what I'm supposed to wear."

Foxx grins sweetly. "You are absolutely beautiful, Bianca. And that has nothing to do with the clothes you have on."

The bridge of my nose pinches like it does just before my eyes cloud with tears. I fan my face to try to ward them off.

"This mascara isn't waterproof, so don't make me cry," I say, sniffling.

"Why would that make you cry?" He laughs, leading me up the steps. "I don't understand you."

"It's a good thing we'll have the rest of our lives to get to know each other, my love."

He pulls open the door, amused as I step inside the house.

A barrage of voices fills the house. Conversations and laughter mix with the sounds of running water. The home is warm—both with spices and spirit.

"Wait." I point at a pillow on the couch and laugh. "Does that say *We had sex here*?"

"Jess."

As if that answers the question, he keeps walking.

My stomach forms the smallest knot as I stick close to my fiancé. We enter the kitchen and dining area, and my jaw drops.

I've heard people comment on how attractive the men are in my family. I've heard it many times. And it might be because I'm related to my brothers, so I don't see what the fuss is about, but they don't hold a candle to the Carmichael men.

They all look so similar—just variations on the same schematic. It's as if God said, *"Well, I nailed it the first time, so I'll make this one slightly taller, that one slightly darker, that one gets a little lighter hair."* They're so beautiful it's hard to think straight, let alone find words.

Kixx and a woman who can't possibly be Foxx's mother reach us first. They both seem delighted to see me.

"Well, there she is," Kixx says, pulling me in for a quick hug. "It's good to see you again, Bianca."

"Likewise."

"You know my dad," Foxx says. "This is my mother, Damaris."

Her bottom lip quivers as she pulls me into a long, warm embrace. "It's so nice to meet you, Bianca. You have no idea."

"It's nice to meet you, Mrs. Carmichael. Thank you for inviting me over for dinner."

"Mrs. Carmichael?" She pulls away, swatting the air. "I'm Damaris. Or Mom. Or whatever you want to call me. But considering you'll be Mrs. Carmichael tomorrow, too, it seems odd for you to call me that."

She beams.

*"You'll be Mrs. Carmichael tomorrow, too."* I take a shaky breath.

Foxx slides his arm around the small of my back. A small gasp escapes my lips at the contact. He presses his fingers into my side, and instead of calming me like I think it's supposed to, it electrifies my insides. *I really wish we would've practiced this before we left his house.*

"Everyone, this is my fiancée, Bianca," Foxx says.

I wave to the people all watching me.

"Bianca, these are my brothers and their girlfriends and wives, depending on the couple. Moss and Brooke, Maddox and Ashley, Jess and Pippa, and Banks and Sara."

*Banks.* I see why his name keeps coming up. He gives me the biggest shit-eating grin I've ever seen.

"Did he tell you he tried to beat me up today?" Banks asks, lifting a brow playfully.

"Tried?" Jess laughs. "You should probably check yourself before he wrecks you. Again."

Damaris puts her hands on her hips. "May I add, Moss is my favorite child today because he stayed and cleaned up a mess that you two"—she points at Banks, then Foxx—"made."

"Foxx, what did you do to Banks?" I ask, laughing.

"I didn't do enough," he says, staring his brother down.

I'm sure he means it. Gannon means it when he says similar things to Tate. But I also know they really love each other—even if it's down *really deep* sometimes. And I can tell by how Foxx and Banks look at each other that it's the same thing.

"Ignore them and welcome to the family," Moss says, his arms tightly around Brooke's stomach.

"We heard there's a wedding tomorrow," Ashley says. "Can we do anything to help?"

"I have to confirm the time with them," Damaris says. "It's not a done deal. Yet."

Ashley grins. "Sorry. I'm just excited."

Chatter breaks out once again, and I sag into Foxx's side. *So far, so good.*

"Thank you for helping us get this together," I say to my soon-to-be mother-in-law. "It's a lot to put on your shoulders with such short notice."

Kixx laughs. "Don't thank her. I haven't seen her this happy since …" He studies his wife. "I shouldn't tell them about what we did last night, should I?"

Foxx scowls at his father. I, however, laugh.

Damaris shushes her husband, but she looks at him with pure, unadulterated love. It takes my breath away.

That's the kind of love I want someday. The kind of love I didn't know really existed. It's the kind of affection I never saw in my parents' marriage. It makes me wonder if that's one of the reasons I've never wanted to marry.

"I have a minister who can come to the house tomorrow afternoon," Damaris says. "Or wherever you want to do it. I shouldn't assume you'll want to do it here."

I glance up at Foxx. He looks at me as if to say *whatever you want*. The look I give him says *too bad that wasn't what you were saying earlier*. He smirks and shakes his head.

"If we could have it here, I think that would be wonderful," I say, leaning my head against Foxx. To my surprise and relief, he tucks me even closer against him. "I'm still trying to get settled at Foxx's—*home*. I guess it's my home now, too."

The words hang in the air. *I guess it's my home now, too*.

Foxx must sense I'm thrown because he takes over.

"Yes, Mom. We'd love to have it here as long as you don't go overboard," Foxx says.

Kixx snickers and joins Foxx's brothers at the table.

"I mean it," Foxx warns her. "We want something quick and basic. Just us. A simple ceremony is all we need."

Damaris holds her hands in front of her. "I understand, and I will do my best." She looks at me. "I think we should talk privately—"

"*Mother*," Foxx says.

"Mother?" Banks snickers. "Why can't we get this Foxx more often?" He looks at me and grins cheekily. "You have done the impossible. You have turned Foxx into a nice guy."

"Banks, shut up," Foxx says.

"I spoke too soon." Banks winces. "It's a work in progress, I guess."

Before I can inject my opinion, the women congregate on us. They are all so friendly and kind with giant, genuine smiles.

I'm not sure what to do with them. I've never been one to really fit in with the girls, and I've never had close girlfriends. My stomach twists as I beg myself not to screw this up.

"We understand that we just met," Brooke says. "And you might have this under control and want us to go away. But we'd *love* to help you with the wedding."

"Damaris said it was a spur-of-the-moment thing," Ashley says. "Do you have a dress and flowers and all of that?"

Damaris smirks at Foxx. He tries to glare at her but can't quite pull it off. I want to laugh, but Pippa pulls my attention away.

"Tell us about yourself, Bianca. Not in some weird interview kind of way. But where did you live before here? What do you do for a living?"

The question is gentle and asked with a sweet curiosity. It's oddly comforting.

"Well, I live, or lived, in Nashville," I say, glancing up at Foxx. "I was the interim president of Brewer Group but have taken a leave of absence since this guy demanded to marry me."

"That's such a Foxx thing to do," Brooke says, laughing. "I wondered how he proposed. A demand seems fitting."

I laugh, laying a hand on his stomach. *My God, the man is made of steel.*

"How did you meet?" Ashley asks.

"Foxx works for my family."

"Doing what, exactly?" Maddox asks from across the room.

"I'm going with she owns a strip club, and he's a stripper," Jess says.

Foxx groans. "Can we not do this?"

"My money is on a spy," Moss says. "And I say that because of the binoculars."

I furrow a brow and look up at Foxx. "Binoculars?"

"I think he's secretly like a children's surgeon or something. And that's why he's always stressed out and in a bad mood," Maddox says.

"I think he inseminates baby goats," Banks says.

"*What?*" everyone says in unison.

"Not … *personally,*" Banks says. "With a syringe or something."

Jess shakes his head. "What goes through your head, Sparkles?"

*Sparkles?*

Banks shrugs much in the same way Foxx does. It's adorable.

"Fascinating guesses. But he's just a part of our security detail," I say. "No baby goats."

The brothers exchange a look. I can't tell if they don't believe me or are bored by the explanation.

"He used to be on my team," I say, hoping context will help them understand the situation. "But he's been on my brother Renn's detail for a while."

Maddox stands, a look of incredulity on his face. "Renn Brewer? Like, the rugby player Renn Brewer?"

"That's him."

"*He's your brother?*" Banks asks.

"Yes." I laugh nervously. "Why? Is there a problem?"

Jess snickers, turning his attention to Foxx. "So that's what you do? You protect celebrities. That makes *so* much sense."

"I feel like I'm missing something," I say.

"We've never known what, exactly, Foxx does," Moss says. "We've had theories. But he sneaks out of here in the middle of the night—with my binoculars. And he won't tell us where he's going."

"I'm under an NDA," Foxx says. "The people I work for don't want everyone knowing their business."

"So you're telling me that Jason Brewer is Renn Brewer's brother?" Banks asks, still piecing things together. "I've had conversations with a famous person's brother and had no idea."

I laugh. "Make sure you tell Jason he's a famous person's brother the next time you see him and see how well that goes over."

Everyone laughs, and the sound is music to my ears.

"We have an idea," Jess says, his arm around Pippa's shoulders. "If you're getting married tomorrow, then you can't stay together tonight."

My heart starts to pound. Foxx squeezes his fingers against me.

"It's tradition," Pippa says. "So why don't we girls have a little bridal shower slash bachelorette party tonight? And Foxx can hang with the guys."

"I don't hang with the guys," Foxx says.

"We'll just stay at my house and have some drinks. Talk shit. Beat up Banks," Jess says.

Banks scoffs. "You can try. He had me pinned behind a table earlier. It wasn't exactly a respectable fight—and it couldn't be a respectable fight because I'd kick his ass."

Foxx lifts a brow. Banks sits back down, angling himself toward the door.

"Or the guys can stay at your house, and Bianca can come to ours," Pippa offers, ignoring Banks. "It would be so much fun. We could get to know each other, and we can help you get ready in the morning. We can do face masks and our nails—all the stuff."

"Pippa, that is such a lovely offer," Damaris says.

My nervousness over the suggestion wanes, and a bubble of excitement grows.

I've never had a girls' night before. I've never been invited to hang out and do masks and nails. And while the prospect is slightly terrifying—especially on the eve of my impromptu marriage—it also seems like fun.

"It might be fun," I say to Foxx. My voice is barely heard over the roar of the room. "What do you think?"

He swallows, eyeing me carefully. Finally, he leans down close to the shell of my ear. "I have to protect you, remember?"

I turn my face to him, nearly brushing my lips against his. I tingle from head to toe and struggle to focus on our conversation.

"I … um …" I take a deep breath. "The houses are close, and it's a dead-end street. You have a security system, and I won't be alone."

He pulls back. "Do you want to do this?"

"*Kind of?*"

Admitting this feels a bit vulnerable for some reason. I just met these women. Do I come across as needy or desperate? But as I glance around the room and feel their energy and kindness—and absorb their excitement, I really want to do it. For the first time in my life, I want to spend time with women who might be able to be my friends.

Hesitation is written all over him. Stress is evident on his shoulders. He closes his eyes briefly before nodding. "Okay. Then we'll make it work."

*Thank you, Foxx.* I don't say it, but I don't think I need to. The crooked smile he gives me tells me he knows.

I lean against him again, taking the contact while I can get it. He adjusts his grip around my waist. The sturdiness of him beside me and his invisible shield around me are new sensations I could get used to.

"Let's fill our plates," Kixx says from the kitchen.

Damaris turns to us, her face lit up like a Christmas tree. "Do you have a time you're thinking for tomorrow?"

"Three?" I suggest. It's a random time, but I need something nailed down so we can move on.

"Fine with me," Foxx says.

"Three it is," Damaris says with a confident nod. "I'll get things rolling. Favorite color, Bianca?"

Foxx sighs.

I giggle. "Vermilion. It's a reddish-orange."

"Love that." She ushers me into the kitchen with an arm around my shoulder. "Now, let's talk about flowers ..."

I glance at Foxx standing by himself in the doorway to the living room. He's watching me with his mother like it's a foreign picture he can't quite understand.

But by his small, shy smile, I think it's one he likes. Maybe even a lot.

# CHAPTER 16

## *Bianca*

A KNOCK HAS ME STEPPING BACK FROM THE MIRROR. "COME IN."

Pippa peeks around the corner of the door. "You sure?"

"Please. I'd like the company."

She walks into Foxx's bathroom with a clear container filled with makeup. It rattles when she sets it on the counter.

"How are you doing?" she asks carefully.

"Great. Just overthinking my entire life, as one does on their wedding day."

She gives me a soft grin.

The Carmichael women stayed the night with me. I imagined we would get to know each other, share a couple of bottles of wine, and talk about me marrying Foxx. And we did that. But we also did so much more.

I've never met a group of people as generous and kind as Brooke, Ashley, Pippa, Sara, and Damaris. By ten o'clock, we were laughing so hard that tears streamed down our faces, ruining the face masks Ashley had brought. By midnight, they had invited Becca, the girl I met at the auction, to join us. She brought leftover pie from her job at Smokey's, a local restaurant. We gave each other manicures. They helped me decide how to wear my hair for the ceremony. They also gave me the rundown on what I needed to know as a Carmichael, where the best shops are, and how they all met their men.

Then they wanted to hear all about my relationship with Foxx.

Creating our love story was more fun than it should've been. I tried to keep it as broad as possible on the rare chance that Foxx shared details with his brothers. They must match, after all. But our relationship must also be believable, so a few specifics were necessary.

The details I shared weren't from a perspective Foxx would understand.

And if there is any goodness in the world, the universe will see that those details come true.

"Are you getting cold feet?" she asks. "Because it's okay if you are, you know. It's completely normal."

I laugh. "How could anyone have cold feet when marrying Foxx?"

My insides twist at my remark. I might not have cold feet, but I am slightly reluctant.

For a girl who never imagined she'd get married, I'm strangely emotional about it.

Things here are so much … warmer than they are at home. Life is so much more laid-back. They focus on the little things—Sunday dinners, inside jokes, caring for one another—and not just contracts and legacies. It's a world I didn't realize existed. I'm also completely smitten with it.

I'm also smitten with my soon-to-be husband.

"I will say, Foxx sneaking over here last night to check on you was very, *very* endearing," Pippa says. "I've never seen him act like this before."

"Really?"

"No. Are you kidding me?" She laughs breezily. "I think I saw him longer and conversed with him more last night than I have the whole time I've known him."

My heart swells.

"The man is crazy about you," she says.

*He is*? I sink back into the chair I dragged into the bathroom from the kitchen.

"Becca and I were talking about it this morning when we picked up our coffee order at Mugger's," she says. "The way he looks at you. His little smile." She squeals. "It's freaking adorable and even more so because it's Foxx. The man *never* smiles."

I pull my arms over my stomach as she gets up to work on my face.

Foxx isn't a *cheerful* person. His generalized demeanor is aloof and a bit cantankerous at times. But when we're together, his demeanor mollifies. It's these moments, happening more and more, that I see the real him—the man who hides his emotions behind barriers of self-built protection.

But protection from what?

My heart softens as I imagine him creating a shield between himself and the world. The man I know—the kind, generous, thoughtful man who will very soon be my husband—seems trapped inside his beautiful exterior, and that makes me sad.

Doesn't he want to be loved? Doesn't he want to experience the world? Experience ... *me*?

I close my eyes as she dabs a sponge over my face.

*You aren't marrying him for love, Bianca. This is an agreement between two mature adults acting from reason and facts instead of impulse or instinct. Don't become jaded.*

"Your hair looks beautiful," Pippa says. "Brooke did a great job."

I check out my reflection in the mirror. "Yes, she did."

"I want to know how she made it so voluminous." She sweeps bronzer over my skin. "I'll have to remember to ask her next weekend at pizza night. Did anyone tell you about pizza night?"

"No. I have no idea what you're talking about."

"Every Friday, we meet at Brooke's for homemade pizzas. They have this pizza oven on their lanai. We set up a bar, eat, and drink some wine. The guys usually end up in the pool at some point." She grins. "Foxx has never been to one of them, so hopefully you can talk him into it. I have a feeling you can talk him into anything."

My cheeks flush, and it's not from the blush she's now applying to my face.

I'm not sure what to think about her observations. I definitely can't talk Foxx into everything, or else I would've had sex with him by now. But I can't tell her that. It would be a big red flag.

But is that what it looks like to everyone else? Is Foxx selling our story that well? I would bet that he can do just about anything well. But acting? Somehow, that surprises me.

A part of me is amused. Another part of me, though, is a little wistful.

It would be so easy to buy into this whole facade. I could lean into being Mrs. Foxx Carmichael, a member of this wonderful family, and escape the reality of my real life. Instead of hiding from my father, I could help Kixx clean up at family dinners. I could hang out with Damaris and learn how to make her pudding pies that everyone raved about last night instead of wishing I could talk to my mother about, well, anything. The only thing I would miss are my brothers.

I miss them.

Tears well in the corners of my eyes.

Even though this wedding is a fraud and it's only for optics, being surrounded by Foxx's family makes me wish for my own. I thought I would be okay. I'm used to dealing with emotional situations alone. But I didn't expect to be emotional, and I didn't expect to long for someone from my family to stand beside me when I take my fake vows to my fake husband.

Pippa pulls back. "Are you okay, babe?"

I dab at my eyes and sniffle. "Yeah. I'm fine."

"Oh, Bianca."

She sets down her brush and pulls me toward her.

The contact breaks me, causing the tears to spill down my cheeks. I don't know why I'm crying or how to save my self-respect after this burst of emotional vulnerability. All I know is that being hugged by this woman I just met means more to me than anything. This is the hug I've been needing.

I pull away, sniffling. "I just screwed up your handiwork."

She takes a tissue and dries my face. "Then it's a good thing I can fix it."

"You're too nice to me."

"You're family." She winks, getting back to work on repairing my tearstained cheeks. "So I'm sure we'll fight it out someday. It's all about balance."

"I was just thinking about my brothers ..." I sigh. "I often think they're the biggest pains in the asses in the world. But, for whatever reason, I wish they were here today."

Her brows pull together. "Why did you say they aren't coming?"

"Oh, *um*, the wedding was a last-minute thing, and they're all busy. It's hard to expect anyone to travel across the country with less than twenty-four hours' notice."

*That and we can't tip off my father.*

"We'll have a party later," I say. "It's probably for the best, anyway. If Tate and Banks were in the same room, it might catch on fire."

She laughs, then fills my lips with pink lipstick.

Damaris taps on the door. "May I come in, ladies?"

Pippa steps back and assesses her work. "You're done and insanely beautiful. Check you out, hottie."

She steps away from the mirror so I can see myself. *Wow.* I look like I usually do, just elevated. I'm ... *pretty.*

"Bianca?" Damaris asks.

"Oh, yes. Please, come in."

I don't know why I suddenly have an overwhelming need for approval, but I do.

I stand, smoothing out the flattering white sundress Astrid found at Halcyon. The tiered-ruffle empire-waist design is finished with self-tie shoulder straps and hosts a swingy hem. With the smocked back panel, it gives me a breezy silhouette that's simple and elegant.

Damaris's hands clasp in front of her. "Bianca. *Oh, my gosh.* You are stunning."

"Really?"

"Absolutely. That dress is divine." She bumps her hips with Pippa. "And you did a tremendous job on the makeup. You can barely tell she has any on, and the way you brought out her beautiful eyes? Amazing."

Pippa beams.

Damaris takes a tissue and dabs her eyes. "*Okay.* I came bearing a gift."

"You didn't have to bring me anything. If anyone owes anyone a gift, I owe you for putting this whole day together."

"Nonsense." In her hand lies a small blue ribbon, only about four inches long. "This is a bookmark from Foxx's baby book. I thought you may need something blue."

I'm unsure what to say as I take the satin fabric between my fingers. *She was planning on giving this to Foxx's actual wife.* This doesn't feel right, but I can't say no. "This is so precious, Damaris. You didn't have to do this."

"I wanted to, sweet girl. Now, do you have the rest of the rhyme? Something old, something new, something borrowed, something blue?"

"This is something old," I say, holding out my right hand. "This pearl was my grandmother's."

"Perfect." Damaris smiles. "Do we have something borrowed?"

Ashley knocks before entering the room. "I'm not late, am I?"

"No." I laugh. "The ceremony doesn't start for another half an hour."

She takes my hand, turns the palm up, and then drops a thin gold bracelet in the middle of it. "It's taken me the better part of the last hour to find this. Maddox *helped* organize my jewelry the other day—which means I can't find anything."

"What is it?" I ask, admiring the delicate piece of jewelry.

"It's your something borrowed," she says. "I mean, if you don't want to wear it—"

"Of course, I want to wear it. Will you help me put it on?"

Ashley smiles and helps clasp it in place.

My emotions are teetering, barely held together by grit and defiance. I don't want to cry in front of them. I don't want to cry at all. I want to be the steeled version of myself I use in the conference room. Impenetrable.

Thankfully, like so much of the past few days, I don't have time to get lost in the details. There's only a moment to appreciate the kindness shown me.

"Oh!" Pippa says. "I have something for you, too!"

There's a hint of mischief in her grin. There's an air of excitement in her tone. Combined, they cause my blood pressure to rise as I watch her walk to the door. Before she opens it, she pauses and turns back.

"I have a message for you," she says, and then twists the knob.

Jason comes in, stopping when he sees me.

*He came.* I hold my hand over my mouth, blinking back the stupid tears I've tried so hard not to shed.

"*Wow, B,*" he says. "You're gorgeous."

My lip trembles as he pulls me into a hug. I didn't know just how much I really needed someone in my family here until this very moment.

"Everyone wanted to be here to witness this momentous occasion," he says, winking as he pulls away. "Especially Renn."

I laugh, knowing what he means. Renn got married while drunk in Vegas, and I'm getting married under threat in Florida. I grew up thinking he and I were so different. Maybe not.

"But I have the plane, so I won." He hands me a small pink box with the coveted *Siggy* logo etched in delicate white script. "We couldn't have you here alone."

"I really appreciate that, Jason." I hold up the gift. "What's this?"

"Open it and see."

I untie the thin white ribbon and discover a filigree heart charm dangling from a safety pin.

"Siggy Mason had this at her pop-up shop," he says. "Ripley thought it was perfect, but we didn't know what you would do with it. Renn got Blakely's opinion, and she said you could pin it to your flowers or on your dress somewhere if you liked it."

"I love it." A lump forms in my throat. "Thank you."

He tucks me against him and whispers, "I'm sorry you have to do this."

Emotions water my eyes. *Again.* "I'm glad you're here."

"My sister is marrying my best friend." He pulls away and smiles for our audience. "I wouldn't miss this for the world. Damaris, our mother, sends her regrets, as do our brothers. Unfortunately, Bianca sprung this on us at the very last minute."

"We cannot wait to meet them," Damaris says, holding her arms out to Jason. "We are so happy to have you in the family, Jason. Welcome."

Jason grins at me as Damaris envelops him in one of her warm hugs.

"There's one more thing," he says, handing me a small black box. "From Mom."

I slip the top off and stare at the sparkling necklace lying against the white fabric. *I can't believe how meaningful this day has become.*

"That's beautiful," Damaris says as Jason helps fasten it around my neck.

How will I get through this day without bawling my eyes out? The gifts. The extremely warm and loving acceptance from the Carmichael family. My mom gifting me this necklace.

I take a deep breath, hoping I can get myself together. *This. Isn't. Real. Breathe, Bianca, even if you hate that you're essentially lying to Foxx's family.*

"It was my grandmother's. She promised me when I was a little girl that I could have it when I got married." I laugh, the sound muffled by my emotions. "I'd forgotten about it."

"Mom wanted to be sure it made its way to you," Jason says.

I look up at him and smile. *Thank you, brother.*

A part of me hates that this is all … false. The treasured Carmichael family heirlooms really aren't meant for me. That Jason didn't show up to support me during my real wedding day. That I'm not really having a wedding at all.

This is so wonderful, so lovely. I wonder if things were different, if this wasn't based on a lie—if Foxx hadn't been transferred to Renn and had stayed with me and allowed himself to fall for me, if all of this could've been real.

"I hate to break this up," Pippa says. "But it's showtime."

A surge of adrenaline spikes through my veins.

Jason flips out his elbow. "May I have the honor of walking you down the aisle?"

"I wouldn't have it any other way."

Ashley hands me a bouquet of the most gorgeous vermilion-colored roses. Apparently, Damaris is friends with the local florist and asked her last night if she could custom-dye flowers for today.

The effort warms my heart.

If I'm not careful, I might fall in love with this family.

# CHAPTER 17

## *Bianca*

"Ease up on that thing," Jason says, nudging my bouquet. "You're strangling it like you want it to die."

*Oof.* I release my death grip on the flowers. "I'm antsy."

"I can tell," he says, chuckling. "You haven't stopped moving since we got here."

Jason and I stand in Damaris's den, waiting for the first notes of the "Wedding March" to play. Per our instructions, we'll exit the French doors leading to the backyard then. Then Damaris says, we follow the path leading to my fiancé.

The shiver of excitement that crept up my spine when she said those words is concerning.

I've stayed cool during billion-dollar mergers. I didn't blink during an audit last year. I was cool, calm, and collected when Dad made *me* fire the CFO. *So why can't I stay composed now?*

I bring my flowers to my nose and inhale the beautifully sweet scent.

*Because this situation involves my heart.*

It's unwise to get caught up in this whole thing. We're playing pretend. We're ensuring Brewer Sports stays within our family and doesn't land in the hands of the Downings. We are not choosing this act out of love.

The telltale notes begin to play, and the doors swing open to reveal a setup far from the fuss-free, simple event Foxx and I requested.

*It's perfect.*

Jason stands tall and tilts his head to me. "You ready, Miss Brewer?"

Goose bumps cover my arms. "Let's do this."

My brother leads me down the aisle of vermilion and white rose petals. His family—his brothers, their girlfriends and wives, Kixx and Damaris—stand as we approach. They aren't sitting on a groom's side for Foxx. They're on both sides of the aisle, supporting us both through our unique event. It tugs at my heartstrings. Although Jason is here, seeing their support makes me feel less alone. It's as if I'm really becoming a part of their family.

"This is amazing," I whisper, taking in the scenery.

The setting couldn't be more beautiful, with a breeze blowing through the trees, rattling the leaves. The grounds are freshly mowed so that the ceremony feels intimate on the larger plot of land. Lights hang from palm tree to palm tree like a highwire of hammocks, and the bougainvillea that Damaris said was fading in the season appears to have bloomed again just for the occasion.

As incredible as this day is in all ways, the sight of Foxx whips the air out of my lungs.

He is always breathtakingly handsome with his lady-killer jawline and those piercing blue eyes. But seeing him in khaki-colored pants and an open suit jacket with a white dress shirt with the top button undone might be the death of me. My heart skips more than one beat.

Dipping his head down, he runs a finger over his mouth as if he's willing a smile to retreat behind his shield.

Jason gently nudges me to keep moving. I hadn't realized I'd stopped.

Foxx looks up, our eyes meeting across the distance. A calmness washes through me. No doubts arise, and no last-minute panic or urge to run away takes over. Instead, I'm confident that this is the right answer. I'll just have to enjoy it while I can and prepare myself for it to be over.

But not yet. Right now, I'm living this up.

Foxx gives me the sincerest smile I've ever seen on his handsome face.

Between the leaves and breeze, it's as if time stands still just for us.

Jason and I stop just before the minister, where he turns to me and wraps me up in a big, brotherly hug.

"I am so proud to be here with you, and I'm so proud you're my sister," he whispers.

"If you don't stop trying to make me cry, I'm going to drop you right here."

He chuckles and places a kiss on my cheek. Then he takes my hand. "Here you go." He offers my hand to his best friend. "You are the only person in the world I'd trust with my sister."

"I won't let you down," Foxx says.

Jason smiles. "Take care of her, my guy." And with that, he finds a seat next to Maddox.

Foxx's fingers lace through mine. They're sturdy and strong. "You're gorgeous, Bianca." He grins bashfully.

The minister welcomes everyone and dives right into the ceremony. I try to pay attention to what he's saying and stay connected to the happenings around me. But it's hard to concentrate on anything besides my soon-to-be husband.

Foxx strokes the top of my hand with his thumb, watching me with the quietest reverence.

I smile at him, wishing we were alone so I could talk to him. I haven't seen him since three this morning when he snuck over to check on me. The girls thought it was wildly romantic, and I played along with that. Really, he just wanted to make sure I was safe.

But despite knowing the truth—knowing Foxx is playing a game of charades right along with me—it would be easy to forget it. The sweet smile. The loving way he's holding my hand. The glimmer in his eyes is so real that I'm impressed he can fake it. It all adds up to a vision of one very real wedding ceremony.

The ring I slip on his finger, thanks to Astrid's quick thinking, is platinum. Foxx's brows shoot to the clear sky as I slide it down his digit.

"How?" he asks, amused.

"Astrid. Don't worry about not having one for me. Blame her."

He chuckles. Then he stares me in the eyes without any resistance in his baby blues. He reaches in his pocket and retrieves a perfect, simple band. He slides it on my finger as he promises to love me for better or worse until death do us part.

"How?" I ask him.

He grins. "Maddox."

"It's perfect, Foxx."

"Do you think so?"

I return his smile. "It's exactly what I would've picked for myself."

"By the power vested in me by the State of Florida, I now pronounce you husband and wife," the minister declares. "Foxx, you may kiss your beautiful bride."

"Jess, get your chicken before it gets in the cake," Banks says from behind us.

Everyone turns to see a big orange bird perched on the back of an empty chair, poised as if it will dive into a cake on a card table. Another one with black in its white feathers, scurries down the walkway nibbling at the rose petals.

"You can't manage to contain your birds for a ten-minute wedding ceremony?" Kixx asks, standing to help Jess.

"I'm not denying them the right to free-range because Foxx decides to get married," Jess says, making everyone laugh.

Everyone except Foxx.

His displeasure over the chickens tightens his jaw. As much as that tic does things to me—things he better be ready to quell as soon as we get out of here—I don't want him tense.

"Hey," I say, touching his face so he'll turn to me.

"I'm sorry Jess's chickens interrupted your day."

"It's okay. It'll make today more memorable."

Out of the corner of my eye, I see an expanse of orange feathers. It's followed by a loud roar of profanities, laughter, and shouting.

I keep my gaze locked with his until his grin returns.

"Actually," I say, pressing my lips together. "It's not okay."

He lifts a brow.

"You're going to need to apologize for that when we get out of here," I say. "And once won't be enough. This hurt me deeply."

Foxx smirks, sliding a hand around my waist and dragging me into his chest. I gasp as reality suddenly gets *real*.

*I'm Mrs. Foxx Carmichael.*

He licks his lips, his face inches from mine. "This won't be the only thing touching you deeply today."

My legs turn to gelatin. "Careful, Mr. Carmichael, or we might not reach our honeymoon."

"I'm sorry, everyone," Damaris says. "Iris gets to keep the cake."

"I'd like everyone to stop for a moment and take note that, for once, it wasn't me who ruined things. It was Jess," Banks says.

A commotion breaks out again, but I lose interest.

Foxx's hands coddle my face like a precious stone. He stares into my eyes as if his heart will stop beating if he loses contact. Slowly, his mouth falls to mine.

His warm and commanding lips own mine as his hands caress my head and lower back equally. I give in and turn over control to my new husband.

Warmth blossoms in my chest as Foxx's lips brush against mine. Dizzy, I lean into the kiss, inhaling the scent of his cologne and absorbing the heat of his breath.

This kiss is a promise of things to come.

Someone begins to clap. It's quickly followed by a lot of clapping and a few whistles and shouts. Foxx's forehead rests against mine as we attempt to slow our breathing. *My God, this man can kiss.* I giggle. *He better do a lot more than that on the honeymoon.*

"What?" he asks.

"I forgot they were watching," I say, laughing.

"I didn't."

*What? What is that supposed to mean?*

He kisses my forehead and then takes my hand, turning us to face his family and Jason. I'm woozy on my feet as he leads me to the house. His mom mentions something about the ruined cake, and Foxx tells her not to worry about it without breaking stride.

We slip inside the den. Foxx quickly locks the door behind us.

"What—*oh!*" I gasp as I'm spun and pinned against the back of the door.

My chest rises and falls as I labor to stay calm.

Foxx's gaze drips down my neck and over my collarbone. He unapologetically drags his eyes down my chest, over my belly, and stopping at the apex of my thighs before returning his attention to my face again.

"You are so beautiful, Bianca," he says, his voice raspy. "But I can't wait to get you out of this damn dress."

My cheeks heat, but I manage to restrain myself from kissing him again. Through quick breaths, I give him an arrogant smile.

He's tortured me for the last day. Thanks to Astrid and the lingerie she sent me last night, I have the upper hand. And he's going to pay for his sins.

"It's too bad we have a whole reception to get through," I say, holding his gaze as I tilt my pelvis into him. "To think that I must sit in these soaked panties while pretending to care about the punch. Your mom will be talking about finger foods, and I'll be thinking about you licking my wetness off your fingers."

His chuckle ends with a growl.

*I want you so bad, but I'd rather have you begging than me throwing myself at you.*

"We better go," I say, batting my lashes. "We have to thank everyone, share in the toast, have our first dance ... It will take a while."

His eyes darken. "One dance. Let's go." He takes my hand, unlocks the door, and tugs me outside.

My laughter trails us.

# CHAPTER 18

*Foxx*

"This is so great," Bianca says, taking in the suite my brothers rented. "Look at the view."

She stands at the windows overlooking Silver Springs State Park. Jess said the views from this hotel were great, room service was excellent, and it was close to a variety of things to do if we wanted to get out and do something fun.

I didn't tell him that everything fun I want to do will be in this room.

The drive to the hotel was quick, thanks to light traffic, and fun, thanks to Bianca's inability to go two minutes without talking. I've never seen her this relaxed or energized. It's adorable. I found myself prodding her to keep her talking about the random shit she'd bring up. We talked about everything from mergers and makeup to contracts and couture. Well, she talked about everything. I occasionally contributed a thought or two. But I was happy to listen to her babble on about the things that interest her.

We talked about everything—besides fucking. But it was all we were thinking about.

I pointedly avoided addressing it outright if for no other reason than to drive her crazy. I want her ready for me, desperate to be touched. It will only make it that much better for her in the end.

"The view has been good all day," I say, sitting on a red leather sofa.

She turns around, pressing her back against the glass.

The tide quickly shifts, going from veiled innocence to blatant hunger. I've wanted this, *wanted her*, for so long that it's hard to wrap my brain around the fact that we're here, and we're going to fuck.

*I'm going to fuck my wife.*

I clench my teeth, fighting the urge to drag her onto my lap and sit her on my cock. There's something so sexy, so alluring about Bianca being my wife. *Being mine.*

"What are you thinking about?" she asks, her nipples straining against the fabric of her dress.

"Do you want a list?"

"Sure."

I lean forward, resting my elbows on my knees. *Patience, Carmichael.*

"I'm thinking about how fucking beautiful you looked today," I say.

Her cheeks flush into the prettiest shade of pink.

"And how proud I was to have you marry me in front of my family," I say. "And I was thinking how much I loved watching you get along with my mom and Brooke and everyone."

She graces me with a shy smile.

"It was an odd experience in a way," I say, watching her listen closely to my every word. "I usually have a stark disconnection with my parents and siblings."

"How was today any different?"

I fight the smile that wants to paint itself on my lips. "Today, I was one of them."

I don't explain it to her, mostly because I can't. How do you explain that you've always felt different from your family without sounding weird? How can you verbalize that you've always felt more reserved and more serious than the rest of them? I've always felt like I was missing a part of their puzzle.

Until today. And that's fucking weird.

"You know, Foxx, I think maybe you're too hard on yourself. You realize how much they love you, right?" She smiles. "Even Banks."

I roll my eyes, making her laugh.

"Are you laughing at me, Mrs. Carmichael?"

Her eyes go wide at the sound of her new title. My heart skips a beat. *I like that more than I should.*

She recovers quickly and shoves away from the window. She eyes me coyly. "I don't know, Mr. Carmichael. Will it get me in trouble if I am?"

Her tone sends a message to my body, setting every cell on high alert.

She saunters over to me and stands behind the sofa. Her fingertips brush up and down my neck before she begins to rub my shoulders.

I shiver against her touch. It's as if my body is electrified, and every contact with her skin sends a shock through me. But I don't pull away. Instead, I let her knead my muscles back and forth.

"Does that feel good?" she asks.

"*Yes.*" I groan. "Damn, that feels good."

"I want you to close your eyes."

I'm not sure where she's going with this, but I do as she requests.

"Now I want you to imagine what it's going to feel like when your cock is sliding between my lips, pushing through my warm, wet mouth."

I groan, palming myself through my pants.

"Pretend I'm licking it—pressing my tongue against the length of your shaft," she says, rolling her hands over my shoulders. "Licking a bead of pre-cum off the tip."

Every muscle in my body contracts as I imagine her kneeling in front of me with my cock in her hand. It's a picture I've imagined many times. But I've never imagined it with her hands on me.

It's a new level of heaven. And a new level of hell.

She bends forward, whispering in my ear. "Imagine my nipples rolling between your fingers." She moans against the shell. The vibrations rattle through every inch of me, culminating in my groin. "And the taste of my flesh as you bury your face between my legs."

I can't take it anymore. I grab her hand and tug, pulling her until she comes over the back of the couch and straddles me.

Her eyes are wide as I lift my shaft against her opening.

I grip her hips with both hands and roll myself against her. Her head falls back, and she pushes down, shifting her weight for maximum contact on her clit.

"Think about what it's going to feel like when I suck that swollen bud into my mouth," I say. "The fire that's going to spread through you so hot it'll burn."

She takes my hands from her hips and moves them to her tits. I palm them both through her dress. They're perfectly round and full, and the moan she gives me as I stroke her nipples with my thumbs has me ready to come in my pants.

"I'm going to slide these soaked panties off you in a minute," I say, kissing the side of her neck. "Then I'm going to lay you down on your back."

Bianca grinds her body against mine, whimpering.

"You're going to spread your legs so you're wide open for me," I say. "And you're going to show me that sweet little pussy that belongs to me."

*"God, Foxx."*

I press a kiss to the side of her neck. "Do you like that? Do you like knowing that your body is mine now?"

She moans, pressing my cock against her clit. "It's not yours until you take it."

"Oh, sweetheart, it's mine. You and I both know it."

I nip at her neck, making her yelp.

"I bought really sexy lingerie to wear for you," she says, breathing hard. "But the thought of putting more clothes on right now sounds like the worst idea ever."

"It's pointless." I lift the hem of her dress and drag it over her body. I gasp a breath. *"Fucking hell, Bianca."*

The fabric goes flying off to the side as I take in the perfection sitting on my lap.

The ways I have envisioned her in the past are nothing close to the sexpot she is in real life.

*Dammit.*

Her tits are covered in a thin, lacy bra. The cups are so full, so round, that they almost spill over.

I run my hands down her sides, feeling the curve of her body against my palms. Her stomach is rounded in the sexiest, most feminine way, and it makes my cock pulse as she grinds against it.

"I have wanted you for so long," she says, running her hands through my hair. Her nails scratch into my scalp. I think I might lose my composure. "Do you know how many nights I went to bed with my vibrator, imagining it was you getting me off?"

"If it is half as many nights as the ones I went to bed, imagining my hand was your tight little cunt milking my cock, then I'm impressed."

I pop her breasts out and sit them on top of the cups.

"What do you want me to do to you, Bianca? Tell me all the things you dream about so I can make them happen."

I pull a nipple into my mouth and cup her ass with my hands. The globes are bubbles—perfectly round and juicy.

She moans, pushing her chest toward me.

I squeeze her cheeks, then trail my fingers down her thong.

"I want you to fuck my pussy and my mouth," she says, rolling a nipple with her fingers. "I want you to come so deep inside me that it rolls down my leg all day."

"Fuck," I mutter against her. "God, that's hot."

"I want you to tie me up and fuck me hard. Eat my pussy until I come on your tongue. Let me ride your face."

This is music to my fucking ears. Bianca wants me—will let me—do all these things to her?

*How did this happen? Who did I please to be favored like this?*

I pull back, flicking her nipple with my tongue as I let it loose. Her eyes are bright and lively as she watches me for my reaction to her admissions.

"You are a dream. Do you know that?" I ask.

She blushes.

"I mean it," I say, squeezing her thick thighs.

"What do you find attractive, Foxx?"

"Logic and common sense."

She laughs, her face lighting up. *She's so beautiful.*

"What do I find attractive?" I ask, letting my hands roam freely over her. "Your mind."

She dangles her arms over my shoulders.

"This delectable body," I say.

She grins.

I bring my lips against hers. *"Calling you my wife."*

Our mouths move together like we've kissed every day of our life. She parts for me, letting my tongue slide over her teeth.

Bianca tastes like sugar and mint, a tingling combination that is intoxicating. She holds my face in her hands as I tease the roof of her mouth. She cocks her head to the side as I lick along her bottom lip. She acquiesces to every move I make.

Everything about this feels so comfortable, so … *right*. In the back of my mind, I remind myself that the only reason this is okay is because it's a part of the job. It's a part of the role I've been asked to play.

But hell if it doesn't feel real right now.

Bianca breaks our kiss, her breathing ragged. Slowly, she climbs off my lap.

She stands in front of me in only her panties and a bra tucked beneath her breasts. Her hair is down, her lips swollen from kissing me. She looks wild and wonderful—fiercely feminine. *And all mine.*

At least, for now.

She removes her bra and tosses it to the side. Then she kneels between my legs, looking up at me demurely.

She holds my gaze as she undoes my belt, and then unfastens my pants. I help her scoot them down my legs. Soon, my pants and boxer briefs join her bra somewhere in the room.

*"Wow,"* she says, taking my cock in her hand. I groan at the contact. "It looks like you're ready for me, *my husband.*"

I clench my teeth together to keep from losing control.

She strokes my length from the head to the base, licking her lips as she watches her hand go up and down. A bead of pre-cum gathers on the tip.

I hiss a breath as she flicks her tongue against the head. The hiss deepens as she takes me in her mouth, licking the cum and polishing my cock clean. I flex my hips into her soft, warm mouth and will myself not to come. Not to lose control.

# CHAPTER 19

## *Bianca*

WATCHING FOXX STRUGGLE TO MAINTAIN HIS COMPOSURE IS THE SEXIEST thing I've ever seen.

Considering that I don't have a ton of experience in this department, I was a little nervous about how this night would go. *Would I freeze up and become self-conscious? Would all the shit I've been talking come back to bite me in the ass? Would I fumble around or be really self-aware?*

The only thing that's happened thus far is that I've never felt as confident, pretty, or sexier than I do tonight.

I position myself between his knees. My chest rises and falls in time with his. We're both anticipating what's coming next.

"This is unreal," he says, his eyes feral.

I palm his cock and gaze up at him, flicking my tongue against his swollen head. "What's unreal?"

"Having you between my legs with my cock in your hand."

"Would it be better if it was in my mouth?"

I pull him between my lips before he can respond. He hisses, his hips flexing instinctively.

"*Fuck, Bianca.*"

I suck the tip, then smile. "Yes, you will. But be patient."

He chuckles mischievously until I take him in again, this time to the back of my throat. He throbs in my hand, swelling even more. The contrast between the hardness of his cock and the softness of my mouth is dizzying.

I worship every inch of him, licking the ridges and veins, the underside of his length. I lick and suck, taking my hand up and down him until his groans become a steady occurrence throughout the hotel room.

Knowing I have this effect on him is powerful. I suck the cum spilling over for me off the tip again, watching him react through my lashes.

He holds the sides of my head with both hands and flexes his hips, thrusting his cock down my throat. I struggle to keep up—to keep licking and pumping my fist, playing with his balls with my free hand.

But just as his balls tighten and a sting of saltiness tints my mouth, he pulls out.

I sit back on my heels, panting. I wipe my mouth with the back of my hand like a true lady.

He stands, picking me up effortlessly, and then his mouth crashes against mine as he carries me to the bedroom. He nips my lip again before tossing me on the bed.

He makes quick work of ridding himself of his shirt, and I only get a quick glimpse of his solid pecs and chiseled abs before he digs his fingers into the waistband of my panties. They're dragged roughly down my legs.

"Let me see that pretty little pussy," he says, bringing my knees up and then spreading them to the sides.

I'm displayed for him. My wet, throbbing clit is there for the taking.

"I'm going to have so much fun with this." He smiles, dipping a finger into my wetness. "You're so damn ready."

"Did you expect anything less?"

He chuckles. "Bianca, I never expect anything from you. You're too unpredictable."

"I can predict with total accuracy—*ah*!" I arch my back as he inserts a finger inside me. "If you touch me for long, I'll come."

He positions himself between my legs. "What if I ..." He flicks my clit with his tongue. "What if I touch it with my tongue?"

"Same outcome."

He blows across my flesh, making me shiver.

"Where is that cocky woman from before?" he asks, toying with me. "Where's the woman who's been begging to be fucked?"

"She's still begging to be fucked. She's just so worked up that words are hard."

He laughs, lowering his face. The laughter fades as he takes a long, slow taste of my pussy.

*My gosh, that feels good.*

He takes his time as if he's relishing the taste of my body. The sound of him sucking and licking rings through the room. I moan his name, threading my fingers through his hair and encouraging him to continue.

He adds a finger, then two, to the mix. They pump in and out as he watches me bask in the flood of sensations.

"Does that feel good?" he asks.

I hum.

"Come on, sweetheart," he says. "You have to tell me what you like. I want to know what my wife enjoys."

He spreads me open, probing his tongue inside me.

"That ... that feels good," I say, struggling to form words.

He presses small circles over my clit as he continues to tongue my opening. The suckling noises, the scent of sex, the brackish taste still on my tongue are all too much.

My legs begin to shake.

I dig my fingers into his scalp as my whole body tenses.

The buildup is slow and steady. It's delicious and divine. The warmth that accompanies the impending orgasm floods my veins, pooling in my already overstimulated pussy. And as he flicks, increasing the pressure on my tingling flesh, I fall apart.

"*Foxx*," I half say, half shout. My teeth clench so hard I'm afraid I'll need a dentist. "*Yes!* My God! Yes! Oh my ... *fuckkkk!*"

He clamps an arm over my belly as I grapple against the force of the orgasm. I try to writhe, try to slip out from under him—but it's no use.

I'm going to lie here and let this burst of pleasure tear me apart.

The intensity surges, and I scream, tears dotting my eyes from the pressure. I can't see clearly. I can't make out any sounds or words distinctly. All I know is that I'm falling apart around Foxx's tongue.

"I can't …" I shiver as I fall gently back to reality. The intensity is nearly painful. "Foxx, I can't. *Please.*"

He eases back, pressing a soft kiss to my opening before lifting his head.

My face is flushed, and my body is spent. My muscles refuse to cooperate as I place the back of my hand against my forehead and watch Foxx climb up the bed and lie beside me.

He strokes my cheek with the back of his hand.

"Can I make a request?" I ask.

He chuckles. "Sure."

I turn my head to face him. "Can we work out some kind of a deal so I get that every day of our marriage? At least once?"

His laughter—loud, deep, and free, is unexpected. But it might be the best sound I've ever heard.

Foxx doesn't laugh often. And when he does, he doesn't laugh like this. *Except for now.*

"I think we can throw it into our vows," he says, his eyes shining.

I giggle. "So what you're saying is that you really said—*to have and to hold, in sickness and in health, promising to make your wife come on your face every day for as long as you both shall live?*"

"Exactly that." He takes my hand and kisses my palm. "That's exactly what I said."

I lean over and kiss him. "I have one more request."

"You're needy tonight."

"Lucky you."

"What do you want?" he asks, lacing our fingers together.

"I need you to go get a condom."

His face breaks out into a smile.

He climbs off the bed and goes into the living room. I hear his suitcase open in the distance.

"What would you say if I told you that I forgot condoms?" he asks.

I ponder that. "For one, you never forget important things. So I'd start to wonder if you might want to knock me up. For two, you'd be taking a chance on knocking me up—although I'm on birth control—because you're not getting out of here until you get off."

He comes back into the room, rolling a protective barrier down his shaft.

"See?" I say, laughing. "I knew you'd be prepared."

He grabs my ankles and, in one quick movement, yanks me to the edge of the bed. "Do you want to lie on your back with your legs up? Or do you want on your hands and knees?"

"I got what I wanted. This one is for you."

"Then get on your hands and knees, and let me watch that ass while I fuck you."

*Why is that so hot?*

I roll over and pop up on all fours. He slips an arm under my stomach and moves back toward the edge of the mattress. I widen my knees and tilt my pelvis to give him better access.

My pussy gets wet all over again.

"This one is going to be fast and hard," he says, massaging my ass.

"Great—*ah!*"

The sound of his hand cracking my bottom flies a split second before the sting of his palm bites at my skin. This is all moments before the force of his cock nailing me from behind jolts me forward. Foxx yanks me back, holding my hips so hard that his fingers burn my flesh.

It's a cacophony of sensations—sounds, feelings, and the faint taste of blood from biting my tongue.

I sag against his cock as he thrusts deeply into me. Each motion is intentional and powerful yet deliciously satisfying.

"You feel so good," he says roughly. "Better than I dreamed."

"Then fuck me."

I squeeze my eyes shut and focus on the way his cock hits the back of my pussy. With every tap the head makes against that spot, I get closer to orgasming again.

His fingers sink deeper into my waist, and he picks up his pace.

"Is this what you asked for?" he asks, cracking me on the ass again.

I yelp, relishing how the burn heightens the pleasure wracking me.

"Can you feel how tight you are?" he asks. "Can you feel how your pussy squeezes my cock? *Damn, Bianca.*"

The buildup begins again.

I tighten my muscles around him and am rewarded with a moan. I do this over and over, clenching down on him until he begins to shake.

He slams into me harder.

I yelp louder.

He grunts deeper.

I shake more uncontrollably.

"I'm going to come, Foxx," I say, the words broken by a shiver.

"Come on my cock."

It takes two more thrusts before I fall apart around him. I begin to fall forward. Foxx holds me in place, driving into me and rolling his hips.

I can feel his cock pulsing into me, spilling his seed into the condom.

I shudder, and my teeth begin to chatter. I shake uncontrollably as the last waves of the orgasm break over me.

Finally, just as my arms are about to give out, Foxx slides out of me. Then he helps me to settle against the mattress softly.

I'm aware that he has moved away from me. I hear the rattling of plastic and something dropping into a trash bin. Shortly after, he crawls onto the bed and lies next to me. He brushes a lock of hair out of my face.

"Are you okay?" he asks, his eyes full of concern.

"Never been better."

His body falls with relief.

I smile at him. "I'm not used to this, so I'll need a minute to recuperate."

"What do you mean you're not used to this?"

"Well, I haven't had sex in a couple of months," I say. "And then it was just a couple of times with my neighbor."

His eyes darken. "It's not a good idea to talk to your husband about who you last fucked."

"Why? You didn't want me."

He rolls over and pulls me next to him. "It was never a matter of me not wanting you, Bianca. It was a matter of it not being the responsible decision."

"And marrying me is responsible?"

"It certainly solved a lot of problems."

I smile against his side. "That it did." I pause. "But what if it creates more problems in the end?"

He moves until he's fully on his side with his top arm draped around me. I'm cocooned against him.

"Want to get cleaned up, and then we can get some food?" he asks, yawning.

I want to call him out for not answering my question but think twice about it. Maybe it's better if we don't talk about it. Maybe we should enjoy this while we have it.

"I'll run the bath. Can you see if any menus are lying around?" I ask.

He kisses my forehead. "Deal."

"Deal."

We climb off the bed, and I search for bubble bath. It feels like it's time to get clean, knowing that my husband will soon be making me dirty all over again.

# CHAPTER 20

## *Bianca*

MOONLIGHT STREAMS THROUGH THE OPEN CURTAINS, CREATING A romantic, sultry glow around the bedroom. Foxx lies in the middle of the bed with his arm curled around me. He holds me tight against him.

I considered joking about him taking up most of the king-sized real estate. But it occurs to me that it might be his way of ensuring I stay close to him. If that's the case, I don't want to ruin his plan, nor do I want to embarrass him.

Foxx has blossomed in front of me tonight. He sat in the bath with me, refilling the tub with hot water twice. He seemed perfectly content to listen to my stories and only interrupted me to ask questions, give thoughtful advice, or tease me. *The teasing was my favorite.*

His chest rises and falls smoothly beneath my cheek. He strokes my arm, occasionally pulling me tighter as if the inch I've fallen away from him is too much. His body is hard yet relaxed. This is the most relaxed I've ever seen him.

"Today has been magical," I say, my eyelids heavy.

The events of the past twenty-four hours begin to accumulate on me. A wedding, reception, drive to Silver Springs. I had sex for the first time with my husband. A long, hot bath with the sexiest man alive and had delicious room service. I feel more seen and treasured than I knew was possible.

He hums. The sound rumbles through his body, tickling my cheek.

"I have to admit that the day started out strong but continued to get better as it went on," he says, trailing his fingertips across my skin.

I smile against him.

"Where do you want to go for our real honeymoon?" His tone is husky from the late hour. The grit of it pulls at my core.

"What do you mean? This is our real honeymoon."

"I suppose to some degree. But this is a generic version of what I want to deliver."

I run my hand down his muscled abdomen. "Mr. Carmichael, there was nothing generic about what you delivered."

He chuckles. "I'm glad you think so. But I fully intend on taking you on an actual honeymoon. I just haven't figured out where that place might be."

"That's unnecessary, you know. I would want to do the same thing we're doing here, regardless of where we were on the planet."

He bends his head and plants a kiss on the top of my head.

My heart flutters at the sweet gesture. I try not to think too much about it. Otherwise, I'll internally spiral about it ending, about the mess at home ... about returning to Nashville.

The idea of going back to Nashville fills me with dread. Things have been so lovely with Foxx—so comfortable and effortlessly easy. It's a version of *the grass is always greener*; we're living in a fictional, idealized world without real-life problems. Still, it's been a breath of fresh air.

And I really like myself here.

"Where would you go?" I ask, cuddling closer against him. "If you could go anywhere in the world, where would it be?"

He laughs softly. I look at him just in time to catch a smile.

"What's so funny?" I ask.

He shakes his head.

"*No*," I say, laughing, too. "Tell me. I'm your wife now. You can't just blow me off."

His eyes darken.

The heat of his gaze coils in my core, and I squirm. "Tell me, and I'll do something about that."

"About what?"

I dip my hand below the sheet and palm his hardening cock. *"This."*

"I was thinking about how I've been to so many places in the world. And none of them have proven to be as amazing as they're supposed to be."

"Really? Like where?"

He nestles his head against the pillows and sighs.

If I didn't have him in my hand and know that his body was ready for me, I would think he was resting after a busy day and readying to fall asleep.

He's so peaceful, so calm. The lines around his eyes have vanished. His shoulders are soft as if he's not on edge, and it's a beautiful sight.

"I was in the military for a while," he says. "That's where I met Landry and Troy Castelli."

"Aw, I like Troy. He sometimes fills in for Calvin."

Foxx pulls back, turning my chin with the tip of his finger. I don't have to look at him, nor do I need a lot of light to read the room.

I giggle, biting my lip as I look up at him.

*"Don't,"* he says. The lines are back in full force.

"Or what?"

He stares at me.

"I already have you in the bag, Carmichael." I press a kiss on his chest. "I don't have to make you like me."

"That's not the point, *Carmichael.*"

He smirks as if he made his point. *Fuck, that's so sexy.*

"What's not the point?" I ask, sliding my leg over his.

"That you already have me in the bag." He grins. "You've had me in the bag for a long time, and you know it."

*What? I have had you in the bag.*

*No, sir. I did not know that.*

I sit up and straddle him, planting my pussy on his cock. He gives me a look, warning me that things might take a *hard* detour. I'm willing to take the risk.

A giddiness I haven't felt in years takes over. I couldn't wipe the smile off my face if I tried.

"What did you just say?" I ask, planting my hands on his chest.

"Don't be coy, Bianca."

"I'm not." I laugh. "I want to hear you say it again—just to be sure I didn't mishear you."

He sets his jaw in place.

*Okay. That's how you want to be, huh?*

I press myself against him, rotating my hips in a slow, smooth circle. Flames flicker in his eyes as his hands find my thighs.

"Come on, *husband*." He licks his lips. "Say it again."

His hands skim across my hips and then up my naked front. "You're so fucking beautiful, *wife*."

My lips part with a small gasp. "Why is it so hot hearing you say that?"

"Because you know I'm yours."

*Good God.*

He lifts his hips into me. His eyes shine in the low light. "I don't know why you're acting surprised."

"Because I am."

He rolls his eyes, making me chuckle. "You know what you're supposed to say now, don't you?"

I hum, relishing in the pressure of his length against my sex.

"You're supposed to tell me that you're mine." He holds me down by my hips and thrusts against me. "*Tell me.*"

"I kind of like where this is headed."

His smirk is dangerous. *And I nearly combust.*

"Tell me, Bianca."

"I might just ride you like this," I say, sliding across his cock. "I don't really need your participation. I could get off from just this."

He slips a hand between us and inserts a finger into my wetness. "I love how wet you get. It's such a turn-on."

"You're about to feel that wetness coat you because I'm going to come."

"That's fun." He lifts a brow as his phone chirps on the bedside table. He reaches for it, pulling his cock away from me.

"What are you doing?" I ask, my frustration growing. "You're not going to check that."

He ignores me and settles back against the pillows.

I smack his chest. "*Foxx.*"

"What?" The glow of the phone illuminates his face. "What do you want?"

"*Put that down.*"

He tilts the phone away long enough to give me a look. Then it goes right back in front of his face again.

"I hate you," I say, squatting harder against him.

"That's quickly becoming a theme in our marriage."

I groan, glaring at him as he pulls his hips away from me and sinks them into the mattress. This was fun at first. Now, not so much.

"You sound agitated," he says, his thumbs tapping the screen.

"You're hilarious. But wait until it's *me* denying *you*. We'll see how entertained you are then."

He doesn't take his eyes off the screen. "Did you know that foxes love to play?"

"Keep it up, and you're going to be one fox playing all alone."

He fights a grin. "Well, that tracks. It says here that foxes can play with other foxes ..."

He drops the phone far enough to see me over the top. His brows are raised. This option is far too entertaining for him.

"I would be very careful before you play with other foxes," I say, raising my brows right back at him.

"They also play with other animals, which really isn't my speed, or they can play alone."

I reach for his phone, but he pulls it away.

"What are you doing?" I ask. "Now isn't the time to be looking up fox facts."

He tosses the phone on the other side of the bed and laughs. "It's that random number again."

"They're still texting you?"

He grips my hips and positions me back over his cock again. "I've only gotten a couple of them." His forehead wrinkles as he rolls my nipples between his fingers. "I have an idea of who it might be, but I'm not sure."

"Who is it?"

He leans forward and grins. "I can't tell you." He swipes his tongue across my lips before capturing my reply with his mouth. I melt into him, my body turning to mush, as he takes command of the situation.

*Like he wasn't in control before. He's always in control.*

He's so hard against my slit that I don't know how he's holding it together. My thighs are sticky, and my pussy's hot as I work my body against his, trying desperately to find the perfect amount of friction that will send me over the edge.

"Are you ready to be a good girl?" he asks, breaking our kiss and lying back again.

He laces our fingers together and holds them in the air. It gives me leverage to work with. I moan as the head of his cock strokes my swollen bud.

*Just a few more times …*

"Whose pussy is this, Bianca?" he asks, shoving his hips into me. "Answer the question, and you can have it."

I close my eyes, wanting to deny him. I love his fierceness when he doesn't get what he wants. I love his passion when he goes after it.

When he goes after me.

"I'm sorry," I say, forming an eight with my hips. "What was the question?"

I squeal as he flips me onto my back before I know what's happening. I'm panting, my heart pounding, as he climbs on top of me.

One hand on each side of my head, he uses his knee to roughly part my legs.

I hiccup a breath, so ready for him that I might fall apart from the look in his eyes.

He leans forward, taking my lip between his teeth. I hiss as he tugs just far enough so it burns.

"Now," he says, positioning himself at my opening. The head teases the hole before he adjusts himself, so it presses against my clit. "You have one last chance to answer my question."

"Or what?"

He grins. "You're going to have to decide whether that's a gamble you're willing to take."

He toys with me, spreading my juices all over my pussy with his cock. All I can think about is how good it's going to feel when he plunges into me.

I grip his shoulders and dig my fingernails into his flesh.

His eyes hood as he senses my willingness to cooperate—that he's on the precipice of winning our little battle.

My legs wrap around his waist. I grin. "Do you feel this?"

He hums in agreement.

"This wet, tight, hungry pussy is all yours—*ah!*" I say, my eyes rolling to the back of my head as he slams deep inside me.

"Are you sure?"

"Yes."

"Say it again," he says, punctuating every word with a hard thrust. "Tell me you're mine, Bianca."

"I'm yours."

"*Again.*"

"*I'm yours.*"

He sinks inside me, rolling his hips. "Again."

"*I'm yours, dammit,*" I say, my voice nearly a scream.

I can't hold back. I can't screw with him or torture myself any longer.

He pounds into me so hard that my head rams into the headboard. The wood bangs into the wall once, twice, three times.

"Open your eyes," he demands. His tone brooks no argument.

My lashes part, and I stare into his eyes.

"Let me watch you come," he says.

He encases my shoulders in his giant palms and shoves me down onto him as he pushes inside me. The pressure is intense. The force exquisite. I'm jetted to the top of the cliff and shoved over the other side.

"*Fuck,*" I say, my teeth chattering and legs shaking.

"Fuck." He tenses. "I have to pull out."

"What?"

"No … *condom,*" he says, barely able to get the word out.

*Oh.* I'm pulled out of the orgasm just enough to realize he's about to come inside me with no protection.

I start to build again. The idea of my husband coming in me has sparks readying to go off a second time. As I feel him start to slide out of me, I panic.

*No. Wait. I want this.*

It's a crazy idea, one that just might be brought on by the need to release the stress of the week and Foxx's naked body. But whatever it is, I want this.

*And he's my husband. So why not?*

I shove him off me. He's startled but rolls onto his back without question. I climb on top of him and grab his cock.

"Now isn't the time to have this conversation, but let's get it over with," I say, desperate for him to be inside me again. "I'm on birth control, and I'm disease-free."

His eyes widen as he realizes where I'm going with this line of questioning. "Are you sure you want this?"

"Tell me you're clean, and I'm going to ride this cock until you come."

"*Fucking hell,*" he says, hissing. "I'm clean. I never would have put you at risk if I wasn't."

I smile mischievously. He returns it.

"Now ride me, baby."

I straddle him and place the head of his cock at my opening. I hold his gaze as I slide onto him slowly, feeling every inch of the smooth, hard rod filling me.

"*God, that feels good,*" I say, taking a moment to absorb the burst of pleasure flooding me.

"You have no fucking idea."

I laugh, disbelief at being at this moment—at being in this life— walloping me. It's crazy and unbelievable. But it's real. *And I'm going to enjoy it.*

"I'm warning you that I'm ready to blow," he says, holding my tits as I start to move. "It's not going to take much."

"Let me watch you come."

His gaze bores into mine as I ride him. I take him deep, swirling my hips and lifting and lowering. He swells, and his body tenses. The veins in his neck pop.

I'm teetering on the edge of another orgasm. I fight the angle I want, avoiding the spot that will throw me into another fit of bliss so I can go off with him.

"I belong to you," I say, finding a rhythm he likes. "This pussy is yours."

He meets me stroke for stroke. "You're damn right it is." His body shakes. "That's it. Right … *there. I'm coming.*"

I rock harder against him.

His Adam's apple bobs. His eyes roll back. He moans my name, sending the word through the room in the most seductive moment of my entire life.

I fall apart around him as his seed spills inside me.

Before I know it, I'm a heap on his chest. Our breathing matches as we fight to regain control of our senses. His arms wrap around me, holding me tight against him.

I wait for the regret—the moment I realize I just let Foxx come in me and what a big mistake it was. But the regret doesn't appear.

I don't know what that means or if it'll happen later. I just know I've never felt this blissful … and I'm in no hurry to end it.

"You're amazing," he says, chuckling. "It's a good thing I didn't know what this was like, or else I would've taken a chance on Jason hating me a whole lot sooner."

I laugh, pressing a kiss to his sternum. "You're lucky I didn't know what it was like, or else I might've offered you a bonus to service me."

His amusement grows as he stretches and yawns.

"Let's get cleaned up and get some sleep," he says.

I groan. "I don't want to get up."

"I know, but you have to." He kisses my forehead. "If you get up and go to the bathroom, I'll have the rest of the cake from dinner waiting for you when you get back."

"Will you feed me?"

He sits up, causing me to sit up, too.

He takes my chin in his hand, his eyes shining, and kisses my lips. "I will do whatever you want me to. Remember that."

My heart expands as I grin at him.

Foxx Carmichael is the best man I've ever known. Sexy. Kind. Loyal. Selfless. Funny. *Mine.*

But if I'm not careful, this fake marriage might not feel fake for very long.

# CHAPTER 21

## *Foxx*

I SLIP OUT OF THE BEDROOM, SHUTTING THE DOOR SOFTLY BEHIND ME.

"Carmichael," I say into the phone, squinting into the late morning sunlight.

"I hate to call you on your honeymoon," Jason says. "But I wanted to do a quick check-in and share some news."

Suddenly, I'm awake. I pull back the phone to check the time. *How the hell did we sleep that long?*

Memories of my wife sitting on top of me, on her knees with my cock in her mouth, bending over the bathtub with her ass in the air throughout the night all come pouring back to me. *"I'm going to ride this cock until you come."*

*Yup. That'll make a man sleep late.*

I run a hand down my face and focus. "All is good here. What's up?"

"Where is Bianca?"

I clear my throat. *This is awkward.* "In bed."

"Okay, good. I was hoping I could catch you alone." He takes a deep breath and blows it out. "Had a call from Landry this morning. The intel came in and was confirmed."

"About what?"

"Originally, we were leaning toward the Downings being the

biggest threat to Bianca—which makes sense. They're the ones who stand to gain from this situation."

"Right."

"But, *and I hate to even say this out loud*, it's Dad."

I furrow my brows, not following along. "What does that mean?" I look over my shoulder. "I'm trying to be discreet on this end."

"I understand. What I mean is that, and we didn't tell Bianca this, but we intercepted an email from an undisclosed IP address that threatened to … well, I'm not going to repeat it. But let's just say it wasn't a good time."

A rush of cold air blows across me, chilling me to the bone. I still, staring across the greenery below, and fight the urge to blow my lid.

I force a swallow. "You're telling me that he was the one who sent the message?" My voice is eerily calm, even to me.

"Yes."

"And where is he now?"

"We don't know."

I look at the bedroom door again, imagining her curled up in bed. She's sleeping peacefully, with a sated smile on her face that she's had all night. The thought of sharing this information with her—telling her that her father threatened to hurt her—is akin to breaking her heart. And that breaks mine.

"Nothing will happen to her, Jason. I will kill a motherfucker for trying, whether that's *him* or someone else."

Saying that to my boss, that I would kill his father, might not be wise. But it's the truth. When it comes to Bianca, I'm not going to play around—not with Jason, not with Reid Brewer, not with anyone.

He pauses. The silence piques my curiosity. *Is he going to try to put me in my place? Is he going to remind me that I'm still on the payroll and currently doing my job? Will he insinuate that I need to remember who's in control?*

The idea of being told that I have no place when it comes to Bianca —a place that isn't her protector—sends a streak of rage through my body. I might be on the Brewer payroll. I might be doing a job. But what happened yesterday … it doesn't feel like a fucking job anymore. It feels personal. It feels like my fight. My responsibility.

*Like my fucking wife.*

I run a hand through my hair, knowing I'm playing with fire.

This situation isn't real; it's a marriage of convenience. I went into this to protect the woman who I couldn't stop thinking about—not to fall in love with her.

My blood turns to ice.

*Is that what this is? Is that what I've done?*

*Oh dear God …*

"Can I ask you a question, Foxx? If I do, I need you to be real with me."

I still.

I know what's coming because I can hear it in his voice. He's going to ask me if there's more between his sister and me.

Panic rises in my chest as I consider what his response might be. *Will he deem me unqualified to protect her? Will he try to assign someone else to watch over her?*

*What if it's worse than that? What if he feels like I've lied to him? What if he feels betrayed?*

Did he mean those words at the wedding?

*"You are the only person in the world I'd trust with my sister."*

He's right to trust me. I would never hurt her. And I will protect her with my life.

My stomach knots. *He knows, doesn't he?*

"Foxx?"

*Whatever he asks, I won't lie to him.*

I clear my throat. "Yeah, of course. What's your question?"

"Are there real feelings between you and my sister?"

*Boom.* There it is.

I shuffle across the floor, nervous energy propelling me to the window. "That's a loaded question, considering I married her yesterday."

He chuckles. "Can I be honest with you? Maybe that will help this conversation go smoother."

I don't answer because if he's honest with me and says he knows how I feel about Bianca, then proceeds to tell me to fuck off—we're better off not going there.

"Foxx, unless I'm way off, and I don't think I am ..."

Sweat dots my forehead. "I'm sorry."

"For what? For being in love with Bianca?"

I sigh, closing my eyes and waiting for the other shoe to drop. For him to tell me that he's sending a plane for her. For Jason to tell me how disappointed he is and to never talk to him or her again.

"I've known for a long time," he says. "Hell, anyone who's ever seen the two of you together knows that. That's why when this started to boil over ... I don't know who I can trust right now, Foxx. I especially don't know who I can trust with my sister."

My chest squeezes hard.

"But I know I trust you—*with my life*. So when Landry asked what I thought we should do with Bianca to keep her out of harm's way, there was only one answer. I had to send her to the man who loved her because he would protect her as fiercely as I would."

A ghost of a smile touches my lips.

"And that man is you," he says. "So what do you say?"

"I think you talk a lot." *Just like your sister.*

He bursts out laughing.

"You really could've wound that up in a sentence or two." *Then I wouldn't have had to sweat buckets over here.*

He settles down. "Does Bianca know how you feel?"

"I don't know." *"Tell me you're mine, Bianca."* I smirk. "She might."

"The sooner the two of you stop playing cat and mouse, the better off we'll all be."

"Well, since you know how I feel, I feel comfortable saying this. She can be a pain in the ass."

"Don't I know it."

I grin. "What do you need from me? What can I do?"

"Right." He blows out a breath. "I don't want to tell her about Dad yet. She tries to play it tough, but I know it'll hurt her. And I don't want her worrying about it until we find him. Then she can deal with it knowing he's put away and can't hurt her."

I pace the room. "But how do we know he won't send someone else? Where are the Downings in all of this?"

"Well, strangely enough, our attorneys reached out to them about the amendment. They sent a formal reply that they weren't aware of the amendment and had no interest in pursuing it."

"And we can believe them?"

"I never believe anyone fully," he says. "But sending a letter via their attorneys is putting it in writing. If something happens to Bianca, they know they'll be one of the first persons investigated. I think this is their way of saying their nose is clean, so to speak."

I lean against the sofa. "So why did your father write the amendment in the first place? I don't understand."

"We don't either. We're still working on it. But if you can keep Bianca busy and out of the public eye until we find Dad, that will help."

I smirk. "I think I can do that."

"I bet you can." He groans. "Let's remember she's still my baby sister, and I will still kick the shit out of you, Carmichael."

Our laughter blends, easing some of the tension that crept back into my shoulders.

"Tell her I called, okay?" he asks. "Tell her she should check the family chat sometimes. Just because she's married doesn't mean we don't exist."

"I will. I'll talk to you later."

"Hey, Foxx."

"Yeah?"

I can almost hear his smile through the phone.

"You should make a real go of this," he says. "You and Bianca. You're the only man I know good enough for her, and she's the only woman who's good enough for you."

*Damn you, Jason.* "Yeah." It's all I can get out without sounding like a moron.

"Ah, the one-syllable answer. There's the Foxx we know and love."

"Fuck off."

He laughs. "Talk to you later."

I end the call.

"What is happening right now?" I ask the empty room.

Before I can attempt to answer my own question, my phone buzzes.

> Mom: Sorry to bother you. But I was just at Smokey's, and they found one of your keys. Becca gave it to me. I set it on your kitchen counter.

> Me: Another one?

> Mom: I know.

> Me: Thanks.

> Mom: Love you. (And it's killing me not to ask questions about your honeymoon, but I won't. Please remember this at Christmas.)

I silence notifications and then toss my phone on the couch.

*"You're the only man I know good enough for her, and she's the only woman who's good enough for you."*

I'm in shock. I'm sure that's what this is. I've heard it described before—low blood pressure, altered mental state, confusion, rapid pulse—but I've never felt it. Not all those things at one time.

Not like this.

As the incredulity starts to fade, another brand of the same emotion begins.

*Could this be the start of something real? If Bianca feels the same way, and I'm not even sure it's realistic to hope that she does, could we really do this?*

*Could she really be my wife?*

I should be backtracking, finding ways to throw up boundaries and keep this thing in a tidy box all on its own. But the idea of keeping her separate from all other things in my life feels wrong. I'd feel cheated. Having her included in my life is the only option that feels right.

"Foxx?"

Bianca's sleepy voice rings through the hotel room. The sound of the slumber still thick in her tone makes me smile. *My wife.* Who I love.

I go to her, opening the door and peeking in. She's lying in the middle of the bed, waiting for me to come to her.

My heart thumps on the heels of my conversation with Jason.

"Hey," I say, slipping into bed beside her. She wastes no time curling up next to me. This is how it's supposed to be. "How do you feel today?"

She laughs. "Tired. Sore. Ready to go again."

My chest shakes as I chuckle.

"What are we going to do today?"

I shrug. "What do you want to do today?"

"Well, I've been thinking about it …" She smiles. "I was thinking we could order room service for breakfast because I saw something about croissant French toast and that's totally my vibe. While we wait, we could exchange some oral just to start the day off nice and easy."

*That's it. She's the perfect woman.*

"Then we could maybe do something outside—just to get some fresh air," she says. "But nothing too outdoorsy. Just because I want to do something outside doesn't mean I want to be an outside girl."

I snort. "Explain that, please."

She sits up. "Okay, it's like this. I like to get fresh air and sun. Hiking is fine if there aren't bugs. Swimming is great if I can see the bottom. We can go camping with air-conditioning and hot, running water. Otherwise, not my idea of a good time."

Bianca's tits are in my face. I have no idea what she just said.

"What?" I ask.

"How did you not—"

I take one of her nipples in my mouth. They're at mouth height. I'm a man.

She pushes me away. "Foxx, I was talking."

"Sorry. I can't help myself."

She sighs. "I'll summarize. I like the outdoors, but don't do bugs."

I shake my head. *You are too adorable.* "That's not how that works."

"I think you can make it happen."

"You have a lot of faith in me," I say.

"So don't let me down." She watches me expectantly. "So you know …"

I flinch. "What? Do you want fucked again?"

"No. I mean, yes," she says, laughing. "But we need to get the food order in because I don't want to get cranky."

I drag her down until she's lying flat against me, then cup her face in my hands.

"Do you think I'm scared of you if you're cranky?" I ask.

"You should be."

I gently kiss her lips.

*"Then we could maybe do something outside—just to get some fresh air."*

Okay, I did hear her. Sort of.

*What can we do outside that's not in public?* I think about it for a second and come up with an idea.

I kiss her again, pulling away as she tries to deepen it.

"Hey!" she protests.

"Food first." I roll her off me and then climb out of bed. "I'm going to order for us. When I get back, be naked and spread out for me."

Her giggles follow me out of the room.

# CHAPTER 22
## *Bianca*

"Don't move!" I grip both sides of the kayak for dear life. "This thing is going to—*ah!*"

He laughs behind me, shifting his weight just enough for the vessel to shake. I recoil from the turtle jetting below us like he's in a race.

"We're not going to flip. Relax," Foxx says from behind me.

My heart pounds as I scan the area for wildlife—mostly wildlife of the carnivorous variety. Since the man at the rental shack warned us to stay out of the vegetation because alligators hang out there, I've been a little on edge.

"Who said this was fun?" I ask, watching a school of fish beneath the glass bottom of the kayak.

"Jess."

"Well, that was your first mistake."

He laughs again. "Why is that?"

I look over my shoulder at Foxx. His white T-shirt sticks to his body, thanks to my handiwork with a water bottle. His legs are long and lean in a pair of green board shorts. I wish his sunglasses were off, though. I'd love to see those blue eyes.

"Jess's chicken ruined our wedding cake," I remind him. "Yet you trusted him to pick our honeymoon adventure?"

"Look around. This is pretty fucking cool."

"Yeah, well, it would've been *pretty* and *cool* to be fucking you right now instead of worrying that the only thing that's going to eat me today is an alligator."

I roll my eyes at his amusement and shove my paddle into the water.

Despite my objections, this is pretty fucking cool.

The crystal clear water is the prettiest shade of turquoise. It reminds me of my favorite beach in Belize. Trees loom large overhead, blocking out the hot Florida sun. Spanish moss drips from the branches and even dangles in the water at some points. It really feels like you're in a whole new world, cocooned away from reality.

Being away from reality with Foxx is my new favorite place to be.

We drift along with the current, listening to the trickling water and occasional animal sounds. I close my eyes and breathe in the fresh outdoor air. The parking lot was virtually empty. Apparently, the park gets slow during the week. We're the only kayakers in sight.

"So what do you think?" Foxx asks, sliding his paddle into the water. "Be honest."

"I'm always honest."

Grasses sway lazily below us, bending gracefully to the water's will.

"As long as I forget about modern-day dinosaurs lurking in the bushes …" I look at him over my shoulder again. "I actually really like this." I face forward again. "I never imagined myself in a kayak floating down a river. It's kind of funny, really."

"Why is it funny?"

I laugh. "I don't know. Last week, I was in a designer suit and heels, threatening to lodge them up someone's ass if a deal didn't come through on time. Today, I'm married, in a bikini, acting like the queen of the jungle."

"Which do you like better?"

"What do you mean?" I ask.

"Do you miss the designer suits and boardrooms?"

My paddle trails in the water, creating a rippling effect on the surface.

I haven't thought about my job in two days. And as the interim president of Brewer Group, that's not a good thing. It's disappointing and irresponsible. This is not who I'm supposed to be, and I'm sure when my brothers told me to stay put for a while and that Gannon would take over until I returned, they didn't expect me not to check in.

But I haven't.

And I don't care.

"Foxx, I think I'm a fraud."

My words hang between us, refusing to dissipate in the thick, humid air. The feeling of them in the world, free from the cage of my mind and available for judgment, is terrifying. But also, it's a relief.

I don't know what I'll say if Foxx agrees. I'm also unsure how I'll respond if he thinks I'm being overly dramatic or blows me off. Because I'm not being dramatic. I'm serious. And the fear of being blown off and not taken seriously has stopped me from admitting this truth to myself—or anyone.

"Why do you feel that way?" he asks, bringing his paddle out of the water.

"I ..." I'm unsure how to put it into words. "I haven't felt like someone I know for a long time. I've made peace with it, telling myself that it's a consequence of being a working woman. That something must give to be the person I want to be." I take a deep breath. "But what if I don't want to be her anymore?"

He sets the paddle across the kayak. "Then don't be her."

I laugh at the simplicity of his answer. "Okay. Sure. Thanks for the tip."

"All right. Then who do you want to be? How is she different from who you are?"

"You see, that's the thing. I think I am her already. I'm just trapped in this world I thought I wanted."

"You're never trapped, sweetheart."

I smile. "What if ... what if I wanted to walk away from Brewer Group? What if the thought of going back there made me ill? And how could I do that to my family—especially when they need me the most?"

"Let's say you don't. How do you justify sacrificing your life? If you're lucky, God gave you one life—a solid eighty, ninety years. How do you take that gift and just throw it away because you think other people expect you to?"

*Oof.*

"Your life isn't less valuable than anyone else's, Bianca."

My chest stretches, filling with an unexpected warmth. *Is it that easy? Should I just value myself and ignore the needs of others?*

*Should I feel guilty if I walk away from Brewer Group?* Because that's what I think I want.

That's what I know I want.

"Look at it like this. If you're not her, *who are you?*" He asks the question as if he already knows the answer. It's curious and hesitant but also hopeful.

I drag my fingertips along the surface of the river. *Who am I when I'm in Nashville? Who am I with Foxx Carmichael?*

*With you, I'm calm. At peace. I'm satisfied and happy.*

*I'm … free.*

"I'm not sure who I am," I say carefully. "But I really like the woman I've been the last couple of days."

He shifts again, rocking the kayak. This time, I don't mention it.

"I've laughed more in the past few days than I have in the past year," I say softly. "I'm in a kayak. I took a spur-of-the-moment trip. I've gotten to know people as humans and not as a contract number or email address. *I got married.* It's been wild."

He chuckles, rubbing his thumb along the back of my neck.

"And do you know the craziest part?" I ask. "It's that I'm here because someone was trying to hurt me. I'm arguably in the most danger than I've ever been throughout my life. Yet …"

I turn around as much as possible without tossing us into the water.

He lowers his sunglasses, giving me the privilege of seeing into his eyes. They're sparkling and beautiful and so clear. If he wants me to see that he's not hiding anything, it's working.

"Yet," I continue, holding his gaze, "I've never felt safer."

He leans forward and carefully, not to freak me out, presses a gentle kiss against my lips.

It's the sweetest kiss he's given me yet. It's also the most powerful. As he pulls away, a realization uncoils deep inside me. It stretches through each part of me and confirms what I was afraid I already knew.

*I love him.*

How could I not?

I want to tell him those three little words and watch his reaction. I want to tell him the many remarkable qualities about himself that amaze me. I want to explain how it makes me feel when he holds me in his arms or calls me his wife like a trophy.

No one has ever come close to making me feel like Foxx Carmichael does.

Yet I'm afraid to tell him because I don't want to ruin what we have. Because if this ends tomorrow and Jason picks me up to go home, I want to remember these few days as the best days of my life.

"Do you want to know something ironic?" he asks.

"Sure."

"While you've spent your life trying to be everything to everyone, I've spent mine trying not to be anything to anyone."

My spirits fall. "Why?"

He sighs. "I don't know, really. It's a multifaceted issue that probably begins with being the eldest of six kids."

"As one of the younger ones out of six kids, I'd love to know why."

"Well, when you're the oldest, it's all on you. If your parents aren't around, you're tasked with keeping the younger siblings in line. You have to watch your mouth, or they'll repeat things, and you'll take the fall. You have to share your stuff. Make them a snack when you get yours."

I've never really thought about that.

"I sort of pulled away in my teenage years because I was just sick of them, to be honest. And then, I went into the military for a while and saw the horrors of the world. I traveled with Mandla. I lost friends who didn't deserve to die."

"Foxx, I'm so sorry."

"Life starts to look like it's out to fuck you. And the more people you're close to, the more ways it can bend you over the barrel."

I hate that he feels this way.

"It makes me sad to think that you spend your life alone," I say, pulling my hand into the kayak as I spot an alligator. I shiver, trying not to make eye contact with it. I also don't want to disrupt this moment with Foxx. "You have so much to offer the world. How do you justify sacrificing your life and withholding the gift of you?"

"I share it with the people I want to share it with."

Chuckling, I put my paddle back in the water to push away from the shrubs. "So, no one, you mean."

"I'm sharing it with you."

My body stiffens. I'm not sure what he means by that. *Does he mean he's sharing it with me right now? Today? This week? Until this situation is resolved?*

*Or does he mean he's willing to share it with me?*

I shake my head, chastising myself for going there when I know better.

"For a long time, I've feared losing the people I love," he says quietly. "I've seen the fragility of life. I wake up sometimes in the middle of the night having dreamed that something was happening to someone important to me, and I can't stop it."

I frown, my heart aching for him. It must be so hard to live with that kind of fear, but something tells me it's even harder for him to admit that to me.

"That doesn't help your desire not to want to be anything to anyone, does it?" I ask.

"No. It doesn't." He shifts again. "But do you know what does help?"

"What's that?"

"*You.*"

*Me?* I'm afraid to look at him. If he's smirking or joking, I might tip this kayak and feed him to the gators. But if he's not …

"You don't have to say it back," he says, his voice wobbling. *Oh my God.* "But yesterday when—"

"Cut to the chase."

He laughs.

The air gets warmer. Thicker. Stickier. I can barely breathe.

*"Say it, Foxx."*

He laughs harder.

My hand shakes around the paddle. "Why are you laughing?"

"What are you doing, Bianca?"

I scoot around in my seat until I face him. The lines around his eyes aren't the severe ones that usually develop when he's irritated or furious. This time, they're crinkled in a different way. Out of happiness, maybe.

The look on his face steals my breath. The dark, mysterious Foxx Carmichael looks relaxed and entertained. I can barely process it.

"Look, you usually say like four words at a time," I say, my blood pressure rising. "And all of a sudden you're Mr. Chatterbox."

His chest shakes as he continues to chuckle.

"Don't get me wrong, I love that you're sharing things with me. *Love that for us.*" I cock my head to the side and point at him. "But if you're going anywhere near where I think you were going, I need you to get back to the old Foxx and get to the point before I have a heart attack. Then you'll have to paddle this thing all the way back alone and then carry me to the car—*ugh*."

His smile stretches from ear to ear. "Are you going to say it back?"

"I don't know," I say, returning his smile. "I don't know what you were going to say."

"We don't have a solid history of you actually repeating what I need to hear."

"*Ooh*, I think that was worth the tussle." I sit up straight, my stomach in knots. "Let's give it a shot. You say it first, and I'll repeat it."

"But will you mean it?"

"I don't say anything I don't mean."

His smile turns cheekier. His eyes darken. I know this look, and it's not the one I want to see.

"*Stop it,*" I say.

"Yeah, I think we should wait and have this conversation later." He pivots the kayak around to head back upstream. "I'd hate to have one of our disagreements on the open water."

"First, this isn't the open water. But, more importantly, our disagreement is going to be much, much worse if you make me wait to hear what you were going to say."

He smirks. "It'll be worth it, wife."

I smirk right back. "Oh, you're right. It will be, husband."

# CHAPTER 23

## *Bianca*

I step back from the mirror and give myself a once-over. "Not bad, Mrs. Carmichael. Not bad."

The sound of *Mrs. Carmichael* makes me giggle. But that's what two glasses of wine, a hot bath, and a solid game plan on how to torture your husband will do to you.

Foxx said he needed to take a little time and make some calls. I think he was just trying to mess with me, but I assured him it was a great idea. I needed a bath and to make some calls myself. He couldn't say no to that. He respects me and my work too much to get in the way. And I think he hoped I was making calls to walk away for good.

I made zero calls. But I did wash, scrub, and shave every inch of my body.

Astrid hit it out of the ballpark with the lingerie selection. The piece I chose is almost too pretty to wear—and I wouldn't wear it at all if I didn't know it would drive Foxx out of his mind.

Beautiful white embroidered lace that's long and flowy. The goddess silhouette accentuates my waist. Long slits are cut from the embellishment nestled under my breasts, which appear fuller and heavier than usual, to the floor. I almost discarded the white thong but decided at the last minute to give the look a shred of modesty.

I laugh. "Modesty. Okay. Tell that to my nipples that may as well not be covered."

Thanks to the hair powder Becca let me borrow for the honeymoon, my hair is voluminous. I created a smoky eye and added glossy pink lips. *Let him think about those being wrapped around his cock.*

Excitement ripples over me in waves. I've tried not to focus on the root of this production—that I think Foxx will tell me he loves me tonight. Instead, I've attempted to play it off like I'm going to make him beg.

And I might.

I open the door to the bathroom. Through the bedroom, I can see him sitting in the living room on the sofa.

"What are you doing?" I ask in my sweetest voice.

"Just figured out who is sending these fucking fox texts."

"Really?" I walk through the room and come up behind him. "Who is it?"

He doesn't turn around, just lifts his phone so I can read the screen.

> Unknown: Taking a Paige out of the wild elephant handbook, foxes in London are domesticating themselves.

"Do you see it?" he asks.

I point at the misspelled word. *Paige.*

"It's your sister?" I ask, laughing.

Foxx chuckles and opens a family chat titled No Girls Allowed. "She'll live to regret this."

"What are you going to do?"

"Just watch."

> Foxx: How are you liking the animal texts?

His phone dings in quick succession.

Maddox: HATE THEM.

Banks: 😠

Moss: I'm contemplating getting a new number. They won't stop.

Jess: Mine have slowed down. I started texting the nastiest shit to them.

Foxx's fingers fly over the screen.

Foxx: It's your sister.

He silences his notifications. But he doesn't put his phone down. Immediately, notifications pop on the screen silently.

Foxx laughs as a new chat is created titled **HOLLIS, COME GET YOUR SISTER** and he's added to it.

"Who is Hollis?" I ask, laughing.

"Hollis is Paige's biological brother. My parents adopted her when she was a baby. Long story short, they found each other in the craziest way."

"That's nuts."

"Hollis is a part of the family. We don't see him a ton because he lives in Savannah near Paige. But he comes for holiday sometimes, and Maddox and Banks went deep-sea fishing a few months ago, and Hollis joined them."

*This family is incredible.*

The No Girls Allowed chat quietly alerts Foxx of a new message. He clicks on it.

> Jess: Okay, Mom's couch will be done for sure next week. The guy just called.
>
> Banks: I believe nothing until I see it.
>
> Moss: What about the loveseat and chairs?
>
> Jess: Those, too. Are you renting the truck to pick them up, Sparkles?
>
> Banks: Yeah, but I'm not paying for it.

"And I'm out." He exits the chat and tosses his phone on the sofa. "Are you going to come around here or hide behind me all night?"

I drag my fingertips across the back of his neck and shoulder as I come around the corner. "Miss me?"

"*Holy shit, Bianca.*" His eyes are wide as his gaze sweeps over my body. "Come here."

I give him a mischievous grin and walk toward the room's bar. I'm aware that the slits in the fabric give him a peek-a-boo view of my bare ass. I might even swing my hips a little to accentuate it.

"I need a drink," I say. "Want something?"

"Oh, okay. I see what you're doing."

I look at him across my shoulder. "What do you mean? I'm just getting a drink."

He swipes his tongue across his bottom lip, positioning his arms along the back of the sofa.

"Did you get your calls made?" I ask as nonchalantly as possible.

"I did. *Did you?*"

I laugh. "I did."

He hums.

It takes every shred of restraint not to climb on top of the man and have my way with him.

He's so sexy without a shirt and only wearing black joggers. His hair is wild, sticking up in a very non-Foxx-like state. But the sexiest thing about him is his grin. It's playful and roguish—and hits me right in the core.

I pour myself another glass of the wine we picked up on the way home from kayaking.

"We go home in the morning, right?" I ask, taking a sip.

He nods, biting his lip.

"That's going to suck." I giggle. "I mean, by the looks of things, that's all that's going to suck for the rest of this trip."

"Nice."

I wink and take another sip.

The alcohol floods my veins with a warmth that pools in the apex of my thighs. I'm so wet for him. My clit aches for his touch. Every part of me is dying for him to put me out of my misery.

But he knows that. *The bastard.*

I take a seat in the chair across the coffee table from him. It's far enough away to keep him from touching me—and me from touching him. Because, right now, I trust my restraint way less than I trust his.

"I talked to Jason tonight," I say, making things up as I go.

"Oh, you did? What about?"

*Um …* "He said he thinks things are settling down, and I should be home by the end of next week."

He nods. "Wow. That fast, huh?"

"Yeah." *Keep going. You're getting to him.* "He asked me who I want on my security detail."

His eyes darken.

*Got ya.* I try desperately to hide my grin. "Troy is finishing up his job in Atlanta, so he's available."

"Huh."

"And I like Troy. He's very, *very* handsome."

Foxx's eyes narrow. He grips the sofa like it offended him somehow.

"But Jason and I agree that Troy probably isn't the best man for the job," I say, watching him as I take a drink.

A slow, devious grin slips across his face. "I'm curious. Who did Jason suggest would be the best man for the job?"

"Well, there are limited options. With everything that's been going on, we don't want to have to get someone new up to date on all the things." *Keep going. You got this.* "So the only other option really is Calvin."

His brows lift to the ceiling. He's amused. *That's never a harbinger of good things to come.*

My heart pounds.

"That's so funny," he says. "I had a call with Jason today, too."

I study him, but I can't tell if he really did or if he's screwing with me back.

"Yeah, he said he talked to you."

I make a show by placing my glass on the table beside my chair. I lift my ass so the lace falls to the side, giving him a look at what he's missing. If only he could break first so we can get on with it.

"Great," he says. "Did he tell you what we talked about?"

*Shit. Shit, shit, shit.*

He's playing me now. I'm sure of it. And I'm even more certain that he knows I'm trying to play him.

"Yeah," I say, playing it as cool as possible.

"What did we talk about then?"

His gaze intensifies. My self-control dwindles.

The wine is gasoline on my libido—and it was a raging fire to begin with.

The longer he watches me, the hotter I become. My face heats. My pussy throbs. And my need to know if he will say he loves me burns out of control.

"I have all night, *wife*."

The cockiness of the sentence blisters through me. And I can't take it anymore.

"He said he's going to hook me up with Calvin—*ah!*"

Foxx lunges at me.

I shriek, scrambling off the chair. I leap across the end table, knocking over my glass of wine and nearly bashing my knee in the process. As I scurry around the room, Foxx is behind me. Somehow, I wind up behind the couch near the door to the bedroom. He's on the other side of the coffee table near the chair that I was just occupying.

My chest rises and falls as I struggle to breathe. Goose bumps spread across my skin. Foxx's smolder makes me shiver.

"You're in a very powerful position right now, Mrs. Carmichael."

*I love it when he calls me that.* "Oh, really? Why is that?"

"Because you hold all the cards."

"What cards?"

"You decide Calvin's fate. You decide whether I'm still friends with your brother." He smirks. "And you decide whether you get properly fucked on the last night of your honeymoon. It's all up to you."

*Damn.*

He moves to the side of the table. I smile, moving to the other side of the couch.

"If I'm in the powerful position, what does that make you?" I ask.

He chews on his lip.

"Oh, come on," I say, teasing him. "If I'm in the position of power, that means you're in the position of weakness. And you can help yourself tonight if you just tell me what you were going to tell me earlier."

His eyes twinkle. "There it is."

I put my hands on my hips. "Tell me."

"Tell you what?"

"Stop it, Foxx."

"Oh, that's right. Tell you what I was going to tell you on the kayak before you *rudely* interrupted me."

I drop my hands. "I got nervous, okay? And excited. And you were talking so much, and it was taking so long, and I just needed to know." I pop out my bottom lip in a pout. "Why don't you talk now? I'll listen."

"Nah. I'm good."

The man has the courage to walk away from me.

"Where are you going?" I ask, gasping.

He grins. "I need a drink. Want anything?"

I gave it my best shot. I really did. But I can't take it anymore.

"Yeah, I need something. Answers," I say. "Fucked. And if you won't give me any, then—*oh shit. Foxx!*"

My giggle breaks through the air as he sweeps me off my feet and tosses me over his shoulder. He bites the side of my ass, carrying me to the bed.

"Now we're getting somewhere—*ah!*" I say, giggling harder as I'm tossed on the bed.

I barely hit the mattress before he's on top of me, straddling me like I do him. I look up at my husband and his beautiful body and handsome face. The tenderness in his eyes.

He takes my hands and holds them above my head. I admire the lines in his biceps as he stretches over me.

"Now that I have you where you can't move, I'm going to tell you something. And if you start to talk," he says, talking over me, "I'll put my cock in your mouth."

"But then we'll both be distracted."

He chuckles before kissing me.

"I was going to tell you today …" His voice softens. "I was going to tell you that I want pizza for dinner."

"No, you were not," I say, kicking my feet to try to toss him off me. Of course, it's a nonstarter.

His smile, free and fun, is the best thing that's ever happened to me.

"Okay." He releases my hands, then rolls onto his side. "Let's try it this way."

I curl up next to him with my ear on his heart. It thumps steadily in time with mine.

I love this man. I love him with my whole heart, and if I'm wrong and that's not what he's going to tell me, it won't change anything.

I'll wait. Because he's worth the wait.

He strokes my hair and blows out a contented breath. "I love you, Bianca."

Tears stack behind my non-waterproof mascara.

"These past couple of days have been the best days of my life. And I knew they would be. I've known that this situation would be my dream come true since the day I saw you. We've done this backward. But I would love for us to see if we could work this out when we get home. I'll date you. I'll spoil you. I don't know how it'll work, but I will do whatever you want. If you want me to relocate to Nashville, I will. I just don't want to lose you. I can't."

Tears trickle down my cheeks.

Not only did he tell me he loved me, but he volunteered to leave his family—his wonderful, magical family—behind for me. And if that doesn't say everything, I don't know what does.

"Don't go to Nashville then," I say.

He stills.

"Because I'll be in Kismet Beach … probably chasing chickens off my lawn," I say.

He pulls me on top of him and kisses the hell out of me. Hard, soft. Short, long. Sweet and seductive. *Always intentional.*

Much to his chagrin, I pull away.

His brows are tugged together, his lips swollen from our kisses.

"Hey, Foxx," I say.

"What?"

I smile at him. "I love you, too."

He rolls me onto my back and makes good on every promise.

*I'm one lucky girl.*

# CHAPTER 24
## *Bianca*



"I'll set up a group call with my family today or tomorrow and let them know that I've decided to stay here," I say.

Foxx reaches across the middle console and takes my hand.

I'm not sure if I'll leave Brewer Group altogether or stay in some capacity remotely. But I'll address that when it arises. It doesn't feel as heavy of a decision as it has before now. Now it's a side note. My marriage is the most important thing.

Last night and this morning couldn't have been better. We stayed up late, sharing stories and snacking on leftover pizza from earlier in the evening. Our conversations were unrushed. It was exactly like it should've been—like we have the rest of our lives to learn about each other. And then this morning, we woke up before our alarm and lazily started our day. Our relationship is now peppered with kisses and touches, smiles and unspoken promises.

This is a fantastic start to our marriage.

"I don't know what to do with my house, though," I say as we turn into Kismet Beach.

The colorful buildings stream by as we make our way through town. It's exciting to think that this is my new home and I'll have time to explore it. To get to know the people. I can have friends.

I'll have a life.

I smile at my husband.

*I'll have a life with him.*

"You don't have to sell it right away," he says, squeezing my hand. "We can take this at whatever speed you want."

"True. But what do you think about having a few pieces of furniture that I love brought down here? I know you have everything, but I would like to have a couple of things."

He laughs. "Bring whatever you want. It's your house now, too, you know."

"Hey." My brow furrows. "Did we sign that prenup?"

His head whips to mine. "No. We didn't."

I shrug.

"Don't shrug at me." He squeezes my hand again before letting it go. "We need to do that as soon as we get home."

"I'm not that worried about it."

"Maybe not. But you're going to protect yourself."

"Why? Are you marrying me for my money?"

He looks at me out of the corner of his eye. "I don't give a fuck about your money."

"Good." I sigh happily. "But I'm bringing it with me. It doesn't make you happy, but it's fun to spend when you're happy."

He laughs, shaking his head.

I know we'll have to have conversations about things like money, and jobs, and whether Foxx will let me be his sugar mama. *A topic I know has no chance of flying.* But we'll have to work all of that out … in due time.

"What are you thinking about?" he asks.

"Just all the things we have to sort through and the decisions we have to make as a married couple." My stomach tightens. "For example, do you want to have children?"

"With you?"

I gasp. "No, with …" I narrow my eyes. "I'm not even joking about that. Of course, with me. Asshole."

He laughs. "Yes, I want to have children with you. I'll have as many as you want. Well, until the first one comes out like Banks or Tate. That'll be it. We're done."

"Fair enough."

We pull onto Honeysuckle Lane. A line of chickens crosses the road in front of us. For some reason, it feels like the perfect welcoming home committee.

"I have to get my car down here, too," I say. "This passenger princess thing is great until it's not."

"Where do you have to go?"

I grin. "Hey, I have friends now. I might want to go see Becca. And I heard there's a pizza night on Fridays around here."

He grips my thigh and gives it a gentle shake. "We need to remember that just because we've decided to stay married doesn't mean that we're in the clear, okay? We still need to be careful and keep our head down for a while."

"I know, I know. Speaking of which, have you actually heard from Jason? I really want to get an update on things so I can get back to my life."

Foxx's face falls. "Yeah. Let's sit down with him soon and figure out where we go from here."

"Sounds good."

Something about the look on his face makes my stomach twist. I don't have time to ask him about it because we pull into the driveway. *Of our home.*

He presses the button, and the garage door rises.

"Welcome home, Mrs. Carmichael," Foxx says, slowly pulling into the bay.

"Is it weird that I'm excited?"

"Considering your house is a mansion and this place ..."

I lean over the console and kiss him. "This place is perfect. It's our home, and I couldn't love it more."

He kisses the tip of my nose before we climb out of the truck.

"How will you handle it when I mess up your organizational systems?" I ask, kidding but also not.

He lugs our suitcases to the ground and fires me a look. "We'll need some boundaries."

"Do you mean like if something needs to be put away out here, you'll do it? Or like I can do it, but if it goes in the wrong spot, you'll spank me?"

He chuckles. "Why do I have a feeling those options were volunteered because you're happy with either outcome?"

"Because you know me well."

We start toward the door when Damaris's voice filters into the garage.

"Hey, kids," she calls.

We poke our heads around the corner. I wave.

"Hi, Mom," Foxx says.

"I'm glad you're back. I'm shopping for a new couch with Brooke tomorrow, Bianca, if you want to come. I have narrowed it down to three. I'm going to pick one, and Kixx can kiss my ass."

Foxx leans back so Damaris can't see him. "The couch is a no. Just try to get her to hold off, if you can."

"Why?"

"I'll explain later."

*Okay.*

"Foxx?" his mother says. "I know you just got back, but can you come over here for a second? I think my water heater is going out, and I can't get your dad to check it for me."

"You have four other sons, you know."

"Yes, but you're my favorite."

I giggle.

Foxx looks at me like he wants me to give him a reason to stay here. Instead, I smile and shoo him across the yard.

"Go. Help your mom," I say. "I'll just make myself at home."

He grins. "Well, you should because it *is* your home."

"Excellent point."

"I'll be back."

"Take your time," I say, calling after him.

I grab my suitcase and go inside.

*Home, sweet home.*

It feels like longer than three days since I was here. *So much has happened.* When we left for our honeymoon, I had no idea I'd come back feeling like I'm actually married. That it would be safe to verbalize my feelings.

That Foxx would love me back.

I stand at the kitchen counter and imagine myself cooking dinner for me and Foxx. I can hear our future children laughing and playing at my feet while I do dishes. I can see little bowls of candy on the island like my grandma used to have and having my family over for holiday dinners.

I shake off the reminder that I have to talk to them about leaving Nashville and potentially Brewer Group. I have faith that they'll understand. *Will they be surprised*? Probably. But they'll accept that I need to do what makes me happy. And Foxx makes me happy. I also know they'll trust my decisions because they've always had my back. They've always trusted me.

Yawning, I stretch my arms over my head. "I need a nap." I laugh as I pass through the kitchen into the living room. "Until Foxx gets back."

"*Hello, Bianca.*"

I freeze in place. My blood runs ice cold at the sound of my father's voice.

*What the hell is happening*? *How did he get in here?*

I turn slowly toward the window and find my dad sitting in a chair by the fireplace with a file of some sort in his hands.

"Have something you want to tell me?" he asks, getting to his feet.

"Why are you here?" I take a step back, my hands shaking. "How did you get in here?"

He paces toward me, unfazed. "You're going to stay very calm and walk back into the kitchen and lock the door. Understood?"

"Dad …"

He stalks toward me like a predator. *And I am his prey.*

I want to scream for Foxx—to scream for help. But I know Foxx will come. He's probably on his way back already.

"*Lock the door, Bianca,*" Dad booms as the door comes into view. "I don't want to hurt you, little girl, but I will if you leave me no choice."

"What are you doing?" I fiddle with the lock until it latches. *Surely,*

*Foxx has his keys with him. Or at least another way into the house.* "Why are you doing this?"

"Because you are going to do two good deeds today." He shoves a gun in my side. I gasp. "Lucky you."

His eyes are wild like an animal. He smells faintly of perspiration and whiskey. His clothes are wrinkled, and his eyes sunken in. *He's not the charming Reid Brewer I remember.*

I try to keep my composure—not to let him see me scared. It's a rule he drilled into my head for years and years. *Don't let them see you squirm.*

The barrel of the handgun is sharp against my ribs. He guides me into the living room and forces me to sit in the chair he just occupied.

"Daddy," I say, trying to appeal to the side of him that I think I once knew. "What are you doing?"

He takes an unfamiliar phone out of his pocket, then hits a few buttons. It begins to ring. Finally, a voice speaks.

"Yes?" the person on the other end says. *Who is he talking to? Why does he have another phone?*

*So he can't be found?*

I struggle to breathe.

"Rory, I'm here with our daughter. Say hi, sweetheart."

"Mom?" I ask, my voice cracking.

"Bianca, are you okay?"

"Mom? What's happening?"

Dad glowers my way. "I'll tell you what's fucking happening. You spoiled brat kids and your worthless mother—"

"Hey!" I say, starting to stand.

He points the gun at me again. So I sit.

"You've taken everything away from me," he says. "You took my life, my home, my money, my job. *My dignity.*"

"No, you took your own dignity. You can't blame that on anyone but yourself."

He laughs angrily. "You think you're so damn cute, don't you? Well, how cute will you be if your mom's head gets blown off today?"

"What?"

Mom whimpers.

My stomach drops, panic shooting through me. *Who has my mother?*

"Yeah. You had to stick your nose where it didn't belong and fuck up my deal with the Downings." His voice rises. "Then you had to run your ass down here and marry that son of a bitch Carmichael just to twist the knife a little more."

My teeth chatter from the adrenaline coursing through me at sonic-level speed.

"I didn't want it to be this way, Bianca. I really didn't."

He moseys my way with a swagger that doesn't compute.

"I tried to warn you, but you didn't listen," he says, standing over me. "You should've listened to the email."

"I didn't get an email from you."

*"Yes, you did."*

*What's he talking about?*

"Here's what you're going to do. You are going to transfer a large sum of money to the Downings, and then you're going to transfer another amount to an offshore account so I can start a new life away from you all," he says, regripping the gun. "And if you don't, your mom will go night-night."

Tears cloud my vision. "Why are you doing this, Dad?"

His chest puffs up. "Because I worked my whole fucking life for you and your fucking brothers and that whore."

*"Don't talk about her like that."*

He grins angrily. *"I* have the gun. Remember?" He shows it to me in case I've forgotten. "Once upon a time, I had to borrow money to purchase our first franchise. Do you remember?"

"Yes. We bought the hockey team."

"Right. Back then, I didn't have the kind of money that we have now. So I borrowed some from the Downings."

*Okay* ... I scramble to keep up.

"Either I'm going to pay them back, Bianca or they're going to fucking kill me," he says, his face turning beet red. "And I figured it out. I figured out a way to pay them back and save my life in one fell swoop. And no one had to know any better."

"But why pin it on me? Why not just transfer the money yourself and be done with it? Why involve me?"

"Because I don't have access to that kind of cash!" His voice rises. "Your mom didn't want me borrowing it in the first place. I figured I could pay it back with no one knowing. No one getting hurt. But then the team took longer to build, and we got delayed … and I was fucked."

*Ah* … "So Bobby helped you secure the Arrows, and you were giving him the stock to pay him off?"

"Exactly. And I tied it to you in case something did go wrong, you'd be the only person involved." He steps toward me. "I thought *you* of all people would have my back. But you didn't. You turned on me just like everyone else." He snarls, coming closer. "My little girl. The one I poured every bit of knowledge and experience I have into. *She* turned on me, too."

*Foxx, where are you? Help me!*

"You're going to initiate the bank transfers. Or I'm going to have Dougie pull the trigger and paint your mom's living room with her brains."

"Don't do it, Bianca," Mom says. "Fuck him."

"You don't want to do this, Daddy," I say, my voice trembling. "Think about it. Think about what you're doing. There's another way. You're not being rational."

He smiles. "Oh yes, I am."

I close my eyes and hear my mother crying softly through the phone.

*Please come, Foxx. Hurry.*

# CHAPTER 25

## *Foxx*

"It's fine, Mom." I flip the light off. "You're just not giving it enough time to heat."

"I hate when you say I'm not giving it enough time to heat like it's my fault. I give it plenty of time."

I roll my eyes.

"So how was the honeymoon?" she asks, following me into the kitchen.

"Great."

"Just great?"

"What do you want from me?" I say, chuckling. "A play-by-play? No offense, Mother, but you don't want to hear that."

She holds her hands together on the countertop and grins. "You look happy, Foxxster. You actually look happy."

"I *am* happy."

"I think the last time I saw you this happy was the year you got that red spy kit for your birthday," she says. "Do you remember that thing?"

*I'd forgotten all about that.* "Yeah. I made Jess's life hell with that."

Mom laughs. "You used to try to set up trip wires across the house. I'd get up in the morning and have to have my wits about me because, if not, I might face-plant on the way to the kitchen."

"Ah, the good old days when you could be a dick, and it was charming."

Her eyes sparkle. "I think you still get away with some of that nowadays."

"I'm offended."

"*Sure.*" She smiles, standing tall again. "So what can I do to help Bianca settle into Kismet Beach? She seemed to get along easily with the girls and Becca. That's good."

My heart swells with happiness and pride. I love how easily she fits in my world and how much she wants to. *Who would've thought a woman like Bianca—wealthy, successful, powerful—would trade it all for life in a small town?* Not me.

"Are you going to continue to work for Landry Security?" Mom asks. "You're gone an awful lot. I thought maybe you'd want to find something closer to home."

"This has all happened so fast. I'll need to think about it before I decide on anything." I reach into my back pocket and pull out my phone. Jason's name is on the screen. "I need to take this real quick."

"Help yourself. Want a glass of tea?"

I shake my head. "No. I'm good. Thanks." I lift the phone to my ear. "Carmichael."

As soon as the call connects, I sense something is wrong. It's a vibe, an exchange of energy—some telepathic way of communicating that Jason and I share.

"What's wrong?" I ask.

His voice is low and controlled. It sends chills down my spine.

"Foxx, listen to me closely," he says.

"Listening."

"I'm at Mom's. No one knows I'm here," he whispers.

"Okay."

My heart pumps so hard that I can feel it without searching for it.

"One perp is in the kitchen with Mom. He has a gun to her head," Jason says.

"*The fuck?*"

That's all it takes for me to slow down and begin calculating ways to eliminate the threat. My breathing is calm. My blood pressure steady. I'm laser-focused on the situation.

"Have you called the authorities?" I ask.

"Negative. There's a second threat."

He doesn't have to tell me what that is. *I already know.* I whip toward the door.

"Where are you?" he asks.

"I'm at my mom's. Fuck!"

Jason growls. "How the fuck did this happen?"

*You took the question right out of my head.*

My brain sorts through a series of events.

*Sorry to bother you. But I was just at Smokey's, and they found one of your keys. Becca gave it to me. I set it on your counter.*

I stop, meeting my mom's fearful gaze. "Quick—did you set my security alarm when you took the key Becca found to my house?"

Her brows pull together. "I think so. Why?"

"*Stay here.*"

"What's the situation?" I ask Jason.

"From what I can gather, if Bianca doesn't do whatever Dad says, the man here is going to shoot Mom."

*Fuck!* "Does your dad have a gun?"

"I don't know."

"Who has a gun?" Mom asks. "Foxx, what's going on?"

I stay focused on my house, trying desperately to evaluate how to get into my house quietly and keep Bianca safe.

"Suggestions?" Even I hear the agony in my voice.

"Dad's the main threat," Jason says. "Eliminate that. *God, I can't believe I'm saying this.* But do it. Do whatever you have to do. I doubt this guy gives a shit. We can't—"

"Alert Reid."

"Exactly."

*Dammit.* I move into the living room and stand off to the side of the window, trying to get a good look at the front of my house. I kick myself for not walking her inside. *What was I thinking not going with her?*

I've failed my wife.

"Can you get inside your house?" Jason asks.

"Yes. I'm figuring that out now. Assuming he hasn't barricaded doors and windows, I should be able to slide in the bottom door."

"From what I can tell, they're in your living room—*fuck! Shit.* Did you hear that?"

I still. The second report of a gun cracks through the air, breaking the silence. Then there's screaming.

*Oh God …*

I have to get to her. If something happens to her, I'll never forgive myself.

"He shot the ceiling," Jason says. "It's all good. All good."

*Fuck my life.*

"See if you can get inside your house," Jason says. "This guy is on speakerphone, so I can pretty much hear everything that's going on. I'll get in position, and if I hear any movements on your end, I'll make one on mine before he can hurt Mom."

"Roger that. I'm sorry, Jason."

"I'm not. If this was going to happen, I'd want it to happen like this. Small favors and all."

"I'm on my way over. Silencing my phone," I say.

"Noted. Doing the same."

"Roger that."

I turn to the door.

"Foxx? *What's wrong?*" Mom asks, pleading with me for an answer. Her hands wring in front of her.

I don't break stride. "Stay here. Stay away from doors and windows and wait for my instructions. I mean it."

"Foxx?"

I pause for a split second with my hand on the doorknob. "It's going to be fine." I hope. *Please God …* "Do what I asked you to do. If you hear anything else, call the police. But not until then."

"Okay."

I duck out of the house and around the side, the hot sun on my face. I jog behind the house and then dash across the open space between them. I take a moment beside the door leading into the hallway downstairs, using the moment to say another quick prayer. Thank fuck I still had my keys on me. Then I creep inside and shut the door behind me.

Chills race down my spine as Reid's voice bellows from above me. *He's unhinged.* I listen closely for Bianca, holding my breath until I hear her respond to one of his rants. *Oh, thank God.*

Her tone is calm and even, barely showing signs of the stress she must be under. She's poised as she tries to talk him down.

I slip through the bottom level and to the base of the stairs. I ensure I'm out of visibility.

"Dad, I can't just call and transfer that kind of money," Bianca says. "You know that, or you would've already done it."

"I don't have the authority to move that much cash. Only you and your mother."

*That's it, baby. Keep him talking.*

"Well, no offense, Dad, but that seems to have been a good idea, doesn't it?" Bianca asks.

*Don't prickle his feathers. Now isn't the time for your smart little mouth.*

"You're turning into her, you know," Reid says. "I used to think you would grow up and be like me. Smart. Ruthless. Strong. But you're really a better-educated version of her."

"Whatever you say, Dad."

"Think about it, Bianca. Think about what your mother would've been capable of if she hadn't stepped away from work to raise you kids. At one point in time, she was a better businessperson than I was. I see her brilliance from back then in you. But you have the same weakness, the same damn propensity not to want it enough—to let your ridiculous dreams get in the way of success."

"What's success to you, Dad? *This*? Is *this* success? You're standing by the fireplace with a gun in your right hand, threatening your daughter to move money to a thug or you'll kill her mother."

*"By the fireplace with a gun in your right hand." That's my girl. Keep it coming, Bianca.*

"What's success?" Reid booms, his voice echoing through the house. "Money. Power. Control."

"Pardon me for being rude, but you don't have much of any of those right now."

"We'll see about that. Get on the phone and transfer the money, Bianca."

"It doesn't work like that, Dad. You know that."

"*Now.*"

Bianca moves by the staircase. She glances quickly to the bottom, catching a glimpse of me.

*I'm here. I'm not going anywhere.*

"Who do you want me to call?" she asks, her voice calm. "The bank? Fine. How much do you want me to transfer?"

"Twenty million to start."

*Play along, Bianca. Keep him talking.*

"Okay," she says, moving through the room. "I need my phone. I'll have to call and get our account number and a number to the main office at the bank."

"Make it quick."

A shadow slips across the stairwell. I duck behind the corner and watch Reid come into focus. His back is to me.

Bianca must keep him in that position because he doesn't move.

"You have thirty seconds to get on the phone before I tell Dougie to have a little fun with your mom."

"You wouldn't," she says. This time, I hear a wobble in her voice—a sign she's growing more uncomfortable.

"Oh, Bianca. *You know I would.*"

It's then that I hear Rory's cries muffled through a speakerphone.

*This bastard is one sick fuck. His own wife. His own daughter.*

*God, I just want to get my hands on him.*

Reid takes a step back, perilously close to the top of the steps. I spring forward, taking the steps a few at a time. My hand is on Reid's gun as I tackle him from behind.

The gun goes off.

Bianca screams.

Reid groans as he smashes against the floor.

I have him pinned beneath me, facing me. I quickly get a knee in the middle of his chest and feed him punch after punch. *I want to kill him.*

Bianca backs up until she's at the couch. In the distance, through the phone, it sounds like Jason scuffles with the hitman.

"Call the police, Bianca," I say through gritted teeth.

"Are you good, B?" Jason shouts.

I glance at her quickly. Tears stream down her cheeks. She looks at me like I hung the moon.

"I'm fine, Jase. How is Mom?"

"I'm fine, Bianca. Are you okay?"

Bianca smiles through her tears. "I'm fine."

Sirens ring through the distance, getting louder as they grow closer. Reid has blood trickling from his nose and lips from my fists and elbows. His weapon is secured across the room. The look on his bloodied and swollen face is nothing other than utter disdain and hatred.

"The feeling is mutual, motherfucker. You're lucky I don't kill you," I say.

"*Do it.*"

I smile menacingly. "Your daughter doesn't deserve to see that. Besides, I bet you'll enjoy prison."

"What happens now?" Bianca asks, holding her arms over her stomach.

"They'll take this motherfucker to jail. You'll have to give a statement. And I'll be right there beside you." I smile at her. "I'm so proud of you. You did one hell of a job, sweetheart."

She smiles, wiping her cheeks with the back of her hand.

The garage door flies open, and footsteps pound against the floor. Banks and Jess stop in the doorway, trying to make sense of the situation.

"What the fuck is happening here?" Jess asks.

"Long story, but this is Reid Brewer. He's Bianca's father."

Banks eyes him. "Nice to meet you."

Reid spits a mouthful of blood on Banks's shoe.

Banks steps on his hand, crunching bones in it as he walks away. "Oops."

"Everyone's okay?" Jess asks. "Someone talk to me. What the fuck is going on?"

"Everyone is fine here." I pick up Reid's phone and listen. "How are you, Jason?"

"Got a busted fucking lip. But this guy will be hurting tomorrow. Where's B?"

"I'm right here, Jason. Mom? Can you hear me?"

Rory whimpers, sobbing quietly. "Oh, Bianca, honey. I'm so sorry."

"Police are here," Jason says. "I'll call you later, Foxx."

"I love you, Jason. Love you, Mom."

"I love you, Bianca. I love you so much," Rory says.

"Love you, B. Talk soon."

The line disconnects.

Sirens pull up to the front of the house. It's not two seconds before someone pounds on the door. "This is KBPD. Open up."

Jess steps to the side as two officers race in, guns drawn.

"Hands up and nobody move," an officer shouts.

"If you get arrested and need to be bailed out, call me," Banks says, his hands in the air. "I owe you one. But I'll let you get a sandwich on the way home because I'm not selfish."

*Now's not the time, Banks.*

I step away from Reid, immediately enveloping Bianca in an embrace. It's never felt so good to hold her and have her in my arms. I make eye contact with Officer Schultz, one of Banks's friends from high school. He nods at me that it's fine to hold my wife.

Bianca shakes as she cries, fisting my shirt with both hands. I pull her closer and vow to never let go.

# CHAPTER 26

## *Bianca*

I HOLD A BAG OF FROZEN CARROTS TO ONE EYE AND THEN THE OTHER. Banks sits across the table from me with a smile stretching from ear to ear at his helpfulness—or so he thinks. As soon as he heard me complain that my eyes were swollen from crying, he ran home and got a bag of frozen vegetables. He said it helped him when he had black eyes so he was sure it would help me, too. I'm not sure it's the same thing, but I can't possibly not give it a try. He's so pleased with himself.

Foxx's chair is pressed against mine, his hand on my leg. He's been this way since the police hauled my father off a few hours ago. He refuses to break contact.

"I must not have turned the security system back on when I dropped off the key." Damaris is pale. "I'm so sorry, Bianca. Foxx ..." Tears trickle down her cheeks. Again. "Please forgive me. I'll never forgive myself."

Kixx stands behind her, massaging her shoulders.

The sky begins to darken. The palm trees sway outside, causing a host of shadows to dance through Foxx's kitchen. It's a somber scene for a somber day.

"Damaris, it's not your fault," I say.

"No, it is. I should've been more careful. Foxx is always telling us to be safe. To lock doors. I didn't listen, and I caused this."

"There could be a lot of fingers pointed today," Foxx says, the smile I've enjoyed over the past few days long gone. "You should've locked the doors, Mom. Set the alarm. But I got careless, too. I should've been in here with her. It was my job. Ultimately, this is my mistake."

"Stop it." I set the carrots down. "I'm all for assigning blame and taking responsibility because that's how mistakes aren't duplicated." I look around the table at the concerned faces. "But this blame sits solely on my father's shoulders. He intentionally set out to hurt me. And every one of you, from Foxx to Damaris to even Banks, has gone out of your way to help me. To care for me." I sniffle, trying not to cry because, if I do, I'm afraid it'll be an ugly sob. "I hate that my father's ugliness spilled into this family. Please, don't blame yourselves."

Foxx pulls me into him. I'm not sure if he's doing it for me, or if he needs the contact, the reassurance. But I do need this. *His hugs. His warmth. His love.*

"I broke his hand for you," Banks says. The words sound serious, but his smirk tells another story.

I laugh. "You're definitely the hero of this story, Banks."

"Well, you know, I do try …"

Slowly, frowns begin to turn up. They aren't quite smiles, but they're better. And that, I've learned, is the magic of Sparkles.

That's still one story, of many, I need to hear.

Gravel crunches outside and we all jump. Banks goes to the window. Car doors shut, the sound echoing through the room.

"Who the fuck is that?" Foxx asks. "I've had enough of unannounced visitors today."

"I'm going to assume you don't mean us," Kixx says, joking with his son.

Foxx doesn't find the humor in it.

"It's Jason." Banks looks at me over his shoulder and then back out the window. "And a woman who looks like Bianca."

My heart springs in my chest. "My mom is here?"

Kixx goes into the foyer and opens the door. I hold my breath, not wanting to be too hopeful—but hopeful, nonetheless.

My brother and mother come around the corner. Both look worse for the wear. Jason's lip is busted, and it looks like he may have a black eye in the morning.

Foxx and I stand. He embraces Jason, and my mother pulls me into the tightest, longest hug of my life.

I can't stop the sobs this time.

My mother shakes as the same level of emotion leaves her. Jason wraps his arms around us both and kisses our heads—first Mom's, then mine. He whispers something under his breath. It might be a prayer; it might just be a universal thanks that we're all okay. But the exact language doesn't matter. I feel it in my heart.

"Mom, Dad, this is Rory Brewer. Bianca's mom," Foxx says, his eyes glistening.

I step away from my mom. We accept a tissue from Damaris, who immediately pulls my mother into a hug.

I laugh through the tears. My poor mother is not a touchy-feely woman. I bet she doesn't know what to think about Damaris. *She'll love her, though. She needs this as much as I do.*

Ever the sophisticate, Mom dabs her eyes and gathers herself. "I'm overwhelmed. I'm sorry."

She sniffles, reaching for my hand. I happily give it to her. Not to be outdone, Foxx takes my other one.

"Today has truly been one for the history books, and I'm sorry that your family was affected by this incredibly horrific situation," Mom says. She looks around the table. "I want to thank you all for taking care of my little girl." Her lip trembles. "She needed you, and you were there. And it's a lesson I've taken to heart today."

Damaris wipes her eyes, too. "We will always be there for Bianca, Rory. And you and Jason, too. And however many other Brewers exist because we're all family now."

Mom places a hand on her chest. "Jason and I had a long talk on the flight down here. Perks of having a son for a pilot." She looks at him and smiles. "I want to truly express my deepest gratitude for your generosity to my daughter. And Foxx ..." Her eyes shine with a new pool of tears. "I've dreamed of Bianca meeting a man like you since the day she was born. And I knew the first time I was in a room with the two of you that this day—well, maybe not *this day*—would happen."

We all chuckle.

"There is no one else I'd rather my daughter fall in love with," Mom says before diverting her attention to me. "I'm sorry I missed your wedding, Bianca. But after getting caught up with Jason and filled in on the details of everything, I was hoping maybe you'd allow me to throw you another one." She looks at Damaris. "Maybe you and I could work together and create something special for them. What do you think?"

Damaris beams. "I do love throwing parties."

"Can someone please explain to Jess that his chickens can't come to this one?" Banks says.

Mom looks confused as we all laugh.

"If the kids don't mind, I'd love to do that," Damaris says.

I look at Foxx at the same moment he looks at me. He grins. I smile back.

This wedding, the new one, isn't just about us. It's about *all of us*. It's a chance for new beginnings, new bonds, and an opportunity to heal wounds. And I think we all need that. We all could use that. And if I know my mother, we'll all get that and more.

"Are you hungry, Rory?" Damaris asks. "I have a pot of chicken and dumplings on the stove."

"And you didn't tell me?" Banks asks.

Mom laughs. "Well, Jason and I did talk about getting a hotel room tonight."

"Nonsense." Damaris slips her arms through my mom's. Mom doesn't stand a chance, and the thought makes me giggle. "You're staying with us. We're family now."

Kixx holds the door for them.

Banks gives us a quick wave. "If they think they're eating without me, they're nuts. And I need to pick up a package delivered there before Mom sees it."

"I already saw it," she shouts from the garage. "Stop hacking my Prime account, you little shit."

Kixx shakes his head and follows them out. Then as quickly as he left, he pops his head back into the house. "Jason, do you want to come? I'm going to watch baseball."

"Sure. I'd love to, Kixx."

Jason squeezes my shoulder and follows him out.

Finally, the house is quiet. Everything is still. There are no uninvited guests, no law enforcement officers, and no family members.

It's just us.

"I feel like today took five years to get through," I say, moseying through the kitchen. "This morning, we were in Silver Springs. Who'd have thought that we'd go through all of this in one day?"

Foxx grins. Although it's not one of his all-encompassing grins that I've to love, he's at least more relaxed than he was thirty minutes ago. I'll take it.

"We've been through quite a lot in one week," he says.

I smile back at him. "That we have." I reach for an orange but notice a bowl of keys next to it. "I need to talk to my mom and Jason about me staying here."

"I'm pretty sure they already know."

"Probably." I pull the bowl to me and take out the keys. "This is what you were talking about before? The keys that aren't yours but are being dropped around town?"

Foxx comes to me. "Yes. I can't figure it out."

"Could it be Paige?" I ask. "She was behind the texts. Maybe this is her, too."

He shakes his head. "I don't think so." He lifts one and inspects it. "I have to be missing something. But I can't find it."

I hop on the counter and pull one out. A label is stuck to the front with Foxx's phone number on it. *Why would someone do this? Why would someone drop his keys all around town?* I pick at the corner of the label and think.

"You don't think it's Banks," I say, remembering what he said to me before about it.

"No. It's too complicated."

"Jess?"

He scoffs. "Chicken Daddy is too busy playing farmer."

I laugh. "Okay, what if it's …" I come up blank. "Who else could it be?"

"Fuck if I know."

I start to set it back in the bowl and take the orange, but the corner of the label begins to peel back. I get my fingernail beneath it and rip it off the key.

*Ooh.* "Okay. Here's a clue," I say.

"What do you mean?"

"Look." I hand him the key. "What does *ninja* mean to you?"

The word is typed in tiny font and was covered by the label.

"*Ninja*? I don't get it," he says.

I grab another key and pull the label back. "*Wyoming.*" I do it again. This time, the word is *top hats.*

"Are these clues for something?" I ask. "Does any of this make sense to you?"

Foxx holds up a key, annoyed. "I don't know. This one says *sourdough,* so you tell me."

"I don't know what this means, but it's fun." I rip off another label. "*The Roman Empire.*"

"*Sun.*"

"*Wrestling.*"

He holds up another one. "*Flannel.*"

I begin to display another one but stop. A look flashes through his eyes, and a small, knowing grin splits his cheeks.

"What?" I ask.

He looks around. "Where is the key she found while we were gone?"

"Um …" I point next to a small candy dish. "It's right there."

He picks it up and pulls the label off it. He starts to laugh.

"What? Tell me. I'm invested."

He lays the key in my palm. *Bianca.*

"I'm confused. Why is my name on here?" I ask.

He nods slowly as if he's still piecing things together.

"Start talking, husband."

He laughs, settling between my legs. "Sometimes you beg me to talk. Sometimes you punish me for it—or try to, anyway."

I press a kiss against his lips.

"My mom said something to me the other day," he says. "I can't remember what her exact words were, but we were talking about Jess and his chicken obsession. And she said something along the lines of one day I'll understand. And it's easy to forget about the things that make you happy." He holds up a key. "All of these random things? They're things I've loved all through the years."

My heart swells.

"And the last one is you," he says softly.

I wrap my arms around his shoulders and bury my head in his neck. "Will you do me a favor, husband?"

"Always, wife."

"Before we go to your mom's and see my mom, will you take me into our bedroom and make love to me?"

He pulls back. "*Our bedroom*. I think I love that just as much as *wife*."

"I love you." I take his face in my hands. "I never doubted you'd come for me. I knew I just had to make it until you arrived."

His face sobers. "Those were the most terrifying moments of my life. I'm so impressed with how you kept it together, Mrs. Carmichael. You amaze me, and I love you. So much."

He sweeps me off the counter, carrying me down the hallway.

We have a lot to figure out—logistics, another wedding, a criminal trial.

Not long ago, I would've been so consumed with work that I would've overlooked my blessings. Because this, being laid gently on a bed with the kindest, smartest, hottest man in the world preparing to show me how much he loves me—this is what it's all about. *This* is the blessing. *Family is the blessing*.

And alongside the vows I made to Foxx, I also vow never to forget this too. No matter what life throws at us or how busy we get or how monumental the day seems, if we have each other, if we keep fanning our flame, we'll be just fine.

# Epilogue

## BIANCA



> Paige: STOP IT WITH THE TEXTS, GUYS. I MEAN IT.
>
> Jess: I'm sorry. What are you talking about?
>
> Banks: What do you mean? Do you want removed from this chat?
>
> Moss: 🙄
>
> Maddox: Stop the texts? What?

I laugh, looking across the table as all of them sit next to each other and text their sister back.

"Hope it was worth it," Moss says.

"What have you guys been texting her?" I ask.

"Different ways to prepare shrimp," Maddox says.

"Facts about rocks," Moss says.

Jess laughs. "Chicken facts."

"Of course," I say, giggling.

"I send her random pages of books. Get it?" Banks says, cracking himself up. "Paige. Pages. I'm so damn funny."

Foxx laces his fingers protectively around my middle and snuggles against me. He doesn't participate in the text war. His notifications are silenced—except for mine.

I'm sitting on his lap at Damaris's table on this beautiful Sunday morning. The rest of the girls went out for brunch, which always included mimosas. Lots of them. Knowing it would be too awkward to pass—and it would invariably draw too much attention to me—I told them that I was meeting Becca before she heads to Savannah. And I *am* meeting Becca this afternoon. But I really just don't want them to know I'm pregnant yet. I want to enjoy the secret with my husband for as long as I can.

"Oh, was that a car door?" Maddox asks.

"Shit! I have to FaceTime Paige," Banks says. "Pick up, pick up, pick up."

"Hey," she says.

"Quick, Mom is coming," he tells her, flipping the camera around.

"Oh, good. I'm not going to miss it. Yay!" she says.

We all exchange a smile and turn toward the living room … and wait.

Kixx's voice is louder than usual. It's the predetermined signal that they're getting ready to walk in. He comes in first, blocking the view. Moss gives him a thumbs-up, and Kixx steps to the side.

"I don't know why you insist on looking there again," Damaris says, frustration thick in her voice. "We've looked at their furniture every month for a year now and they never—*oh, my God.*"

"Surprise!" everyone shouts.

She covers her mouth. Her shoulders slump. Her eyes nearly fall out of her head as she takes in her new furniture.

"Obviously they prioritized correctly," Banks says. "Because my wrestling singlet is front and center."

"You paid extra for them to do that, didn't you?" Moss asks.

"*No.* It's just obviously the coolest piece of merch we sent."

"It's not merch, you fool," Jess says, rolling his eyes.

"It's your jerseys," Damaris says, dropping her hands. "Guys! *Oh, my*. How did you do this? I'm … speechless."

"We knew you'd miss the sentimental aspect of the old couch," Banks says. "I mean, my SpaghettiOs stain has made it all these years. So we wanted to give you something that still made you think of us."

Moss gets up and joins her in the living room. We all take his lead and join them, too.

They take turns pointing out different pieces of fabric and laughing about related stories associated with that particular garment. There are baseball shirts, pieces of singlets, and football jerseys. A hockey jersey, too. But hidden among those pieces of fabric are swatches of their baby clothes. I think those hit the hardest for Damaris.

"Do you think she thinks this is the couch?" Kixx whispers, leaning against the wall beside us.

I grin. "It kind of looks like it."

He watches her proudly go through each section of the material. "I'll let her revel in this one for a while. Then we'll go downstairs and bring up the one she really wanted."

I move back to the table, fighting a wave of nausea. Foxx is at my side, holding my hand, looking at me like I might burst into tears or vomit. *Probably because I've done both lately.*

The man has been a champ. He installed a mini fridge beside the bed so I can keep water and snacks close by. Eating and drinking a little something before I get up has helped. So far. Things seem to change every day.

But they change for the better in every way. I fall deeper in love with Foxx. Our baby grows bigger inside me. Our family bonds get stronger.

I haven't been to Nashville in three months. Astrid organized all the things I wanted to be sent to me. I donated the rest to charity. And my house is on the market, waiting for a buyer.

But that doesn't mean I don't see my family. We're actually closer than ever. Mom bought a house on the beach, and she's been spending a lot of time here. I think it's good for her to start fresh in a place that doesn't remind her of my father. At least the divorce is final, and he's tucked safely away behind bars. I'm sure that helps. She hasn't sold her home in Nashville just yet, but she'll do what's best for her in her own time.

Foxx took time off from Landry Security to spend with me. I'm not sure what he'll do now, but we're figuring it out. In the meantime, my brothers are all too happy to come golf with him … and to eat Damaris's home cooking.

The last year, even before I got married to Foxx, has been a roller coaster of emotions and situations. It's really run the gamut. But if there's one thing I've learned, it's this—have faith that every situation can end in your favor. It's wild what can happen when you open your mind … and your heart.

"Do you wanna sneak out of here and go home?" Foxx asks.

I look at him and smile. Silly man. He doesn't realize that *home* is wherever he is.

"Yeah, let's go," I say.

He takes my hand, and we slip out the back door—and almost trip over a chicken.

Continue to swipe for the first chapter of The Proposal, the first book in the Brewer Family Series. You're going to love Bianca's family!

# The Proposal

BLAKELY

"Could you die quietly?" Ella sighs, pulling her sunglasses down and squinting into the sunlight. "And maybe do it over there, please?"

Two quintessential frat boys, a label I'd bet my life on yet feels like a disservice to fraternities everywhere, cease their constant complaints about being hungover. Their whining is a show, a pathetic effort to gain attention, and one we're over—especially Ella.

They fire a dirty look at my best friend. She cocks a brow, challenging them right back, and waits.

Lying on the chaise next to her, I smirk. *How many seconds will it take for them to realize they're outgunned by a five-foot-three pistol with bubble-gum pink toenails?*

*Eight … Nine … Ten …*

They gather their things quietly, watching Ella like she might toss them into the pool if they don't act quickly enough.

I wouldn't be shocked if that happened, either.

Ella St. James doesn't surprise me much anymore. She carried a tray of freshly baked snickerdoodle cookies when she rang my doorbell three years ago. She was adorable, wearing an apron with embroidered cherries and a white silk ribbon in her hair while welcoming me to the Nashville neighborhood. It starkly contrasted with the following weekend when she took me out so I could *get acquainted with the city.*

That night ended with Ella jacking some guy's jaw for trying to grope me on the dance floor and me picking her up from the police station in an Uber at three in the morning.

"Thank you," she says, sliding the glasses up her nose and returning to her book.

Las Vegas is sweltering. Blue water sparkles just inches from our feet, and I swear it only amplifies the sun's rays. We should probably get a massage or go shopping to beat the unbearable heat, but I didn't fly for almost four hours to stay inside.

I could've celebrated my new job and birthday like that in Tennessee.

"How do you think I would look with red hair?" I ask, stretching my legs in front of me. "Not bright cherry red, but a more purple-y, crimson-y red."

"No."

I furrow my brows. "That wasn't a yes or no question."

"I was cutting to the chase." Her fingertip trails along the bottom of the paperback. "That's not the question you were really asking."

*It wasn't?* I settle against my chair. *Yeah, it wasn't.*

*It was a last-minute attempt at being young and reckless before I turn thirty tomorrow.*

This whole birthday crap has been a bit of a mind fuck.

I've lived the past ten years with little abandon. I've traveled, dated, and swam with sharks. Went on a ten-city tour with a rock band. Attended a movie premiere, got engaged (and unengaged), and ate pizza at the world's oldest pizzeria in Naples. *Check that off the bucket list.* And with every year of fun, I assumed I had nothing to worry about—that I would have my shit together before I turned thirty and became a real adult.

That was an incorrect assumption.

By all accounts, I should be in a stable relationship and burdened with a mortgage and enough debt to bury my soul until Jesus returns. Appliances should excite me. I should have a baby. *I should understand life insurance.* Instead, I just broke up with *another* bad boy with commitment issues, re-upped the rental contract on my townhouse, and refilled my birth control.

But that all ends in six hours. I have to turn over a new leaf when the sun comes up. It's time.

Ella's book snaps closed. "This is not a tri-life crisis, Blakely. It's just a birthday."

"I know that."

"But do you?"

"*Yes, I do*," I say, mocking her. "I'm not in crisis mode. I'm just transitioning into this new era of buying eye cream and freezing my eggs, and it's a little … terrifying."

She sighs. "You've been buying eye cream for years."

"Yeah, as a hedge against the future. This *is* the future."

Ella rolls onto her side, brushing her dark hair off her shoulder. "While I can't relate because I have a solid two years before I'm thirty—"

"Was that necessary?"

She laughs. "You're freaking out for no reason. Tomorrow is just another day."

"I know. *I really do*. There's just this pressure to get my ducks in a row and start making serious progress, or else I'll be fifty with no husband or kids. And I want both."

"All I ask is that you be a little more selective on the husband part because the last few guys you've dated …" She whistles. "Not good, Blakely."

*Yeah, I know.*

"I know you feel your biological clock ticking or whatever it is, but you *have* been doing big things," she says. "You're the new artist manager assistant at Mason Music Label. Remember, you little badass? That's impressive."

I shrug happily at the reminder. That's true—a dream come true, really. *And even more of a reason to get my shit together.* "But would I be even more impressive as a redhead?"

"The answer is still no."

I groan. "*Come on.* I want to go out on something big. Something fun. Something wild that I'll remember while I'm taking vitamins and going to bed before ten."

Ella reaches for her water. "Fine. But let's find something else. Red doesn't suit your skin tone."

"Like what? I'm not getting anything pierced, and I don't think I'm ready to commit to a tattoo."

"You've been wanting a tattoo since the day I met you. As a matter of fact, weren't you looking at tattoos when I brought over those cookies?"

I laugh. "Yes. But it's so permanent. What if I don't want it next week?"

She rolls her eyes.

"What else is there?" I ask. "Let's think."

"Well, you could find a man with money and get a quickie wedding on the Strip."

I laugh again, turning over onto my stomach. "At this point, that's the only way I'll get married—inebriated and to a stranger." *The guys I date aren't marriage material. I'll probably be alone forever at this rate.*

"Hey, people find love in all sorts of ways."

"True, but the odds that I'll find a marry-able man in the next few hours is incredibly low." I fold my arms under my head. "In lieu of sexy strangers with an engagement ring in their pocket, what else do you suggest?"

She taps a finger to her lips. "We could go to a show tonight. A male striptease or something like that. It might be a way to get your juices flowing—"

"Ew!"

"*While lacking permanence.* Then just see where the night takes us. Be free-spirited."

"You just want to go because it's one more way to needle Brock."

Her grin is full of mischief. "So? What's your point?"

Ella and my brother have been *a thing* for almost two years. *What kind of thing?* I'm afraid to label it, although I'm fairly certain they're exclusive without declaring exclusivity.

On the one hand, Ella is a lot to handle. She's smart, opinionated, and doesn't need a man—and she knows it. She also has a propensity to make decisions and weigh the risks after. That drives Brock nuts.

On the other hand, dating Brock would be a nightmare. Women

throw themselves at him wherever he goes. Men stop him for autographs and to *man-swoon* over him. And during the season, he's focused and mostly unavailable. That doesn't always work for Ella.

I watch this back-and-forth and vow never to get into a relationship with a player—an athlete or otherwise. *Again.* I've done that before, and it didn't end well.

"I'm taking it you two are still fighting," I say.

"We aren't fighting. There's nothing to fight about." She lifts her chin to the sky. "I'm right, and he's wrong. That's all there is to it."

"I agree. You're right this time."

Her eyes widen. *"You're damn right I'm right.* I'm not putting up with him taking off to Miami with his friends and not even mentioning our anniversary."

"How can you have an anniversary if you aren't in an official relationship?" I snicker. "Isn't that what you always tell me? That you aren't in an official relationship with him?"

She waves a hand through the air, dismissing my question. "It's a prelationship, but that doesn't change anything in this circumstance."

"A *what?*"

"A *prelationship.* The formative stage where boundaries and expectations are established so you can determine if the other person is willing to abide by them." She pauses. *"Brock isn't."*

I roll my eyes and let it go. They'll settle this before Brock returns from Miami and we're home from Vegas. I've seen it too many times to count.

"Then fine," I say, sitting up. "Let's go to a show. But if my brother asks whose idea it was, I'm not taking the blame."

"Tell him it was mine. *I want him to know.* A little competition never hurt anyone."

"Competition for your non-boyfriend?" I ask, grinning.

"Precisely."

I shake my head as a bead of sweat trickles down my face. I wipe it away with the back of my hand. "I'm ready to go in and grab a shower."

"And I need to make reservations for dinner." She sits up, slipping on her flip-flops. "You owe me, you know."

"What do I owe you for?"

"For depriving me of my right as your best friend to throw you the most outrageous, amazing birthday party that Nashville has ever seen." She stuffs her water bottle in her bag. "I'm known in certain circles as the girl who throws the best bashes. I can only wonder what everyone is thinking about this."

I laugh at her ridiculousness, slipping my cover-up over my head. "You've thrown me a huge birthday party every year I've known you. You can miss this one. It won't hurt."

She frowns. "Maybe it won't hurt *you*, but it pains *me*. I have a reputation to uphold."

"You'll survive."

I drop my phone, towel, and water bottle into my bag. I skim the area around me to ensure I have everything.

"Ready?" she asks.

"Yeah." A bubble of excitement fills me. *Let the birthday festivities commence.* "Let's go find trouble."

Ella shares my smile as we slide our bags on our sun-kissed shoulders. I spot my book under her chair and grab it. *How did it get there*?

As I stand, my gaze falls on Ella. Her wide eyes are twinkling. I've seen this look enough times to know things are about to get real.

"What?" I ask, frozen in place.

Her grin pulls wider. "I think trouble just found us."

*Oh no.*

The Proposal is live now on Amazon, Audible, and free with Kindle Unlimited.

# *Acknowledgments*

*Wow*. Foxx Carmichael made me work for it. But, honestly, I didn't expect anything less.

I'd like to start, as I always do, by thanking my Creator. I'm grateful that I can bring a bit of joy and happiness to lives through the art of storytelling.

My family has brought dinner to my desk, checked on me before bed, and cheered me on over the writing of this book. Thank you to my husband and our four incredible sons. I love you guys so much.

I'd like to thank my bonus parents, Peggy and Rob Williams, for their love and support. You are the greatest. It's true, because I said so.

I have to shout out my sweet nephew, Foxx. You have brightened so many lives. Your smile spreads joy. Your antics, *oh, my, your antics*—they keep us laughing. You are so loved. And if you grow up someday and wonder why your auntie used your name in a romance novel, I used your sister's name a long time ago and I wanted to be fair. (I also want to be the cool aunt.)

There's one person I'd like to call out specifically, and that's Debbie Doo. Your excitement over my stories energizes me. You are an absolute delight and a gift to all who know you. Thank you for reading my books, my sweet friend.

My oldest "book world friend", Kari March nailed this cover. She always does. She knows what I mean when I'm not even sure, and she doesn't get (too) frustrated at my creative attempts to show her (terribly) want I want. (Which is never what I really want.) I love you, Kari.

Big thanks to my assistant, Tiffany Remy, and my team of beta readers that pull through for me. Authors Kenna Rey and Anjelica Grace—you are the absolute best and I appreciate you more than words can describe. Michele Ficht is always ready to cheer me on and helpfully uncover all my mistakes. What would I do without you?

My dear, sweet editors, Marion Archer and Jenny Simms—I am impressed with your talent and humbled to work with each of you. Thank you for dealing with my timelines, plot holes, and for being patient when I have characters in unreasonable positions. No one should be sitting on a cactus. Ha!

I would be remiss if I didn't thank the team at Valentine PR. Kim deserves a medal for having the patience of a saint. Christine, Kelley, Meagan, Ratula, and Sarah are fairy godmothers. And a huge thank you to Nina, my publicist and agent, for always being there to help me figure things out (and ease me into scary things).

I'm honored to be working with Blue Nose Audio for the audiobook production of this title. I can't wait to hear it!

There is no list if my closest friends aren't on it. Author Mandi Beck—thank you for being you. For crying with me, cursing alongside me, and cheering with me. I love you forever. Author S.L. Scott—when I say I couldn't have done this without you, I mean it. You know why. You are a bright spot in my life and I love you so, so much. Author Jessica Prince—thank you for bullying me into my office every day. *winks* Seriously, without you, I'm a lonely procrastinator. I prefer doing it with you.

Thank you to Stephanie Gibson for always having my back, Katie Reister for being pure sunshine, and Bailey Boughton for delivering motivation and inspiration to my inbox every single morning.

Last but certainly not least, thank you to my readers. Chatting with you, laughing with you, and obsessing over book boyfriends with you is the best part of my job. I love you. Thank you for being here.

# About the Author

USA Today Bestselling author, Adriana Locke, writes contemporary romances about the two things she knows best—big families and small towns. Her stories are about ordinary people finding extraordinary love with the perfect combination of heart, heat, and humor.

She loves connecting with readers, fall weather, football, reading alpha heroes, everything pumpkin, and pretending to garden.

Hailing from a tiny town in the Midwest, Adriana spends her free time with her high school sweetheart (who she married over twenty years ago) and their four sons (who truly are her best work). Her kitchen may be a perpetual disaster, and if all else fails, there is always pizza.

Join her reader group and talk all the bookish things by clicking here.

<www.adrianalocke.com>

www.ingramcontent.com/pod-product-compliance
Lightning Source LLC
Chambersburg PA
CBHW011142310726